PRAISE FOR DOROTHY SIMPSON

"Dorothy Simpson never disappoints."
— *The Boston Sunday Globe*

"Dorothy Simpson's . . . series featuring Inspector Luke Thanet of the Sturrenden CID is . . . imaginatively conceived and skillfully executed. . . . Simpson is an adroit storyteller with a talent for creating complex and intriguing characters, not the least of whom is Thanet himself."
— *The San Diego Union*

And for **WAKE THE DEAD**
"A solidly satisfying, eminently readable and well-plotted detective story."
— *London Evening Standard*

"An engaging murder mystery with depth and humor."
— *Booklist*

DOOMED TO DIE
"Inspector Luke Thanet and sidekick Sergeant Mike Lineham score another hit. . . . Fans . . . are sure to enjoy this layered, thought-provoking tale."
— *Publishers Weekly*

DEAD BY MORNING
"Red herrings strew the path that leads to the novel's clever ending, which has undeniable shock value. . . . An adroitly written mystery."
— *The New York Times Book Review*

BY DOROTHY SIMPSON

WAKE
THE
DEAD

DOROTHY SIMPSON

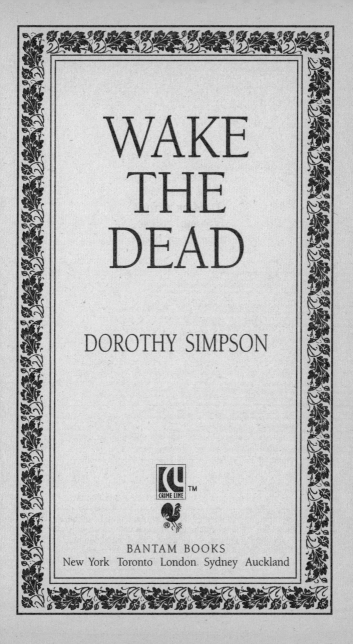

BANTAM BOOKS
New York Toronto London Sydney Auckland

This is a work of fiction. Names, characters, places, and incidents either are the product of the author's imagination or are used fictitiously. Any resemblance to events or persons, living or dead, is entirely coincidental.

This edition contains the complete text
of the original hardcover edition.
NOT ONE WORD HAS BEEN OMITTED.

WAKE THE DEAD
A Bantam Crime Line Book / published by arrangement with
Charles Scribner's Sons

PUBLISHING HISTORY
Charles Scribner's Sons edition published 1992
Bantam edition / November 1993

CRIME LINE *and the portrayal of a boxed "cl" are trademarks of Bantam Books,*
a division of Bantam Doubleday Dell Publishing Group, Inc.

All rights reserved.
Copyright © 1992 by Dorothy Simpson.
Cover art copyright © 1993 by Jack Unruh.
Library of Congress Catalog Card Number: 92-19962.
No part of this book may be reproduced or transmitted in any
form or by any means, electronic or mechanical, including
photocopying, recording, or by any information storage and
retrieval system, without permission in writing from the publisher.
For information address: Charles Scribner's Sons, Macmillan Publishing
Company, 866 Third Avenue, New York, NY 10022.

ISBN 0-553-56252-5

Published simultaneously in the United States and Canada

Bantam Books are published by Bantam Books, a division of Bantam
Doubleday Dell Publishing Group, Inc. Its trademark, consisting of the
words "Bantam Books" and the portrayal of a rooster, is Registered in
U.S. Patent and Trademark Office and in other countries. Marca Reg-
istrada. Bantam Books, 1540 Broadway, New York, New York 10036.

PRINTED IN THE UNITED STATES OF AMERICA
RAD   0 9 8 7 6 5 4 3 2 1

To Margaret and Brian,
whose courage and devotion were an
example to us all

WAKE
THE
DEAD

1

They were all three pretending to watch television while they waited. It was a sitcom, but none of them was laughing.

Thanet glanced at his watch. Eight-thirty. Enough was enough. 'Come on, let's eat.'

Ben jumped up with alacrity. 'Good. I'm starving.' He followed Joan into the kitchen.

'I'll open the wine.' Thanet crossed to the window for one last glance down the empty street before going into the dining room where the bottle of 1986 Chablis Leclos which he had been saving for just such an occasion stood in the cooler on the festive table. Snowy-white tablecloth, best cutlery and crystal glasses had been brought out for this special meal to celebrate the end of Ben's O level examinations. Where on earth were Bridget and Alexander, this new boyfriend of hers they'd heard so much about?

By now anger at their lateness was beginning to give way to anxiety. They should have been here long since—between seven and eight, Bridget had said. How safe a driver was Alexander? On a Friday evening the motorway from London was always crowded, but surely by now the traffic should have eased. Thanet hoped the meal was not spoiled. Joan had taken so much trouble over it. With Bridget a newly fledged Cordon Bleu professional cook working in the directors' dining room of a firm of London stockbrokers, her mother always felt she had to try to match her daughter's standards on occasions such as this.

The phone rang. Thanet got there first.

'Dad? It's me. Alexander's only just arrived, he got held up at the office. We're leaving now, so we should be there between half past nine and ten. Thought I'd better let you know, in case you were worried.'

'Right.'

Something in his tone must have alerted her. 'There's nothing wrong, is there? Dad?'

'No, not at all.'

But try as he might the note of false assurance came through. And Bridget, of course, knew him only too well.

'You haven't waited supper for us, have you? Oh, don't tell me Mum cooked a special meal!'

Thanet knew he shouldn't say it, but he couldn't stop himself. 'Well, Ben took the last of his O levels today . . .' There was no need to say any more. Bridget, he knew, would immediately envisage the whole scenario.

'Oh, no . . . Dad, I am sorry.'

'We should have told you. But you were so sure you'd be here between seven and eight . . .'

'And of course, Mum wanted it to be a surprise.'

Thanet now felt guilty at having made Bridget feel guilty. It wasn't her fault, after all. He tried to ignore the small, critical voice which insisted, *She could have rung earlier.* 'Never mind. As long as you're all right. We were just beginning to get a bit concerned, I must admit.'

'Oh, Dad, I'm sorry, I really am. I should have rung earlier. It's just that I thought there wasn't much point until Alexander actually got here.'

'Not to worry. We'll keep something hot for you.'

'No, don't do that. It'll be so late. Alexander said we'll pick up something on the way.'

'Right. See you later, then.'

Thanet recounted the conversation to the others.

'She could have let us know earlier,' grumbled Ben.

'She realises that now. She said so.'

'And why couldn't Alexander have rung her, if he knew he was going to be late?'

'Food!' said Joan, whisking plates into the dining room.

The prospect cheered them all up, the reality completed the process. Joan had excelled herself and Thanet couldn't help wishing that Bridget had been here to appreciate the fact: home-made pâté with wafer-thin curls of crisp melba toast; baked salmon stuffed with monkfish mousse in lobster sauce; bite-sized new potatoes in their jackets; mangetout peas, fresh broad beans and a delicious *mélange* of peppers, courgettes and mushrooms; then, to crown it all, a summer pudding stuffed with raspberries, blackcurrants and redcurrants, served with that most delectable of forbidden delights, fresh cream. And the wine was, they all agreed, superb.

By the time they heard a car pull up outside the mellowing process was complete.

'There they are.' Ben jumped up and went to the window. 'Wowwwww,' he breathed, his eyes opening wide in astonishment and admiration.

Thanet and Joan looked at each other with raised eyebrows. Ben was at an age when it was considered sophisticated to remain unimpressed by more or less everything.

'What?' Curiosity drove them both to join him at the window.

Ben was still gaping. 'A Porsche! She didn't tell us he had a Porsche!'

Thanet blinked. Ben was right. There it was, a sleek red low-slung schoolboy's dream, parked incongruously in their suburban drive behind the modest Astra provided for Joan by the Probation Service. And just getting out were Bridget and the much-vaunted Alexander. Thanet had no more than a fleeting impression of someone tall and fair before Joan tugged both him and Ben away from the window. 'Come on, stop goggling, you two! Your eyes are sticking out like chapel hat-pegs!'

They all went into the hall to greet them and a moment later the two young people came in in a flurry of apologies.

Hugs all round from Bridget and introductions made, Alexander handed Joan the tall gift-wrapped package he had been carrying in the crook of one arm. 'I'm terribly sorry to have inconvenienced you, Mrs Thanet. Brig tells me you cooked a special dinner.'

A plummy accent, Thanet noted, as Joan's eyes lit up with surprise and pleasure. And 'Brig'! Thanet suppressed the irrational spurt of indignation that this boy had already coined a special nickname for Bridget.

Alexander listened to Joan's It-really-doesn't-matter murmurs before turning to Thanet. 'I really must apologise, sir. Something came up at work and it simply couldn't wait until Monday.'

Sir! Thanet couldn't recall ever having been addressed thus before by the various young men Bridget had brought home over the past eighteen months. His hand was taken in a firm grip and two piercingly blue eyes met his in a gaze of unwavering sincerity. He could see why Bridget was so taken by Alexander. He was tall, well built and undeniably handsome, with regular features, fresh complexion and a thatch of golden curls. His clothes were casual but elegant: designer jeans and Boss T-shirt. He was older than Thanet had expected, twenty-seven or -eight, perhaps. Thanet suppressed a qualm of unease: altogether too experienced and sophisticated for Bridget, surely? He murmured an appropriate response.

Alexander turned to Ben. 'I do hope we didn't ruin your celebration. You took your last O level today, I gather?'

Bridget waited for Ben's reply and then said, 'Go on, Mum, open it!'

They all watched while Joan removed the wrapping paper. 'Oh, look!' she breathed. 'Isn't it beautiful!'

And there was no denying that it was, a handsome deep blue hydrangea with five blooms so perfect that they looked almost unreal.

Bridget and Alexander beamed.

'I've got a plant pot exactly that colour,' said Joan. 'It's in the cupboard under the stairs.'

The pot was produced, the hydrangea placed ceremonially in the centre of the hall table and then they all moved into the sitting room. Coffee was poured and they settled down to talk. Over the next hour or two Thanet's misgivings intensified. Alexander was patently out of their class. He was, as Thanet knew, a stockbroker, and it now emerged that he had been to Winchester and Oxford, having taken a year out (financed by 'the parents', as he put it) to travel around the world. You name it and it seemed that Alexander had done it, from crossing the Sahara in a jeep to backpacking in the Andes. Thanet watched Bridget listening to these traveller's tales with shining eyes and wondered: was this self-possessed and confident young man what he wanted for his daughter? Not, he acknowledged with an inward sigh, that it would make any difference what he wanted. Bridget would make up her own mind and they would have to go along with it.

Are you kind? he said silently to Alexander. *Are you considerate? Would you be faithful to her, good to her when things go badly? What sort of values have you got?*

He confided his unease to Joan later, when they were in bed.

'You're rather jumping the gun, aren't you?'

'I can't help thinking that way, whenever she brings someone home.'

'There's no reason to believe they're serious. To be honest, he struck me as the sort of young man who enjoys having a good time. I shouldn't think he'd be ready to settle down yet. And Bridget is only nineteen, far too young to be thinking about getting married.'

'And that's another thing. He's much older than I expected.'

Joan rolled over to kiss him. 'Stop worrying!'

'You haven't told me what you thought of him, yet.'

She sighed. 'I can understand what she sees in him, of course, but . . .'

'So there is a "but"!'

'Can't we talk about this in the morning, Luke? I'm so tired.'

He was immediately contrite. Joan had worked all day, then produced that wonderful meal . . . 'I'm sorry, love. Of course. At least I haven't got to go to work tomorrow, so I won't disturb you getting up early. You can have a lie-in.'

'I've heard that one before,' she said sleepily.

But for once it looked as though his free weekend really was going to be free. They all got up late, had a leisurely breakfast, then Bridget and Alexander announced that they were going to Rye for the day. Ben had plans of his own and Thanet and Joan had arranged to go along that afternoon and support the annual village fête in Thaxden, where Joan's mother lived. She had made an excellent recovery from her heart attack the previous year and as usual was helping on a stall.

'Wonderful day for it,' said Joan as they set off.

And it was. The sky was an unbroken blue and the July sun sufficiently strong for heatwaves to shimmer above the tarmac.

Thanet nodded. 'They should get a lot of people there.'

The Thaxden Fête was held annually at Thaxden Hall, home of the local MP, Hugo Fairleigh. As village fêtes go it was an elaborate affair, and usually raised large sums of money. The previous year over four thousand had been donated to various local charities and this year they were hoping to exceed that sum. Thanet thought they had a good chance; the proposed hospice in Sturrenden was a popular cause.

By the time Thanet and Joan arrived at 2.30 the fête was in full swing. No-parking cones lined the road through the village and a uniformed policeman was directing the traffic into a large field opposite the Hall. Hundreds of cars were already parked there and more were arriving all the time. Families were heading purposefully for the tall gates across the road, where gaily coloured bunting fluttered above a huge sign slung from tree to tree over the entrance. 'THAXDEN FETE. IN AID OF THE STURRENDEN HOSPICE APPEAL.' The blaring music of a fairground organ added to the general air of festivity.

'Looks promising,' said Joan.

'Certainly does. What time did it start?'

'Two o'clock. Jill Cochrane was opening it.'

Jill Cochrane was a well-known local television personality who was always generous of her time in supporting charitable events.

Pausing for a moment to admire the gaudily painted organ which stood just inside the gates, they strolled up the drive towards the front of the house, whose originally classic Georgian façade with five windows above and two either side of the porticoed front door below had, in Thanet's view, been spoiled by the later addition of two wings of unequal size at each end. He said so, to Joan. 'If it were mine, I'd have them down.'

'I don't suppose you would, you know. Very few people will actually sacrifice existing space, unless they have to.'

'Possibly. I don't know ... Look at that!'

In front of the house a lovingly restored World War Two Spitfire was surrounded by an admiring crowd. Its owner stood alongside, answering questions. Two old metal firebuckets stood nearby and people were tossing coins into them. Thanet admired the plane for a while, added his contribution, and then he and Joan began to work their way around the stalls and sideshows which encircled both lawns on either side of the drive and spread around the back of the house.

'Look, there's Mum.' Joan waved and headed for the WI stall, where Margaret Bolton and two other women were doing a brisk trade in home-made cakes, biscuits, jams and chutneys.

'Just as well I saved one for you,' she said, bending down to pick up a luscious-looking chocolate gâteau. 'We've practically sold out of cakes already.'

'Wonderful!' said Joan. 'Makes your mouth water to look at it, doesn't it, Luke?'

'Mmm?' Thanet was abstracted. He had just spotted Hugo Fairleigh, who was clearly fulfilling the host's duty of escorting Jill Cochrane around the fête.

'She looks stunning, doesn't she?' said Joan, following his gaze.

Jill was wearing a beautifully cut sleeveless linen sheath in a pale cucumber green.

'Yes.' Thanet's reply was automatic. Eye-catching though she was, it wasn't Jill who had captured his attention. He was wondering why Hugo Fairleigh was looking so—what was the word?—disconcerted, yes, that was it. The MP was watching someone or something intently and Thanet tried to work out who or what it was, but it was hopeless, there were so many people milling about.

Joan was handing over money for the cake. 'Could you hold on to it for me, Mum?'

'Yes, of course.'

'See you afterwards, then.'

They had arranged to go to Mrs Bolton's house for supper.

Half an hour later Thanet was trying his hand, unsuccessfully, at the coconut shy.

'Inferior *biceps brachii*,' murmured a voice in his ear, just as he released his last ball.

It went wide of its mark.

'Thanks a lot!' he said, turning around. He knew who it was, of course.

Doctor Mallard, the police surgeon, and Helen his wife were standing beside Joan. All three were smiling.

'I challenge you to do better!'

Mallard shook his head. 'I'm past it, I'm afraid. Twenty years ago I'd have taken you up on that. But now, well, a nice cup of tea would be more in my line. What do you say?'

Joan and Helen consulted each other with a glance, smiled and nodded. 'Lovely.'

'Good.'

The small marquee where the teas were being

served had been erected on the back lawn, presumably so that water was readily available from the Fairleighs' kitchen, and tables and chairs had been set up in front of it.

'Looks as though we'll have to wait,' said Thanet. 'They're all full.'

'No, look.' Joan pointed. 'Those people there are just going. And the table's in the shade.'

'We'll go and sit down,' said Helen. 'You get the tea.'

'What would you like to eat, love?' said Mallard.

'Oh, just a scone, I think. What about you, Joan?'

'The same.' She grinned. 'But you two men can indulge yourself in cakes, if you like.'

There was a short queue and Mallard insisted on paying. 'My invitation, my treat.'

They carried the tea tray across to the welcome shade and settled themselves with the women. Mallard took an appreciative sip. 'Ah, this is the life,' he said, sitting back in his chair. 'Beautiful day, beautiful surroundings . . .' He glanced from Joan to Helen. 'Beautiful women . . .'

'My word, you are in a good mood today, James,' said Joan, smiling.

'And why not? What more could I want, I ask myself?' He patted Helen's hand and they exchanged smiles.

So did Thanet and Joan. They never ceased to marvel at the transformation in Mallard since his second marriage. During the years following the death of his first wife from a slow, lingering cancer, they had wondered if Mallard would ever recover. The cheerful, dapper little man who sat with them this afternoon was scarcely recognisable as the testy, scruffy figure who at that time seemed certain to live out his life entrenched in a bitterness from which nothing could save him.

Until Helen had come on the scene, that is. Thanet,

who had known Mallard since childhood, would always
be grateful to her for rescuing his old friend—and
grateful, too, for what she had done for Bridget. Helen
Mallard was a well-known writer of cookery books and
throughout Bridget's adolescence had helped and encouraged her in her ambition to follow a career in
cookery.

It was as if she had tuned in to his thoughts.

'How's Bridget?' she asked.

Thanet noticed Hugo Fairleigh come out of the
house and hurry on to the lawn, looking about him
purposefully. He seemed agitated.

It was Joan who answered. 'Home this weekend, as
a matter of fact. With the latest boyfriend.' Joan pulled
a face. 'Luke's not too keen.'

'Why?' said Mallard. 'What's wrong with him?'

Thanet shrugged. 'Too—' He broke off. Fairleigh's
gaze had focused on Mallard and now he was coming
towards them.

Mallard, Helen and Joan turned to see what had
captured his attention.

'Doctor Mallard . . .'

Thanet had been right. The MP did look agitated—
distinctly upset, in fact.

Mallard rose.

'I'm so sorry to interrupt your afternoon, but I wonder if you could spare a moment?'

'Yes, of course.' Mallard glanced at the others. 'Excuse
me, will you?'

Fairleigh put a hand under Mallard's elbow, drawing
him away towards the house and stooping to murmur
in his ear. Then their pace accelerated.

'Wonder what's wrong,' said Joan.

Helen sighed. 'I knew he shouldn't have said that—
about everything being perfect. It was tempting fate.'

'It's one of the hazards of being a doctor, I suppose,'

said Joan. She glanced at Thanet. 'Rather like being a policeman. You're never really off duty.'

Helen smiled. 'I know. Even on holiday . . . James never lets on that he's a doctor, you know, not if he can help it.'

'I read an article by a doctor once, on that very subject.' Thanet grinned. 'It said that if there's an emergency on the beach, all the men sitting with their heads firmly down reading newspapers will be doctors. One quick glance to check that it's not their nearest and dearest involved and that's it, they just don't want to know.'

'I can believe it,' said Helen.

'Would you like some more tea, while we're waiting?' Thanet rose, picked up the women's cups as they nodded and said, yes, a good idea. Then he paused. 'Ah, there he is now.' He had just spotted Mallard come hurrying out of the back door, alone. The little doctor looked grim, he noticed. What now?

'Look, I'm sorry about this'—Mallard's gaze encompassed all three of his companions—'but I'm afraid I'm going to have to ask you, ladies, to excuse both of us.'

'Why? What's happened?' said Thanet. He put the cups down.

All three of them instinctively glanced around to see if they could be overheard and leaned forward as Mallard lowered his voice.

'It's Mr Fairleigh's mother. She died this afternoon.' Mallard patted Helen's arm and glanced from her to Joan. 'This is confidential, of course, but . . .' He looked squarely at Thanet. 'There's no doubt in my mind that she's been murdered.'

2

As he and Mallard hurried towards the house Thanet had already begun to make a mental list of priorities: call for assistance, contact Lineham, contact Draco, put someone on the gate to take down names and addresses. Thanet groaned inwardly as he tried to estimate how many people were here this afternoon—a thousand, fifteen hundred? Fifteen hundred possible suspects; no, you could cut that down because a lot of them were children, say seven hundred and fifty, then, or . . . He shook his head to clear it. What was he doing, counting suspects? There were a lot of them, that was the point. But before doing anything else and certainly before making an appropriate announcement over the loudspeakers he would have to check for himself that there was a strong possibility that old Mrs Fairleigh really had been murdered. Not that there was any doubt in his mind. The police surgeon was, after all, the very person they normally called in to confirm just that. For himself, he would have taken Doc Mallard's word without question, but he would have to play this by the book. Hugo Fairleigh was an important man and Super-intendent Draco might cast off his current lethargy and revert to normal, in which case he would have Thanet's guts for garters if anything went wrong.

'You mean to say you informed over a thousand mem-bers of the public that you would require them to give us their names and addresses without even bothering to check for yourself that there was good reason?'

'I knew I could rely on Doc Mallard's word, sir.'

'Just listen to me, Thanet. In my patch you never take the word of anyone who is not a trained member of this force without checking. No matter who he is.'

'But—'

'No one is infallible, Thanet, remember that. How did you know he wasn't joking?'

'He wouldn't . . .'

'And it was a hot day, wasn't it? Very hot. Hot enough to give someone sunstroke, especially if, like Doctor Mal-lard, you happen to be bald.'

'He was wearing a hat, sir. A Panama.'

'I don't care what sort of hat he was wearing! Are you being deliberately obtuse, Thanet? I'm simply making the point that a policemen can't afford to take anything for granted. Ever. Is that clear?'

'Yes, sir.'

They had almost reached the house and with an effort Thanet switched Draco off and stopped. There were one or two points he wanted to get clear before they went in. He noted that there were two doors in the back façade of the house: one at the far end of the central block which was the original house, one in the project-ing right-hand wing. This was the one to which Mallard had been leading him and was also the one through which helpers had been going in and out to fetch fresh supplies of water for the tea urns. 'Who did you leave with the body?'

'Don't worry, no one.' Mallard's hand dived into his pocket and produced a key. 'This was in the door, so I used it.' He grinned at Thanet over his half-moon spectacles. 'I watch television too, you know.'

'Where is Mr Fairleigh now?'

'With his wife. We ran into her on our way in and she came up with us.'

'Have you told them what you suspect?'

Mallard shook his head. 'I wanted to have a word with you, first, let you see for yourself.' He pulled a wry face. 'I suppose I was being a bit of a coward, really, wanted some moral support when I broke the news.'

'But you're certain, aren't you?'

Mallard nodded. 'I'm afraid so.'

'How did you explain coming to fetch me?'

Mallard looked shamefaced. 'Just said I wanted to fetch a colleague. Fairleigh seemed to accept it.'

'I'm surprised.'

'I don't think he was thinking straight.'

Fairleigh had looked pretty agitated, Thanet remembered. Even MPs are human, after all, and finding one's mother dead is a shock to anyone. And of course, if he had brought about that death himself, he wouldn't have liked to query anything Mallard suggested, however much he wanted to, in case it brought suspicion upon himself.

'What about locking the bedroom door? Didn't he find that a bit odd?'

'He doesn't know I have—or didn't, anyway. His wife was upset and he took her off somewhere.'

'So how did the old lady die?'

'She was smothered. A pillow over the head, I imagine. She was in bed, of course, and considerably weakened by the stroke Fairleigh told me she'd had about ten days ago. I suppose someone decided it was a good opportunity to finish her off.'

'Any sign of an intruder? Anything taken?'

Mallard shook his head. 'I don't suppose it would have entered Fairleigh's head to check. He seemed to take it for granted that the death was natural—it's the attitude you'd expect him to take whether he did it himself or not.'

So the murderer was almost certainly a member of the family, thought Thanet, as it usually was in such cases. Of course, the police would have to go through the motions, take all those names, conduct perhaps hundreds of interviews, but it would all be a monumental waste of time.

'Right, let's go in.'

The back door opened into a short quarry-tiled corridor leading off to the left. They could hear voices and the clatter of crockery coming from an open door a few yards along. A moment later a woman came out carrying a tray of clean cups and saucers. She frowned when she saw them.

'Can I help you?'

'No, thank you. We're on our way up to see Mr Fairleigh,' said Mallard.

Apparently satisfied she nodded and they flattened themselves against the wall for her to pass.

'Good thing you look so respectable,' said Thanet when she had disappeared through the back door. 'She might have thought we were burglars.'

But it wouldn't have been too difficult for someone to have waited until the coast was clear and then slipped in and up these stairs, he thought as he followed Mallard up a narrow staircase which had once, he guessed, been used exclusively by servants to gain access to the first floor.

He was relieved to find that, strangely enough, he

was not experiencing his usual apprehension of the first sight of the corpse. Normally he dreaded that moment, had to brace himself for it to the degree that for several minutes before he was almost incapable of coherent thought. It was a weakness with which he had never quite come to terms and he was grateful that this time he seemed to be getting off lightly. Was it perhaps because he knew that old Mrs Fairleigh's death had involved no obvious violence, that it had apparently appeared sufficiently peaceful to deceive her son—or allow him to hope that he could deceive others—into thinking that it had been natural?

They had almost reached the top of the stairs and Mallard turned. 'To the left,' he whispered, laying a finger on his lips.

Thanet understood at once, and nodded. Mallard didn't want Fairleigh to hear them.

Fortunately this upper corridor was thickly carpeted and their feet made no sound as they moved silently along. There were several doors set at intervals along the right-hand wall and windows spaced out along the left, overlooking the paved terrace and the tea tent on the lawn beyond.

This is ridiculous, thought Thanet. We look like a couple of conspirators. But he could understand Mallard's caution. The police surgeon wanted to be certain that he had the backing of the police before facing Fairleigh.

This was the calm before the storm.

Mallard had the key ready in his hand and now he stopped, inserted it and turned it as quietly as he could.

The bedroom was light and spacious, with pale green fitted carpet and floor-length chintz curtains at the tall sash windows. Thanet had no time for more than a fleeting impression; his attention was focused on the still figure in the high, old-fashioned mahogany bed. He and Mallard advanced and stood side by side looking down at the old woman. The pillow beneath her head, he noted, was slightly askew.

Even in death her strength of character was evident in the firm chin, jutting prow of a nose and deeply etched frown lines on her forehead. She must, Thanet thought, have been a rather formidable person; intolerant, probably, and uncomfortable to live with—ultimately, perhaps, her own worst enemy. Which of her nearest and dearest, he wondered, had finally found her living presence intolerable?

What did you do, or say, that drove someone over the edge? he asked her silently.

What had she thought or felt in those final moments when she must have realised that a familiar face had become filled with murderous intent? If only, he thought, we could wake the dead and hear what they had to tell us. How much simpler it would all be, how much pain could be avoided for those innocent bystanders caught up in the merciless searchlight of a murder investigation.

Apart from the pillow—and its position could so easily be taken for normal that in itself it would certainly not have alerted anyone to a suspicion of foul play—he could see no sign that she had met a violent end, but Mallard was bending forward, pointing out this and that, lifting an eyelid to reveal the burst blood capillaries in the eyes. Thanet's sense of smell had already drawn his attention to a further common sign of suffocation, the voiding of bladder and rectum.

Mallard straightened up. 'So, you see what I mean.'

'Now you've pointed it out, yes. Otherwise I'd never have suspected.' He sighed. 'I wonder just how often murder is committed and no one ever does suspect.'

'More often than we'd care to think, I'm sure, especially in circumstances like this. GPs are busy people, and if a patient has had a major stroke, as she had, death would come as no surprise, her doctor would be half expecting it.'

'So you're saying that if Mrs Fairleigh's own doctor had been called in, instead of you, he would probably have issued a death certificate without a second thought?'

'Highly likely, I should think. Not that I'm casting doubt on the competence of her GP, I don't even know who he is.'

'Unlucky for whoever did this, then, that Mr Fairleigh happened to alight on you. I gather he knew you're a doctor. Did he also know you're a police surgeon?'

'Not to my knowledge. He might, I suppose. I only know him slightly, we've met a few times at local Conservative functions.'

'But why fetch you? Why not send for Mrs Fairleigh's own GP?'

Mallard shrugged. 'I assume he wanted to get a doctor to her as quickly as possible just in case anything could be done, unlikely as that seemed. It was a perfectly understandable reaction, in my view. She was still warm, you see, very recently dead.'

'So you'd say she died within the last hour, say?'

'Yes. I don't think I could narrow it down further than that.'

Thanet glanced at his watch, made a mental note. Four-ten. He made up his mind. 'Right, we'll get going, then. We'd better have some photos before you make any further examination.'

The door had opened as he was speaking and Hugo Fairleigh came in. 'I thought I heard voices.' He gave Thanet a searching look and said to Mallard, 'Who's this? What further examination? What's going on?'

The MP was tall and well groomed, with straight fair

hair brushed back and Cambridge blue eyes. He had inherited his mother's firm chin and strong nose. He was immaculately dressed in cream linen suit, white shirt and discreet tie. He possessed, as Thanet knew, considerable charm, which at the moment was conspicuously absent. The blue eyes were frosty, the jutting chin more prominent than usual.

Thanet did not envy Mallard the task of breaking the news.

The little doctor had obviously decided to waste no time beating about the bush. 'I'm afraid I have some bad news for you, Mr Fairleigh.'

Fairleigh's eyebrows rose.

'I have good reason to believe that your mother did not die a natural death. I therefore felt it my duty to call in the police before proceeding any further. This is Detective Inspector Thanet of Sturrenden CID. I knew he was at the fête, I'd seen him earlier.'

There was a moment's silence. Fairleigh blinked, then his eyes travelled briefly over Thanet's off-duty attire of cotton trousers and pale blue T-shirt.

Something would have to be done about clothes, Thanet realised. He could hardly launch into a murder investigation dressed like this, especially in a house like Thaxden Hall. He must remember to ask Lineham to bring something more appropriate out with him. Fortunately he and the sergeant were roughly the same build.

'You can't be serious.' Fairleigh's tone was icy.

'I'm afraid I am. All too serious.'

Fairleigh glanced from Mallard to Thanet and then advanced to look incredulously down at his mother's body. 'But she was ill. Seriously ill. I told you, she had a severe stroke ten days ago, and we were told then that she could well have another one that could be fatal. So this came as no surprise. A shock, of course, but no surprise.' He turned back to Mallard. 'I'm sorry, I'm afraid I must insist on a second opinion.'

'That is your right, sir,' said Thanet politely. 'But before you proceed perhaps I should inform you that Doctor Mallard is our police surgeon, and is very experienced in such matters. If you could listen, first, to his reasons for having come to this conclusion . . .'

Fairleigh's eyes narrowed and he hesitated.

Thanet watched him closely. He could understand the man's dilemma. If he was himself the murderer he must be kicking himself now for not having called in his mother's own doctor, and especially for having called in one who turned out to be a police surgeon. So what should be the best course of action? Should he play the outraged innocent, make as much fuss as possible, invoke perhaps the influence of higher authorities? Or would it be better to try to hush the whole thing up as far as possible? Guilty or innocent, it would be in his own interest not to antagonise the police, and in either case he would want to be seen as a right-minded citizen, anxious to cooperate with the authorities and detect his mother's murderer as soon as possible.

Yes, Fairleigh would now back-track, Thanet decided.

He was right.

Fairleigh's lips tightened. 'Very well,' he said stiffly. His eyes focused on Mallard in fierce concentration as the little doctor began to talk.

When Mallard had finished Fairleigh turned away and walked across to the window, his hands clasped behind him. The knuckles, Thanet noticed, were white. The man was restraining himself only by a considerable effort of self-control and was no doubt thinking furiously.

Thanet and Mallard waited.

Finally Fairleigh took a deep breath and let it out slowly in a long release of tension. Thanet saw the rigid shoulders relax, the grip of his hands slacken. He turned to face them.

'Very well,' he repeated. 'You've convinced me.' He shoved his right hand in his trouser pocket and began to jingle the coins or keys in it. 'My God, it's against all belief or reason, but you have convinced me. You'd better get on with whatever you have to do.' The chinking sound betrayed his agitation and he must have realised because he snatched his hand out of the pocket and rested it inside on the windowsill. He glanced out at the crowds below. 'You're going to have your work cut out, aren't you?'

The implication was obvious. Fairleigh was trying to ensure that from the outset it was accepted that the crime had been committed by an intruder.

Thanet decided to play along for the moment. It would be to his advantage to allow the murderer, if he were one of the family, to be off guard, think himself safe.

'You may already be too late, of course. I shouldn't think he'll have hung around.'

Thanet became brisk. 'I'll get things moving, then. First, we'll have to put someone on the gate to take names and addresses.'

'Our local bobby is outside, directing traffic,' said Fairleigh.

Thanet nodded. 'Fine, we'll get him to do it. I'll put out an announcement over the loudspeakers, say there's been an accident and we'll be looking for witnesses. Then I'll call in my team. Meanwhile, we'll have to lock this door.'

'Right. If you don't mind using the phone in here for your calls, as you know the way . . . I must get back to my wife. This has all been rather a shock for her, of course, and I can't imagine how she'll react when she hears . . .'

Thanet would have liked to watch young Mrs Fairleigh's reaction himself, but he really had to get someone on the gate as soon as possible, just in case. 'As soon as I've got things organised I'll want to talk to the rest of the family. I'll need to find out if anyone saw anything.'

'Right. We'll be in my mother's sitting room. It's the room next door to this.'

'I'll fetch my bag, and tell Helen not to wait,' said Mallard in Thanet's ear as they followed Fairleigh out of the room. 'She can take the car, no doubt someone will give me a lift home. What about Joan?'

'Ditto. Tell her I'll get Lineham to drop me at her mother's house. If I'm later than 10.30, I'll go straight home.'

There was a buzz of excited conversation after the announcement as people speculated as to the nature of the accident. Then Thanet returned to Mrs Fairleigh's bedroom. It wasn't the place he would have chosen to make his phone calls, with the old lady's body lying there awaiting the indignities to which it would shortly be subjected, but Fairleigh had given him no choice. Spreading a clean handkerchief across his palm before picking up the receiver he rang Lineham first. Fortunately the sergeant was on duty this weekend.

Lineham's whistle down the phone when he heard the news made Thanet's ear ring.

'No need to deafen me, Mike.'

'But Mr Fairleigh's mother! Is this going to cause a stink! Does the Super know yet?'

'No. I'm just going to ring him.'

'Isn't he in London again this weekend?'

Angharad Draco was undergoing treatment for leukaemia, which involved regular trips to a London hospital. Draco always drove her up and fetched her and, whenever possible, stayed there. He adored his wife and the change in the dynamic little Welshman since the diagnosis had been dramatic. The man who had once said that he wanted to know if anyone so much as sneezed in his patch now merely kept things ticking over, an automaton whose attention was more or less permanently engaged elsewhere. More or less, Thanet reminded himself. With the Fairleighs involved this might well be a case of less rather than more.

'I'd forgotten. Yes. I'll give him a ring at the hospital.'

'I'll just get the SOCOs organised, rustle up some reinforcements, and I'll be on my way.'

'Right. Oh, Mike, just one more thing. Could you make time to call in at your house on the way to pick up some clothes for me?'

Lineham understood at once. 'Yes, sure. What would you like?'

'A shirt, a tie, and a lightweight jacket.'

'Trousers OK?'

'They'll do.'

'What colour are they?'

'What does it matter? Fawn.'

'Just wanted to make sure the jacket matched.'

'Mike, I'm not taking part in a fashion parade. Just bring me something more suitable, that's all.'

'OK, sir. I'll see what I can do.'

Thanet tried the hospital but Draco had gone out. He left a message and then went along the corridor to the sitting room. Here he found Mallard, Fairleigh and a third person, a woman. It wasn't Fairleigh's wife, Thanet knew Grace Fairleigh by sight. This was a stranger.

3

'Ah, Inspector,' said Fairleigh. 'This is my aunt, Miss Ransome. She and my mother share—shared—this flat. Letty, this is Inspector Thanet.'

No one would ever have taken them for sisters, thought Thanet. Apart from the age difference—Miss Ransome, he guessed, was a good five years younger than Mrs Fairleigh, in her late sixties, probably—this woman would have faded into the background anywhere. She was slight, dowdily dressed in a long-sleeved limp summer dress in floral pastels. She wore no make-up and her straight brown thinning hair streaked with grey was scraped back into a bun, untidy wisps escaping around the sides and at the back of the neck. She was clutching the wooden arms of the chair in which she sat as if to prevent the foundations of her world from rocking. As she glanced up at Thanet and murmured an acknowledgement to the introduction she kept her head down and raised only her eyes, as if expecting to be browbeaten or reprimanded. Had this been her habitual reaction to the woman who lay dead in the next room? Thanet remembered the arrogance of that profile and wondered: had Mrs Fairleigh put down her younger sister once too often?

Miss Ransome had now taken a wisp of lace handkerchief from the pocket of her dress and was dabbing at the tears which had begun to trickle down her cheeks.

'I just can't believe it. Such a terrible shock. We were half expecting her to go, but to think that someone . . .' She shook her head, looked in despair at the useless scrap of material in her hand and accepted with gratitude the immaculately folded white handkerchief which Fairleigh now took from his breast pocket and handed to her.

'Thank you, dear.'

'Miss Ransome,' said Thanet gently, 'I'm afraid I shall need to talk to you at some point, but I can see that you're very upset at the moment. A little later on, perhaps?'

She blew her nose and nodded. 'Yes, of course.' She glanced up at her nephew. 'Perhaps it would be better if I joined Grace?'

'A good idea. My wife,' he explained to Thanet. 'She has gone to wait in our own drawing room, away from . . .' His eyes flickered in the direction of his mother's bedroom. 'I thought it would be best. Understandably, she is very upset. A friend of hers is with her.' He bent solicitously over his aunt. 'Caroline is with Grace, Letty.' He put a hand under her elbow to help her up. 'Let me take you down to join them.'

'You'll come back up, sir?' said Thanet.

Fairleigh nodded. 'I'll only be a few minutes.' He put an arm around his aunt's shoulders and ushered her gently from the room.

Thanet used the time to fill Mallard in on the arrangements he had made and to look around the room, which was comfortably furnished with faded oriental rugs, curtains and loose covers in floral chintz. There was rather too much furniture for his taste, though, all of it antique and polished to a mirror-like gloss, each piece cluttered with ornaments, pieces of porcelain, photographs in silver frames and table lamps.

The room was on the side of the house and Thanet crossed to look out. The crowds had thinned considerably and one or two of the stallholders were beginning to pack up. Mallard had ensconced himself in an armchair beside the fireplace and seemed quite content to wait, tapping his fingers on the arm of the chair in time to a tune he was whistling softly between his teeth. Thanet had just worked out that it was 'The Skye Boat Song' when Fairleigh returned.

'Oh God,' he said. 'What a day! I still can't believe this is happening.' He sat down and waved Thanet to follow suit. He took out a packet of low-tar cigarettes and offered it around before lighting one. He inhaled deeply. 'Now, what did you want to ask me?'

'If you could just give me a general picture of what's been happening here today? I imagine it's been fairly hectic.'

Fairleigh took another drag at his cigarette and groaned, the smoke issuing from his mouth in a thin stream. 'I don't know why we do this every year, I really don't. We must be mad.'

Thanet thought he knew why. It was because it was good for Fairleigh's public image, to be seen to be prepared to put himself to considerable effort and inconvenience for the sake of charity.

Fairleigh contemplated the glowing tip of his cigarette. 'Well, let me see. It got off to a bad start with the day nurse ringing to say that she was sick and wouldn't be in today. The night nurse had just gone home and the agency couldn't supply another at such short notice so we decided we'd somehow have to manage to look after Mother ourselves.'

'That was at what time?'

'Around 8.15, I should think.'

'And "we" being . . . ?'

'Well it had to be my wife, chiefly, as far as this afternoon was concerned. The rest of us—my aunt and I, that is—would be fully occupied. I had to be present at the opening to introduce Jill Cochrane and then to escort her around the stalls and so on, and my aunt was helping to run one of the stalls. We had deliberately left my wife free to deal with any last-minute emergencies that came up, there's always something on an occasion like this. And whereas we'd normally be able to get someone from the village in to help, everyone was involved with the fête. We did manage to find someone to sit with Mother this morning, fortunately, a Mrs Brent, but she was helping with the teas this afternoon, so my wife said she'd take over after lunch. She couldn't stay with Mother all the time, but we decided that if she looked in on her every half an hour or so that should be sufficient. It wasn't as though she needed constant attention.'

'I gather she had a stroke around ten days ago.'

'That's right. On 30 June.'

'Was it serious?'

'Pretty severe, yes. Which was why I wasn't surprised when I looked in this afternoon and found her dead.' He compressed his lips and stubbed out his cigarette with more force than was necessary. 'I never dreamed . . . Anyway, yes, the stroke left her paralysed down one side and unable to make anything but unintelligible noises. She seemed to understand what was said to her, but she had to be fed, washed, looked after like a baby, really. She must have hated the indignity of it all.'

'Did she go into hospital?'

'Oh yes, for the first week. But when there had been no noticeable change in her condition by then, it seemed that it was likely to be a long slow process and she had made me promise that if anything like this ever happened to her, that I would make sure she was nursed at home. She wanted to die in her own bed, she said.' He grimaced. 'Well, she did, didn't she? It would have been better if I'd disregarded her wishes and left her in the hospital. At least there she would have been safe.'

'Had her condition improved, since coming home?'

'A slight improvement only. Over the last day or two she had begun to regain a little movement in her fingers.'

'What about the side that was not paralysed? Was she able to move her arm?'

'Yes. But she didn't, much.' He frowned. 'She just lay there.'

'So she wouldn't have been able to put up much of a struggle, you think.'

The muscles at the side of Fairleigh's jaw tightened as he clenched his teeth and shook his head. 'I shouldn't think so, no.'

Mallard cleared his throat and crossed his legs and Thanet glanced at him, raising his eyebrows in case the doctor had something to say, but Mallard shook his head.

'Perhaps we could go back to this morning, then. What happened after the nurse rang?'

Fairleigh shrugged. 'My wife and I had breakfast, then she went up to see to my mother, I believe my aunt helped her. Mrs Brent arrived at about 9.30 and took over. We had a pretty busy morning, as you can imagine, getting ready for the fête, and I was outside most of the time. Around one we all had a sandwich lunch.'

'All?'

'My wife and I, my aunt, Mrs Brent and Sam.'

'Sam?'

'Samantha Young, our housekeeper. She'd been working outside most of the morning too, she mucks in with everything, she's practically one of the family. Perhaps I should explain that although we all live under the same roof, we run two entirely separate establishments here. My mother and my aunt have their own entrance, their own housekeeper, and take all their meals here in their own wing. We used to see each other, of course, but not much more than if we'd been next-door neighbours.'

'Are there any internal connecting doors?'

'Yes, two, one upstairs and one down, but they are very rarely used ... Look, is all this relevant, Inspector?'

'I'm just trying to get the general picture. It's important for me to understand how one gains access to your mother's room.'

'Yes, I see. Well as far as this afternoon's concerned, there was only one way.'

Thanet raised his eyebrows.

'Through the door by which you came in, downstairs near the kitchen. For security reasons we always lock the front and back doors of the main house on occasions such as this, and shut the downstairs windows and draw the curtains. It makes sense, don't you agree?'

'Very sensible.' But members of the family would presumably have keys, Thanet thought, and if there was a connecting door upstairs it would have been easy to slip through and into old Mrs Fairleigh's room with none of the women coming and going in the corridor downstairs any the wiser.

'So, you all had lunch at around one. Then what?'

'I went back outside for a last-minute check before going up to change. A few minutes before two Jill Cochrane arrived. At two she opened the fête and after that I was with her most of the time until I came in for a pee.'

Fairleigh was rubbing the side of his nose. Thanet was instantly alerted. This was an unconscious gesture frequently indulged in by someone who was being evasive or, more importantly, lying. And yes, Fairleigh was looking directly at him, holding his gaze as if to demonstrate how transparently truthful he was being.

If they were trying to hide the truth, rogues and villains would often become defiant at this point, as if challenging the interviewer to disprove what they were saying, or else they would find themselves unable to meet his eyes and would look shifty. But many people believed that direct eye contact was tantamount to proof of innocence, unaware that there were other ways in which they were simultaneously betraying themselves. Also, of course, the experienced policeman learned over the years to trust his instinct. Yes, he would certainly have to go into that 'most of the time' in more detail later, thought Thanet. But for the moment he let it pass.

Meanwhile his face betrayed none of his suspicions. 'What time was that?'

Fairleigh thought for a moment. 'It must have been . . .'

There was a knock at the door.

Fairleigh turned his head. 'Come in!'

It was Lineham, Thanet was glad to see, carrying a small suitcase which presumably contained the promised change of clothes. Thanet wished the sergeant could have arrived just a few minutes earlier, to confirm his impression that Fairleigh was lying. He and Lineham had worked together for so long that without the sergeant he felt as though he were operating on three cylinders. Lineham was his extra eyes and ears when his own had too much to assimilate, his second pair of hands in times of crisis, the sounding board against which theories were tested, the stimulation he needed to see possibilities unthought of.

He introduced Lineham to Fairleigh. 'Mr Fairleigh was just telling me what happened this afternoon. You were saying you came in at . . . ?'

'About half past three, I suppose, or a little later.'

The blue eyes still held Thanet's, unwavering. If he were lying, was it because he wanted to cover up what had happened before half past three, or after?

'I could have used the downstairs cloakroom, but to be honest I was glad to get away from the crowds for a bit, so I deliberately spun out my time inside by going up to our own bathroom. Then I thought, while I was in I might as well look in on Mother. So I came in through the connecting door and found her'—he shook his head grimly and waved his hand in the direction of the bedroom—'as you saw her.'

'That would have been, what? Around twenty to four, then?'

'Something like that, yes.'

'During the time that you were in the house, did you see anyone else?'

Fairleigh shook his head.

'Any sign of disturbance, anything in the least unusual?'

'No.' Fairleigh suddenly stood up and took a few agitated steps towards the window before turning. 'I just don't understand it! I suppose he was making for my mother's dressing table, where she kept her jewellery, when he realised she was there. But why do what he did? I mean, it was obvious she was helpless, for God's sake. And with all that din going on outside no one would have been able to hear her if she did call for help.' He took his cigarettes out and lit one with angry puffs. 'The whole thing is my fault, my responsibility. I should have made damned sure that someone was with her all the time.'

If Fairleigh were innocent this was something he would always reproach himself with, Thanet knew. But if not, well, he was putting on a fine show.

'Or if I'd been just a few minutes earlier . . . My wife says she came up to check on Mother at ten past three, and everything was all right then.'

If that were true, the period during which the murder had been committed had now become reduced to half an hour.

'Later on, after the Scenes-of-Crime officers have finished, we'll ask you to check whether or not anything is missing.' Thanet glanced at Lineham. 'I imagine they'll be here soon?'

'Any minute, now, sir, I should think.'

Fairleigh nodded. 'Right.'

'There's just one other point, then. Is there anyone who perhaps had a grudge against your mother? An ex-employee, for example, who might consider himself unfairly treated? Someone whom she might have antagonised in the past?'

Fairleigh looked horrified. 'You're not suggesting this might have been planned, *deliberate*? Good God, Inspector, she was a helpless old woman. Who could possibly have had any reason to wish her harm?'

Who indeed? *Cui bono?* thought Thanet. Who benefits? The old lady might well have been a wealthy woman, and Fairleigh, to his knowledge, her only son and heir—a point he would have to check. And then, however much Fairleigh pooh-poohed the idea, there was another classic motive, revenge. Who knew what harm or injury the old woman might have committed in the past? If someone had long held a grudge against her, what better time would there have been to execute vengeance than now, when she was helpless to defend herself and there was no nurse on duty to act as watchdog? Sooner or later it was going to dawn on Fairleigh that the police investigation was concentrating on the family, and Thanet had no doubt that that was when the storm would break. But for the moment it would be easier all round if he allowed the MP to go on thinking that his suggestion of an intruder was accepted by the police as the most likely possibility.

Thanet rose. 'Well, thank you for being so patient, sir.'

'What now, Inspector?'

'First, I'd like to change. Sergeant Lineham has brought me more suitable clothes.'

'There's a bathroom next door.'

'And then I'd like a word with your wife and your aunt. I must check if they saw anything suspicious during the afternoon. They'll have had a little time to compose themselves and think about it.'

If he was right, and one of the members of Mrs Fairleigh's family had seized the opportunity to finish her off, the circle of suspects was small: Fairleigh himself, his aunt, his wife.

He was eager to find out what the other two had to say for themselves.

4

The clothes fitted reasonably well and, feeling more comfortable now, Thanet emerged from the bathroom to find Fairleigh and Lineham waiting for him in the corridor outside. Fairleigh led them to a door which opened on to a broad landing in the main house with a white-painted balustrade overlooking the spacious hall below. The carpet was soft, the walls hung with prints and paintings, the air faintly scented by a huge bowl of pot-pourri on a sidetable and the fresh flowers in an arrangement near the top of the curving staircase. The effect was of carefully maintained luxury. Samantha was evidently an efficient housekeeper.

Fairleigh led them down the stairs and across the hall.

'In here,' he said, pushing open a door.

The room was large, square and elegant and seemed to swim in a dim, sub-aqueous light. The curtains, drawn for the afternoon against prying eyes, had been pulled back only a few inches and the delicate greens, turquoises and creams of curtains and upholstery melted into each other, blurring the outlines of the furniture. The shadowy forms of the three women in the room briefly lost definition as they turned towards the door.

'God,' said Fairleigh, striding across to the windows, 'it's like a morgue in here.' He froze, briefly. 'Sorry,' he muttered. 'Not the best choice of word, in the circumstances.' He fumbled at the side of the curtains and they rolled smoothly back. The movement attracted the attention of a passerby, who turned his head and glanced curiously at Hugo. Beyond him a lorry was backing slowly towards the house, cars and vans edging around it. Fairleigh clicked his tongue impatiently and narrowed the gap between the curtains. Then he adjusted those at the other window, too.

'That's better. Grace, this is Inspector Thanet and Sergeant—Lineham, was it? Yes. Inspector, this is my wife.'

Grace Fairleigh was sitting beside another woman—her friend Caroline, presumably—on the sofa. Caroline had an arm around her shoulders. Thanet had seen the MP's wife before of course, at public functions with her husband, and had glimpsed her here and there earlier on. She was tall and slender, with a cloud of black hair and regular, well-formed features. Her eyes were especially beautiful, large, dark and lustrous. This afternoon she looked very tense, her lips compressed, hands clasped tightly in her lap. She acknowledged her husband's introduction with a tight nod at Thanet.

'And this is Miss Plowright, a friend of my wife's.'

Not 'of ours', Thanet noted. He had seen Caroline Plowright before, too, around and about in Sturrenden. He noticed that Fairleigh made no move to approach his wife and comfort her, seeming quite content to leave her to Caroline's ministrations.

'My aunt, Miss Ransome, you have of course already met. And now, Inspector, if that's all you want of me at the moment, there are a hundred and one things I ought to be attending to outside.'

'By all means go and see to them.'

'If you want me you know where to find me.'

And Fairleigh hurried out with almost indecent haste. Was he being unfair to the man? Thanet wondered. It was true that there must, indeed, be a great deal to see to outside, but nothing, surely, that was so urgent as to prevent a husband staying to give moral support to a distressed wife in circumstances such as these?

Caroline Plowright was watching him with a slightly sardonic expression, as if she knew what he was thinking. She was the complete antithesis of her friend— short, solidly built, with meaty arms and shoulders and legs almost as thick at the ankles as at the calf. Her face was broad, with an almost Slavonic tilt to eyes and cheekbones, her short fair hair cut in a square, uncompromising bob. In contrast to Grace, who was wearing an elegant suit of lemon-coloured linen, Caroline's dress was a straight up and down white shift patterned with huge scarlet poppies. She was not wearing a wedding ring. An interesting woman, Thanet thought, not afraid to be noticed despite her physical disadvantages, and with a mind of her own. Observant, too, and therefore potentially useful.

The question now was, how to proceed? Once again he was faced with the perennial dilemma: how to treat a possible suspect who could well be innocent?

'Mrs Fairleigh, I know you must be very upset by all this and I'm sorry to trouble you but I'm afraid that in the circumstances I have to ask you a few questions.'

It was Caroline Plowright who responded. She was watching Grace Fairleigh's reaction anxiously and spared Thanet only a brief glance. 'Is it absolutely necessary to do this now, Inspector? Can't it wait?'

'It's best to deal with it while today's events are fresh in people's minds, Miss Plowright.'

Grace Fairleigh gave Caroline's arm a dismissive pat. 'It's all right, Caroline, really. The inspector is only doing his job. I don't see how I can help, but . . .' She gestured. 'Please, go ahead. And do sit down.'

Automatically, Thanet and Lineham chose seats where they could see the faces of everyone present.

'If you and Miss Ransome could just fill me in on some background information?'

He gave Letty Ransome a questioning glance and she sat up straighter and nodded. He was pleased to see that she was looking much more composed.

'Of course. Anything we can do, to get this dreadful business cleared up as quickly as possible. Though, like Grace, I don't really see how we can help.'

'I'm just trying to get a general picture of the household, what has happened here today. And of course, I especially want you to try to remember if you saw anything, anything at all, however trivial, out of the ordinary.'

They consulted each other with a glance and shook their heads.

'Well, something might come back to you as we talk.'

Neither of them had yet begun to relax, he thought, as he took them through the events of the morning, Grace Fairleigh sitting bolt upright with hands still clasped in her lap and Letty Ransome tugging nervously at one corner of the handkerchief which her nephew had lent her. They both confirmed what Fairleigh had said. After the phone call from the day nurse and an unsuccessful attempt to get another nurse from the agency, Grace had spent some time ringing around to try and find someone to sit with her mother-in-law during the morning. Eventually Mrs Brent had agreed to come in at 9.30. Grace had then gone across to the other wing to tell Letty what had happened and together she and Letty had attended to the old lady and given her breakfast. As Grace was the only person in the household without a specific task at the fête, she had volunteered to check on her mother-in-law every half an hour or so during the afternoon. Letty had given her sister lunch at 12.30, before going down to join the others for sandwiches at one, in the main house.

Now that they were approaching the time of the murder Thanet's interest quickened.

'So what happened after lunch? Mrs Fairleigh?'

Grace shrugged. 'I went up to change. Then I went along to check that my mother-in-law was all right.'

'What time would that have been?'

'About a quarter to two. I made her comfortable, then left, saying I'd be back in half an hour or so to see if she wanted anything.'

'She understood you?'

'Oh yes, certainly. Not for the first few days after her stroke, perhaps, but then she gradually began to respond to simple questions. She had movement on one side, you see.'

'We'd hold her fingers,' said Letty eagerly. 'And she'd give one squeeze for yes, two for no. And over the last day or two the movement was beginning to come back in her paralysed hand. We all thought she was on the mend.' Tears began to flow again and she wiped them away with the crumpled ball that was now Hugo's handkerchief. She shook her head. 'Oh, I know the doctor said she could have another stroke at any time but this . . . Oh, it's dreadful, really dreadful.'

Was he imagining it, or had she peeped at him over the corner of the handkerchief to see what effect her tears were having on him? If so, was it coincidence, he wondered, that Letty Ransome had broken down just as they were approaching that crucial mid-afternoon period?

Grace rose and went to perch on the arm of Letty's chair, putting her arm around the older woman's shoulders and patting her arm. 'Try not to upset yourself too much, Letty. It won't help us find out who did this, will it? We must try to stay calm.'

Caroline had that sardonic look in her eyes again. Why? Thanet wondered. Was it because she didn't believe Letty Ransome's display of grief to be genuine? Yes, he must arrange to have a private word with Miss Caroline Plowright as soon as possible. If anyone could help him to understand this family, she could.

Letty was blowing her nose and sniffing. 'Yes, yes, you're right, of course you are. I'm sorry,' she said to the room at large. 'Making an exhibition of myself . . .'

'Understandable, in the circumstances,' said Thanet, somehow managing to sound both sympathetic and brisk. 'But I'm sure we all want to clear this up as soon as possible. So if we could go back to what you were saying, Mrs Fairleigh?'

With a final glance to check that Letty was now sufficiently composed Grace returned to her seat beside Caroline.

There was a knock at the door. Reinforcements had arrived, including the SOCOs. Lineham went off to deal with them.

'So,' said Thanet, trying to pick up the threads yet again, 'on that occasion you must have left your mother-in-law at about ten or five to two?'

'At five to. I kept an eye on the time because I wanted to be there for the opening at two. I just made it.'

'So when did you go up next?'

'At 2.30.'

'And Mrs Fairleigh senior was all right then?'

'Yes. Fine—well, just the same as usual. I gave her a drink, plumped up her pillows and so on.'

'So you stayed, what, five minutes or so?'

'Yes. Then I went up again at about ten past three. And yes, she was still all right. I was going to go up again at a quarter to four—in fact I was actually on my way when I ran into my husband, with Doctor Mallard. He told me he'd looked in on her a few minutes before, and found her . . . found her dead. It could only just have happened, he said, she was still warm, so he'd fetched a doctor, just in case anything could be done. I . . . I couldn't believe it, I'd only left her half an hour earlier. So I went up with them. And when I saw her she . . . she looked so peaceful, we had no idea there was any question of . . . anything wrong.' She took a deep breath, let it out in a sigh. 'However prepared you are, death always comes as a shock, doesn't it? And when it's . . . when there's . . .' She shook her head. 'It's difficult to take it in.'

Caroline was watching her friend with a curiously assessing look.

What was she trying to assess? Thanet wondered. The truth of Grace Fairleigh's story, or the sincerity of her reaction to the old lady's death? Isobel Fairleigh couldn't have been the easiest of mothers-in-law, he thought, remembering that proud, arrogant profile, the determined lines etched into the dead face. And although the two households had, according to Fairleigh, existed independently, their proximity must have caused problems at times, made the relationship between husband and wife more difficult. Who knew what humiliations Grace may have suffered in the past, the degree of suppressed resentment she may have bottled up for years? Perhaps the temptation of having the old woman at her mercy had proved too much for her? On the other hand, even if old Mrs Fairleigh had been difficult when active, her stroke would surely have eased the situation. A helpless invalid, though an inconvenience, would have been far easier to deal with than an interfering battle-axe, especially when the day-to-day drudgery of looking after her was dealt with by trained nurses. Watching Grace Fairleigh, he wondered if she was in any case capable of the degree of cold-blooded vindictiveness necessary deliberately to finish off someone unable to defend herself. The same applied, of course, to Letty Ransome.

'And what about you, Miss Ransome?' he said, switching his attention. 'What did you do after lunch?'

She was composed again, had listened intently to Grace's account of the afternoon. She looked startled when Thanet addressed her.

'Me? Oh, I, well, I went straight out into the garden to see if any more stuff had come in for my stall and needed pricing. I was on the white elephant stall, you see, people kept on bringing things in all morning, and it's so difficult to decide how much to charge. Some of it was quite good stuff, but you know what it's like on these occasions, people expect to be able to pick things up for next to nothing, and judging exactly the right amount to ask, well, it takes time.' She flushed, ugly red blotches appearing on the sallow skin of face and neck. 'I'm sorry, you don't want to hear all this . . . Anyway, I went outside and stayed there.'

'All afternoon?'

'Yes.'

Thanet noticed Grace's eyes widen slightly at this unequivocal affirmative. Was Letty Ransome deliberately lying, or had she forgotten some errand which had briefly taken her away from her stall?

'We were very busy,' Letty was saying. 'I don't know

how much we made yet, of course, but . . . Oh dear, it all seems so trivial, now, in comparison with what's happened.'

'You said "we." Someone was helping you?'

'Yes. Mrs Bennet. We usually do the white elephant stall together.'

'And neither of you took a break? For a cup of tea, perhaps?'

'No, someone usually brings us a cup, halfway through the afternoon. Oh, just a moment, I forgot. Yes, I did come into the house briefly, to—'

The door opened and Lineham came in.

They had worked together too long for it to be necessary to speak. *Everything organised?* asked Thanet's slight lift of the eyebrows. *All under control* said Lineham's brief nod.

'Miss Ransome was just telling us that she came into the house briefly this afternoon, Sergeant,' said Thanet. 'What time would that have been, Miss Ransome?'

The red splotches on the scrawny neck were appearing again. 'About . . . um . . . a quarter past three, I should think.'

A quarter past three. Thanet's scalp tingled. If Grace Fairleigh were telling the truth and her mother-in-law had still been alive when she left her at around 3.15, and Fairleigh had found her dead at 3.40 . . . Letty Ransome wouldn't be able to risk lying about the time, of course, not in the circumstances, with hundreds of potential witnesses about. He kept his face impassive, however, as he said, 'Now I want you to think very carefully. This could be important. What, exactly, did you do and see?'

This time the tide of colour which began at the neckline of her dress and spread up into her face was so pronounced as to engulf the red patches completely. Thanet watched with interest. What was coming?

Her reply, however, was a distinct anticlimax.

'I simply went to the cloakroom, just inside the back door, then came out again.'

Could maidenly modesty have been responsible for that blush? wondered Thanet. Was that possible, in this day and age? Just, he conceded. On the other hand, if Letty Ransome had something to hide perhaps that betraying flush was something more than embarrassment. Guilt, perhaps, if she had lied. She didn't strike him as the sort of person who was an habitual liar.

'You didn't go upstairs at all?' he persisted.

She shook her head, one of the escaping wisps of hair floating across her mouth with the passage of air. She brushed it away impatiently. 'No.'

And she *was* lying, Thanet was certain of it now. He could tell by the even more pronounced flash of surprise which crossed Grace Fairleigh's face. She had seen her husband's aunt not only inside but upstairs, Thanet was certain of it. She noticed Thanet watching her and looked away.

'There was something you wanted to say, Mrs Fairleigh?'

She met his eyes squarely. 'No.'

So family solidarity was the order of the day. It looked as though there wouldn't be much point in persisting but he decided to try again. 'You must have been coming away from your mother-in-law's room at around the time your aunt came into the house.'

'I expect she was in the cloakroom as I went by.'

Thanet did not miss Letty Ransome's relief.

'Now I must ask you both to think very carefully. Did either of you see anything or anyone in the least suspicious while you were indoors?'

They shook their heads. But he caught the brief flicker of a memory recalled in Letty Ransome's eyes before she lowered her head and again plucked at the handkerchief.

'Miss Ransome?'

She shook her head again, compressed her lips. 'No.'

So she wasn't going to tell him, not at the moment, anyway. Perhaps she wanted to think about it, first, decide in her own time.

He caught Lineham's eyes. No, he hadn't imagined all this. Lineham had seen it too, he could tell. The sergeant's slight shrug confirmed his own opinion. There was no point in pursuing the matter at the moment. Neither woman was going to change her story at this point. Wait, then, for further leverage.

Experience had taught him that sooner or later he would find it.

5

'We looking for anything in particular?' said Lineham, peering into one of the drawers of Mrs Fairleigh's desk.

Thanet shrugged. 'Not especially. Anything and everything.' He leaned forward to try to decipher the signature on an indifferent watercolour of the house. It was signed E. Fairleigh, 1878. Hugo Fairleigh's great-grandmother? He tried to work out the dates, then gave up. What did it matter? He resumed his prowling around the room.

It was much later. The SOCOs had been and gone, the old lady's body had been taken away and Thanet and Lineham had been left in sole possession of this, her most private domain. If Isobel Fairleigh had had any secrets, this must be where she had kept them, thought Thanet, looking around the bedroom. The sitting room shared with her sister was too much a joint territory. He wondered how it had felt for old Mrs Fairleigh to give up being the mistress of the entire house and retire to one small section of it. Had she been angry, resentful, or resigned, accepting? No, never resigned, he thought, remembering that proud, decisive profile. Isobel Fairleigh had not been the type to lie down and let life dictate its terms to her. If she had chosen to withdraw, to abdicate in favour of her daughter-in-law, it could only have been a deliberate choice, the result of careful consideration. So, he wondered, why that particular option? Why not move out altogether, to a cottage in the village, perhaps? He couldn't believe that it was because she hadn't been able to afford to buy another house. No, much more likely that she wanted to stay near Hugo. Thanet doubted that there were any other children. It was always Hugo who gazed solemnly out of the framed school, team and undergraduate groups which hung upon these walls, smiled out of the elaborate silver frames disposed about the room. There were just two exceptions, a head and shoulders shot of an officer in First World War uniform—Isobel Fairleigh's father, he guessed, by the resemblance—and a wedding photograph of Isobel and her husband. Thanet picked this up to study it more closely. They had been a handsome couple, Fairleigh tall and well built with the same sleek fair hair as his son, Isobel a classic English beauty, her abundant hair framing a face in which the glow of youth eclipsed the ominous firmness of jaw and mouth. There was no photograph of Hugo and Grace's wedding, he noted.

'Seems to have been pretty well organised,' said Lineham. He was systematically sorting papers into piles: business correspondence, personal letters, bank statements, chequebook stubs, dividend slips.

'That doesn't surprise me.' Thanet's reply was abstracted. He had picked up an envelope which he had noticed earlier on the bedside table. It had already been opened and he took the letter out and glanced at it. Nothing interesting, just an estimate from a local builder for some proposed decorating. 'This is post-marked yesterday. Someone must have brought it in and read it to her.' He put it back on the table. 'Any sign of a diary, Mike?'

'Not so far.'

'Probably in her handbag.' Thanet looked around. He couldn't see one. Someone had probably tidied it away during the old lady's illness. The obvious place was the wardrobe, an elegant Edwardian serpentine-fronted affair of inlaid satinwood. It was full of expensive clothes crammed in so tightly that it must have been difficult to extricate them. Well-polished brogues and high-heeled shoes of sleek, soft calf were neatly lined up on the floor and the long shelf above the hanging rail was stacked high with hats and handbags. Thanet guessed that the one Mrs Fairleigh had been using when she had had her stroke would have been kept apart from the others. Yes, that would be it, on the floor at one end, a pigskin handbag with single handle. He fished it out and sat down on a chair to open it. And yes, here was a diary.

Lineham glanced across. 'Found it?'

'Mmm.' Thanet was already engrossed. What sort of a life had she led?

A busy one, he discovered. Until the last week or two there were entries for most days, sometimes two or three in a day. There were a number of regular weekly commitments. On Mondays, Wednesdays and Fridays Isobel Fairleigh had helped serve meals on wheels at lunchtime. On Tuesday and Thursday afternoons and on Wednesday evenings she had played bridge. On Friday mornings she had had her hair done. In between she had served on various committees, attended coffee mornings and fund-raising events for charity, gone to WI and NADFAS meetings.

And on the first day of every month, regardless of

which day of the week it was, she had written a capital B.

Thanet pointed it out to Lineham. 'Wonder who B is?' He turned to 1 July, the day after Isobel had had her stroke. Yes, there it was, an appointment which had never been kept.

'One of the family might know.' Lineham was running his finger down a piece of paper. He whistled, a long drawn out sound of wonder and awe. 'Just look at this! Half-yearly statement from her brokers. She had close on a half a million tucked away here and there. Is Mr Fairleigh's face going to light up when he sees this! Or perhaps he's already seen it, and thought it might be worth his while to give his mother a helping hand, speed her on her way.'

'Half-yearly statement, you say? Sent out when?'

'Dated 3 July.'

'After her stroke, then. In that case, as it's obviously been opened, someone's seen it, that's certain. I wonder who's been opening her letters for her.'

'And who she's left it all to.'

'Quite. Find out who her solicitor is, Mike. Incidentally, I haven't had a chance to tell you before, but I'm pretty certain Fairleigh was lying earlier, about his movements this afternoon.'

'He wasn't exactly shedding too many tears over his mother's death, either, was he, sir?'

'So far as I could see, nobody was.'

'Except Miss Ransome.'

'I didn't think that was grief, did you?'

'Either shock or panic, you mean? She was definitely lying, wasn't she?'

'About not coming upstairs, you mean? Yes. Through her teeth.'

'Young Mrs Fairleigh knew it, too, didn't she? She must have seen her.'

'But had no intention of giving Miss Ransome away.'

'You think Miss Ransome knew she'd been spotted?'

'My impression was that she didn't. And I think she was concentrating so hard on her own performance and its effect on us to notice Grace Fairleigh's reaction.'

'So d'you think Miss Ransome might have done it, sir?' Lineham tapped the broker's list with his fingernail. 'She's probably had a good look at this, and no doubt her sister will have left her a tidy chunk in her will.'

'I agree. Still, we mustn't jump to conclusions, Mike. You know as well as I do that every time we're involved in a murder investigation we find that people start lying right, left and centre, trying to cover up grubby little secrets which have no bearing whatsoever on the case.' Thanet stood up. 'Come on. Bundle all that stuff up into an envelope and we'll take it back with us, study it at our leisure. I want to have a word with Mrs Kerk before we go home.'

This was old Mrs Fairleigh's housekeeper. She had been working in the kitchen all afternoon, supplying hot water for the teas and supervising the washing-up, and Thanet wanted to ask her if she had noticed anything suspicious. He had assumed she lived in, like Hugo Fairleigh's housekeeper, but she didn't and by the time he got around to asking for her she had already gone home.

The address they had been given was on a small new council estate on the edge of the village, an attractive mix of houses, old people's bungalows and maisonettes which was a far cry from the rows of dreary, identical council houses thrown up all over the country in the post-war years. Some of the tenants had obviously taken advantage of right-to-buy schemes encouraged by the Conservative government, pride in their homes demonstrated by porches, extensions and refinements such as wrought-iron gates.

Mrs Kerk's house sported no such embellishments but the council would no doubt consider her a good tenant: the windows sparkled, paintwork shone and the front garden was neatly mown and ablaze with a dazzling display of summer bedding plants.

An expensive motorbike was parked outside by the kerb and as Thanet and Lineham walked up the path the front door opened and a youth came out carrying an elaborate crash-helmet.

'Mrs Kerk?' said Thanet.

The youth hesitated, then pushed open the front door, which he had been about to close behind him. 'Mum!' he yelled.

There was a brief blare of sound from the television set as a door opened and closed and a woman came out. 'Yes?'

The lad ran off down the path, fastening on his helmet as he went. He jumped on to his bike and kick-started the engine. Thanet waited for him to move off before introducing himself and Lineham.

'Oh,' said Mrs Kerk nervously. She glanced back over her shoulder at the door from which she had emerged, then up and down the street. She stepped back. 'You'd better come in.'

She led them down a short passage into a neat modern kitchen well-equipped with gadgets such as microwave oven and food processor. 'Um . . . Would you like to sit down?' She gestured at the small pine table and chairs.

'Thank you.'

Thanet studied her with interest. Isobel Fairleigh couldn't have been the easiest of employers and he suspected that anyone with too much spirit would quickly have come to grief. Mrs Kerk was middle-aged, buxom, with a round placid face and neatly permed brown hair. She wore no make-up and was wearing a flowered cotton skirt and a short-sleeved white blouse which displayed her solidly fleshed upper arms. She folded her hands together on the table in front of her and waited, only the whitening of her knuckles betraying her tension.

He set out to put her at ease. He might need her cooperation later, when he began to probe more deeply into the relationships within the Fairleigh family, and at this initial meeting he didn't want to frighten her off and make her clam up. 'Just some routine questions, Mrs Kerk, no need to worry, this shouldn't take long. How long have you been Mrs Fairleigh's housekeeper?'

His conversational tone reassured her and they chatted for a few minutes before edging nearer the purpose of his visit.

'There were just one or two small points I wanted to clear up with you. The first is this. What were the arrangements for letters, in the household? How did Mrs Fairleigh get her post?'

The factual nature of the question made her relax further and she became quite voluble.

'All the post for the house was delivered to Mr Fairleigh's side. That Bert—our postman—couldn't be bothered to walk all the way around the back to deliver ours separately. It used to make Mrs Fairleigh so mad, time and again she complained about it and for a few weeks he'd do it, and then he'd go back to delivering it all in one bundle. Said it were the post office that didn't separate it out.' She gave a sniff which expressed scorn for all the people in the world who couldn't be bothered to do their job properly.

'And what happened to it after that?'

'Miss Letty or Mrs Fairleigh would go down and fetch it.'

'And since Mrs Fairleigh has been in bed?'

'Sometimes Miss Letty went down for it, sometimes young Mrs Fairleigh would bring it up.'

'And who would read it to her?'

'I don't know. One or the other of them, I suppose.'

'What happened to it today, do you know?'

'No, I'm sorry. We was all so busy, with the fête . . .'

'Yes, of course . . . I wonder, did Mrs Fairleigh usually tell you where she was going, when she went out?'

Mrs Kerk looked blank, shook her head. 'She'd tell me she was going to be out for lunch or dinner, that's all.'

'Only we've been checking through her diary . . .' He fished it out of his pocket and showed her the entry for 3 July. 'And she seems to have met someone with the initial B on the first of each month. Do you have any idea who that might be?'

Another shake of the head. 'Sorry. I really haven't a clue.'

'Her friends never came to the house?'

'She didn't—' She stopped, abruptly. 'Only for the bridge.'

Had she been going to say, 'She didn't have any friends'? 'And who were they?'

'Well, there was Mrs Fairlawn, Mrs Crayford and Mrs Pargeter, mostly. And sometimes Miss Highstead or Mrs Porter, if one of the regulars couldn't come. But it was mostly them three.'

'And do you know their Christian names?'

'Mrs Fairlawn is Edith, I think, and Mrs Pargeter is Margaret. I don't know the others. Miss Letty might be able to help you.'

'Miss Ransome didn't play bridge herself?'

A smile, for the first time. 'No, not she. Said it was beyond her and she wouldn't dare, they all took it so serious, like. It could get quite nasty at times, she said.'

'Right. There's just one other point I wanted to raise

with you. You were working in the kitchen off the downstairs passage all afternoon, I understand?'

'That's right, yes.'

'Now I want you to think very carefully before you answer my next question.'

She immediately looked apprehensive, the broad forehead creasing into vertical lines.

'Did you at any time this afternoon see anyone other than those who were helping you come into the house?'

'I was busy.' She was defensive. 'I didn't have much time to stand around watching comings and goings.'

'Yes, I realise that. I just thought you might have happened to notice? If you could think back?'

Silence, while she considered. And yes, she had remembered something, Thanet could tell.

'There was someone,' she said slowly.

'Yes?'

'A woman.' She stopped.

'Someone you knew?' Thanet was encouraging.

'No, I'd never seen her before. Said she was looking for the toilet. I told her toilets for the public were outside.'

'There is one, though, isn't there, just inside the back door?'

'Yes, but they wasn't supposed to use that. We couldn't have half the village tramping through the house, could we?'

'Where was she?'

'Coming back along the passage towards the back door.'

'From the direction of the stairs, then?'

'Yes. I'd just been out to collect some crockery to wash up. I came in through the back door and she was coming towards me.'

'And what did she say, exactly?'

'Something like, oh, sorry, I was looking for the loo.' Mrs Kerk hesitated. 'She seemed in a hurry.'

'What do you mean?'

'Well, anxious to get out, like. A bit breathless. I thought she just wanted to go bad, you know, and I did wonder whether to tell her to use the indoor toilet, but I thought no, do it for one and before you know where we are we'll have them queueing up outside the back door. So I didn't.'

'Did she seem upset, would you say?'

The housekeeper shook her head. 'I don't rightly know . . . You're not thinking she had anything to do with Mrs Fairleigh's . . . well . . . with what happened, are you?'

'I'm not thinking anything at the moment, Mrs Kerk. At this stage all I'm trying to do is gather information. This woman, could you describe her for me?'

Mrs Kerk frowned with the effort of recollection, screwing up her eyes and pursing her mouth. 'Not young, but not what you'd call middle-aged, either. Early forties, perhaps? Not slim, not fat, sort of plumpish, I suppose. Dark curly hair.'

'Height?'

'Middling. Bit taller than me. Nicely dressed, but not a lady.'

'What do you mean?'

'Her accent. She was well-spoken, but she didn't speak like Mrs Fairleigh or Miss Letty.'

'What was she wearing?'

'A navy dress with little white flowers on it. Long sleeves.'

'I must congratulate you, Mrs Kerk. You are very observant. That is an excellent description.'

Mrs Kerk looked pleased.

Now for the crucial question. 'What time was this, do you know?'

Another frown. 'Sorry, I don't. I didn't think it was important.'

Pity. 'Of course not. But was it early in the afternoon, or later?'

'Must have been getting on, because we was so busy washing up, and people didn't really get going on the teas till about three. I tell you what, though, it wasn't that long before I saw Mr Hugo come hurrying into the house with another man.'

'A smallish man, with half-moon spectacles and a bald head?'

'That's right!'

Doc Mallard. So whoever the woman was, she had been in the house during the crucial period. 'How much time do you think elapsed between your seeing this woman and then Mr Fairleigh?'

'I'm not sure. We had a bit of a rush on about then.'

'If you could think, I'd be grateful.'

She frowned with concentration. 'Ten minutes?' she said, eventually. 'I couldn't swear to it, mind.'

'But it was something like that.'

She nodded.

'Mrs Kerk,' said Thanet, 'there's no doubt about it. You are a gem.' He waited for her gratified smile before saying, 'Now, are you sure you didn't notice anyone else come in? Miss Letty, perhaps?'

A shake of the head.

'Or young Mrs Fairleigh?'

'Oh, yes, I did see her once, now you mention it. Early on, before we got busy.'

'Mr Fairleigh?'

'Only that once, I told you about.'

Thanet rose. 'Well, perhaps you'd have another think. And if you remember anything else, I'd be grateful if you'd let us know.'

'So,' said Lineham as they got into the car. 'Could this be a case of *cherchez la femme*?'

'Drop me at my mother-in-law's house, would you? I told Joan I'd meet her there ... Who knows? In any case, with all the people there this afternoon it'll be like looking for a needle in a haystack. All the same, we'll take a good look at the names and addresses taken by the men on the gate, show it around to the family. Someone might recognise a name.'

'If this mystery woman had anything to do with the murder, she wouldn't have hung about. She'd have been gone long before you got that organised.'

'You could say the same of anyone, if it wasn't one of the family.'

'True,' said Lineham gloomily. He brightened up. 'But with all that loot lying around waiting to be inherited, I bet you anything it was.'

Thanet laughed. 'I won't take you up on that, it could prove expensive.'

6

'Ah, that's better.' Thanet laid down his knife and fork with a little sigh of contentment. Joan and her mother had eaten long since, but had saved supper for him: thick, succulent slices of ham on the bone, new potato salad with chives, a salad of apple, celery, walnut and yoghurt, and crusty home-made rolls. Now, comfortable in his own clothes again, he leaned back in the capacious basket chair and relaxed.

They were sitting on the little paved terrace at the back of his mother-in-law's house. Margaret Bolton was a keen gardener and the scent of nicotiana and old roses hung in the warm, still air. Although it was ten o'clock it was such a lovely evening that they had all been reluctant to go indoors and shut the windows against marauding insects.

'Delicious supper, Margaret.' Thanet took out his pipe and began to fill it.

Margaret Bolton smiled. 'I should think you were ready for it.' She ran a hand languidly through her hair, raising it a little from her scalp and letting it fall gently back into the soft curls which framed her face. 'Lovely to be able to sit outside so late, like this.'

Joan nodded. 'We could almost imagine we were in France.'

She and Thanet exchanged affectionate smiles, remembering their first joint holiday in France many years ago, on their honeymoon. They had loved the Dordogne, revelled in the delight of lingering outside on many an evening such as this, and had since returned time and again to savour the unique pleasures of rural France.

'Let's hope it lasts,' said her mother. 'More coffee, anyone?'

'Yes, please,' said Thanet.

'Just half a cup for me, Mum.' Joan waited until her mother had poured out the coffee and then said, 'Anyway, how did it go today, Luke?'

'So so. As well as could be expected, I suppose.'

'How are they, the Fairleighs?' said Margaret Bolton.

'Oh, all right. Shocked, of course. But not exactly devastated.' It occurred to Thanet that his mother-in-law might be able to give him an outsider's view of the family. She had lived in Thaxden for years, was a member of the local Conservative Association and no doubt came into contact with them fairly frequently at local events. 'I shouldn't think the old lady was too easy to live with.'

'You can say that again! Her poor sister, the way she bossed her about . . . I don't know how Letty put up with it.'

'Perhaps she didn't have much choice,' said Joan.

'You're right,' said Mrs Bolton. 'She used to keep house for her father and the way I heard it, he was a pretty improvident type. When he died the house had to be sold to pay off his debts and Letty was left with virtually nothing. I don't think she was ever trained to do any kind of job and I expect she was only too glad to accept Isobel's offer of a home.'

'When was that?' said Thanet.

'Oh, ages ago. A couple of years after you were married.'

'Somewhere around 1965, then?'

'I should think so, yes.'

'I imagine the Fairleighs could well afford to have her live with them.'

'Oh, yes. I think they're pretty well off. I don't know how long the family has been living in Thaxden Hall, but for two or three generations, anyway. They had a town house in London, too, but that was destroyed in the Blitz during the war. It was rather tragic, really, Hugo's grandparents were staying in it at the time, and they were both killed. His father was their only son and presumably inherited everything.'

'What was he like?'

'I didn't know him as well as I know his son. He didn't mix in village affairs as much as Hugo. He was also the MP for Sturrenden, if you remember. Hugo followed in his father's footsteps.'

'Yes, I know. Didn't he die unexpectedly, of a heart attack?'

'That's right, two or three years before the Conservatives got back into power in the 1979 election. It was the year before Hugo got married, I do remember that. It was a great shock to the family, he was what was commonly called a fine figure of a man and seemed very fit, walked a lot, played tennis and so on. I believe he was tipped for Ministerial Office, if he'd lived.'

'But Hugo Fairleigh didn't stand for election immediately after his father's death, did he? I seem to recall that we had another MP in between.'

'Yes. Arnold Bates. No, when Hugo's father died

Hugo was only just launching into politics. He'd been to Oxford and been called to the Bar and presumably Central Office thought he ought to have some more experience before offering him a safe seat. So they let him cut his teeth on a tough Labour by-election and then, when Arnold Bates also died unexpectedly only a couple of years later, Hugo was selected to fight the Sturrenden by-election. He made a very good showing, got in with a slightly increased majority. That was in 1978. Then the following year there was a General Election and he increased the majority still further. He's been our MP ever since.'

'He's pretty well thought of as an MP, isn't he?'

'I think so, yes. He works hard, and he's very conscientious, listens to what people say and tries to do something about it. I think he's definitely on the way up. And of course, the first time he fought the seat there was a lot of sympathy for him locally. His son died halfway through the by-election campaign and people admired the way he managed to carry on. All the local associations really put their backs into helping him.'

'Ah, yes, I remember now,' said Joan. 'A cot death, wasn't it?'

'Yes. It really was a tragedy. It was the only child they've ever had, and it was a Down's syndrome baby. It was born in the spring of that year, 1978, and died in September. It was a terrible shock for his wife. Despite the fact that it was mentally handicapped she absolutely adored that child and almost had a nervous breakdown when it died. It took her years to recover—in fact, I'm not sure that she ever has, not properly.'

'Was she looking after the baby herself?' said Joan.

'No, there was a nanny. Rita something. There was an inquest of course and she was completely exonerated, but I think Grace always blamed herself, felt that if she had been looking after the baby herself all the time as a proper mother should, it would never have happened. You know how it is in such cases, there's such a lot of irrational guilt around.'

They nodded. Joan as a probation officer and Thanet as a policeman had both come across cases of sudden infant death syndrome as it was officially called; had had to comfort distraught parents whose immediate reaction, however careful and loving they had been, was to blame themselves for their child's death.

'How did Hugo Fairleigh feel about the baby?' said Thanet. He found it difficult to imagine Fairleigh with a Down's syndrome child. He had a feeling that had the child lived it would have been hidden away in an institution as soon as it was old enough to be separated from its mother. And if Grace Fairleigh had, as Margaret seemed to think, been really attached to the child, there would have been all kinds of problems ahead.

'I don't really know. I'm sure it's been a great disappointment to him, since, that there have been no more children. It always must be, when there's no future generation to inherit a family home like Thaxden Hall.'

'I imagine old Mrs Fairleigh was pleased he won that by-election,' said Thanet.

'Oh, delighted, I'm sure. I think that when her husband died so unexpectedly she just transferred her ambitions for him to her son.'

Now Thanet put the question he had been wanting to ask all along. 'What was she like?' He was fond of his mother-in-law and respected her judgement. He awaited her reply with interest.

Margaret Bolton was silent for a while, considering. 'Well,' she said at last, 'as you've no doubt already worked out for yourself, she was a pretty formidable person, really. Bossy, managing. Liked to get her own way. She was on lots of committees, and usually managed to manoeuvre herself into being chairman and running the show.'

'Doesn't sound as though you liked her much,' said Joan.

'No, I didn't. She always behaved as though the world should be organised to suit her and was prepared to go to any lengths to make sure it did. And people usually gave in to her because she was so overpowering. Mind, she could be charming when it suited her. She was very manipulative. I've seen her persuade people into doing things they didn't want to do without their ever realising how she'd managed it.'

'She liked power, then,' said Thanet.

'Yes, I've never thought of it quite like that but yes, she did. I remember she once told me her father had wished she was a boy so that she could have gone into politics—he was a politician too, did I say? Though he never got very far.'

'Why didn't she, I wonder? Go into politics, I mean,' said Joan.

Margaret Bolton shrugged. 'Women didn't so much, in those days. Perhaps, as a woman, she was encouraged rather to aim for marrying a promising young politician and becoming the power behind the throne. Well, we all know that happens, don't we? And certainly she was always very much in evidence as the MP's wife.'

'She must have found it hard to take a back seat, after her husband died and before Hugo was elected.'

'Yes, she must. Though she soon adjusted. She simply rechannelled her energies into local organisations and charities. And she's always kept them up, since. She had an amazing amount of energy, you know. It made us weaker mortals feel exhausted just watching her, sometimes.'

Thanet grinned. 'She certainly sounds a doughty old bird. But not the easiest of people to get on with at close quarters. How do you think her daughter-in-law coped?'

Margaret Bolton shrugged. 'I don't really know. I don't know either of them well, only the faces they showed in public. I wouldn't say there was any affection between them, but neither did they show any animosity, either. I imagine Isobel Fairleigh was a rather difficult person to be fond of, and Grace just made the best of it.'

'Hugo Fairleigh and his wife don't seem particularly close, either.' Thanet knew that he was getting very close to the realms of gossip, of which his mother-in-law fiercely disapproved, and he wondered how she would react to this feeler.

As expected, she gave him a reproving look. 'I wouldn't know. I do think, though, that it must be very difficult for people in their position. They live their lives so much in the public eye that they have to erect a façade behind which they can retain some privacy.'

Thanet held up his hands. 'All right, all right, I stand corrected. Let's change the subject!' He looked from Joan to Margaret. 'I don't suppose either of you saw anything that struck you as odd, this afternoon?'

'We talked about that, over supper,' said Margaret. 'And I'm afraid I was just too busy on my stall to have noticed anything much. But Joan did, didn't you?'

'Well,' said Joan slowly. 'I'm not sure if it's worth mentioning, but there was one little incident I did notice. You wouldn't have seen, you were doing something at a sideshow nearby at the time. I was just standing around waiting for you, near the white elephant stall.'

'Miss Ransome's stall?'

Joan nodded. 'That's right. Well, while I was there a funny little man went around to the back of the stall and whispered something in her ear. She gave him a sharp look, they exchanged a few words, then she glanced at her watch and nodded. He went off and a second or two later she said something to the woman who was helping her on the stall and hurried off towards the house.'

'Any idea what time that would have been?'

Joan shook her head. 'Sorry, no. Some time in the middle of the afternoon. I wasn't exactly keeping an eye on the clock.'

'No, quite.'

'From Joan's description I think I know who the man was, if that's any help,' said Margaret. 'I think it was Ernie Byre, the Fairleighs' gardener and stable hand.'

'That's why I wondered if it was worth mentioning,' said Joan. 'He might well have been on some errand to do with the fête.'

But if so, and as a result Letty Ransome had had to go into the house, why hadn't she mentioned it? Though the fact that she left the stall a few moments after this reported conversation didn't necessarily mean that her departure had anything to do with it. 'You say she went off towards the house?'

'Well, in that direction. But she could have been going to speak to someone about something, pass a message on, whatever . . .'

'Quite. Well, thanks for mentioning it, anyway.'

It was time to go. It was definitely getting cooler now and his mother-in-law, he noticed, was rubbing her bare arms. He stood up. 'You're getting cold, Margaret. Time we were on our way.' He picked up his plate, cup and saucer. 'We'll just give you a hand with these . . .'

'No, leave them. There's hardly any washing up anyway. Joan and I did it earlier.'

As they wound their way home through the quiet

country lanes it occurred to Thanet that Joan seemed unusually preoccupied.

'Anything the matter?'

She shook her head half-heartedly.

'Come on, what is it? Not Bridget?'

'Oh no. No, nothing to do with the family.'

'One of your clients?' It was unusual for Joan to bring anxieties about a client home with her, but he knew that even an experienced probation officer occasionally came across a case which was difficult to switch off.

'It's Michele.'

'The battered girlfriend?' Joan had talked about this case before. Michele, who was in her mid-twenties, had first been placed in Joan's care after being picked up joy-riding with her boyfriend. Apart from the fact that she had been driving at the time, she had been well over the limit. As it was a first offence she had been let off relatively lightly, being put on probation and having to attend a drink-driving course once a week for a year. It hadn't taken Joan long to discover that the boyfriend—with whom Michele was living—was regularly beating her up. Thanet remembered their first conversation about her.

'It's a classic case, Luke. She positively invites him to hit her. She provokes him, goads him, until he loses control. And she won't bring charges against him. I think she feels it's only right that he should beat her, that she deserves it.'

'As a punishment, you mean?'

'Exactly.'

'For what?'

'Well, that's what we were talking about today. Apparently, when she was in her early teens, her father walked out on her and her mother. She'd been giving them a lot of trouble at the time—playing truant from school, staying out at night until all hours, the usual sort of thing, and there'd been a lot of rows at home. So when he went she was convinced it was because of her, that she'd driven him out.'

'As you say, a classic case. She's blamed herself ever since, feels a thoroughly bad lot, makes sure everyone else gets the message, and picks a man who'll punish her for being what she is. And is she?'

'A bad lot, you mean? No, I don't think so. In fact, I'm sure she's not. She has a lot of good qualities, only she seems incapable of acknowledging them.'

'Think you're going to get anywhere with her?'

'I can only try.'

Joan had been trying ever since, almost a year, now, and had failed dismally. The girl's image of herself was fixed, and whatever approach Joan tried got her nowhere.

'So, what's happened?'

'You remember I told you her mother died?'

'A couple of weeks ago. Yes.'

'Well, she had a letter from her father yesterday. He wants to see her.'

'Ah. And is she going to?'

Joan was silent for a while, considering. 'She's dithering, of course, but I think she probably will. I don't think she'll be able to resist the temptation.'

'She's never heard from him before, in all this time?'

'No. Of course, it's possible that this could be the breakthrough we need.'

'Unless, of course, she finds she's been right all along. That he did leave because he couldn't take any more from her.'

'Oh come on, Luke. We both know that when two people split up it's very rarely because of the children. It's almost always because the parents' relationship has broken down beyond the point of recall.'

'True. But you have to face the possibility.'

Joan sighed. 'I know.'

They had arrived home. Alexander's Porsche was parked outside and lights were on all over the house.

'They're back, then,' said Thanet. 'And they're still up.' He was tired and had hoped that he and Joan would be able to slope quietly off to bed.

His tone had not escaped her. 'Come on, darling,' she said, getting out of the car. 'Better come and be sociable for a little while at least.'

He followed her reluctantly up the path to the front door.

7

When Thanet left home next morning the rest of the household was still sunk in Sunday-morning slumber. He drove through the deserted streets enjoying his after-breakfast pipe—Lineham hated him smoking in the office and he had long since capitulated except in unusual circumstances. It was another glorious summer morning, the sun hot, the sky a clear, unblemished blue.

As he expected, Lineham was already hard at work. The sergeant was very much an early bird and it was rare for Thanet to be there before him.

'Anything interesting, Mike?'

'Not really. I was just going through this list of people at the fête yesterday.' Lineham waved a batch of closely typed sheets.

Someone had been hard at work last night.

'Nothing rings a bell, though.'

'Didn't think it would. Still, it had to be done and we'll take it with us today, get people to glance through it. Did anyone think to list the helpers?'

'Yes. There's a separate section, at the end.'

'Good.'

'Oh, and a reporter from the *Kent Messenger* rang up.'

The first swallow, thought Thanet. No doubt others would come flocking along soon enough now. He was glad he'd eventually managed to get hold of Superintendent Draco at the hospital and let him know what was happening, though Draco had obviously been anxious and preoccupied with Angharad's treatment. After a few perfunctory questions he had simply said that he relied on Thanet's discretion and would see him at the morning meeting on Monday, as usual.

There was a knock at the door and Mallard came in.

'You're about bright and early for a Sunday, Doc.'

The little doctor beamed. 'Had an early call, so thought I'd pop in on the way home to breakfast.' He crossed to the window and stood looking out. 'Lovely day, isn't it? Helen and I thought we might go on a picnic.'

Thanet and Lineham groaned.

'Don't rub it in,' said Thanet. 'Anyway, how can you if you're on call?'

Mallard turned around and twinkled at him benevolently over his half-moons. He patted his pocket. 'Beep, beep. The wonders of modern science, Luke. We'll stay within easy reach. Anyway, I thought you might like to know, I had a word with old Mrs Fairleigh's doctor—Dr Beltring, do you know him?'

'Know of him.'

'Yes, well he's a nice chap, good reputation, conscientious. He just confirmed what we already knew, really. He wouldn't have been in the least surprised if Mrs Fairleigh had had another stroke.'

'What did he say when you told her she'd been suffocated?'

'He was shocked, naturally. Couldn't believe it. Said he'd like to see the PM results.'

'He was querying your judgement, you mean?'

'No. Just out of interest.'

'Do we know when the PM is?'

'I managed to fix it for first thing tomorrow morning.'

'Thanks . . . Doc, there really isn't the slightest doubt in your mind, is there?'

At one time Thanet would never have dared ask Mallard such a question. The police surgeon would have gone through the roof. Now, Helen's mellowing influence was such that he just smiled and said, 'I won't take offence, Luke. I know you're just asking me to confirm it again, not implying that I could be wrong.' He held up his hand as Thanet opened his mouth to verify this. 'After all, we can all make mistakes. But in this case, no, I'm certain. The evidence was there, plain as a pikestaff to anyone who knew what to look for.'

Thanet felt bound to justify himself. 'It's just that . . .'

'Really, Luke, say no more. I can just imagine how you-know-who would react if we'd started tossing the word "murder" at people like the Fairleighs without justification. I assume you think that one of them is involved?'

'More than likely, don't you think?'

'But you haven't actually said so to Fairleigh yet?'

'Not yet, no.'

'I'm glad it'll be you not me in the firing line this time.'

'It must have crossed his mind though, surely,' said Lineham.

'True,' said Mallard. 'But crossing his mind is one thing, having it spelled out to him is another. Well, must be off. Let me see, what did Helen say was on the menu this morning? Ah yes, fresh croissants.' He gave a cheery wave as he disappeared through the door. 'Have a nice day' floated back at them.

'All right for some,' said Lineham.

'Come on, Mike. You're a workaholic and you know it. Tell me truthfully, now. Which would you prefer, a day at the beach with the family, or a murder investigation?'

'I don't like traffic jams,' said Lineham with a grin. He nodded at the window. 'And today the roads to the coast will be solid with traffic.'

'Now that we've got that straight, we'd better get on. First thing I want to do is have a chat with Caroline Plowright, get a bit of background on the family.'

'Doesn't miss much, that one,' agreed Lineham.

'Exactly. Think it's too early to ring her?' Thanet glanced at his watch. 'It's nine o'clock.'

'I'd say give it a try.' Lineham was already riffling through his notebook, reaching for the phone.

'I think I'll speak to her myself. Might be more diplomatic. She's not directly involved, after all. What's the number?'

Thanet dialled as Lineham read it off.

She answered on the second ring.

'Detective Inspector Thanet here, Sturrenden CID. We met yesterday at the—'

'Yes, I remember. What can I do for you?'

'I'm sorry to trouble you on a Sunday morning, but I wondered if you could spare us a little of your time.'

'Why?' The monosyllable was uncompromising.

Thanet was equally blunt in reply. 'Because you know the Fairleighs well. I think you might be able to help us.'

'If it's dirt you're looking for, no. Not that there is any anyway, but . . .'

'I'm not looking for dirt, as you put it, Miss

Plowright. Just a little straightforward background information.'

She was silent for a moment. 'Very well. But it'll have to be at the shop. I'm just leaving.'

'The shop?'

'Big is Beautiful. In the High Street.'

'Ah yes, I know it. Right. What time?'

'As soon as possible, before I get started on my work. Then I won't have to break off. In fifteen minutes?'

'Fine. Thank you.'

Big is Beautiful was at the Market Square end of the High Street. It had opened a couple of years previously and specialised in clothes for larger women. As Joan was an average size fourteen she and Thanet had never had occasion to go in and he'd had no idea who its owner was.

'Remind me to ask Mr Fairleigh for the name of his solicitor,' he said as he and Lineham left Headquarters.

'We're going out to Thaxden next?'

Thanet nodded. 'I want to talk to them all again, today.' He was enjoying the fresh air and sunshine, and the rare experience of a walk along Sturrenden's picturesque High Street without the crowds which usually thronged it. At this hour it was too early even for the weekend window-shoppers who came to gaze into the antique shops even though they were closed on Sundays.

They paused outside Caroline Plowright's shop.

'Looks as though she's expanding,' said Lineham, nodding at the premises next door. These had been empty for some time and now Thanet noticed that the façade had just been painted to match the green and gold façade of Big is Beautiful. The words 'COFFEE SHOP' had been outlined above the arched windows, some of the letters already filled in by an expert hand. 'OPENING SOON', announced a notice on the door.

'Very clever,' said Thanet. 'Tempt people in with a cup of coffee and hope they'll drift next door to spend.'

'I see you're admiring my new venture,' said Caroline Plowright, unlocking the door to let them in. This morning her generous proportions were masked by a silky straight skirt and shift top with three-quarter length sleeves and flattering cowl neckline. The bold abstract pattern in muted blues, greens and turquoise suited her colouring.

She was a good advertisement for her wares, thought Thanet.

'Come and see. I'm very proud of it.'

'We were just saying what a good idea it is.'

Inside the preparations were virtually complete. A generous archway had been opened up in the wall which divided the two premises and the green and cream colour scheme carried right through. The effect was spacious, elegant and congenial. The coffee shop had a conservatory-like air, with tall plants in big cream ceramic pots, comfortable sturdy wicker chairs designed to accommodate the bulk of prospective customers and glass-topped wicker tables well spaced out to allow the passage of substantial bottoms without embarrassment.

'Very nice indeed,' said Thanet admiringly.

'And good for business, I hope.' Caroline ran her hand lovingly over the smooth cane of a nearby chairback. 'A substantial investment, I can tell you.'

'I can imagine. Still, it'll pay off, I'm sure.'

'I hope so! There are just a few final details to sort out, and we'll be launched. I don't suppose you happen to know any large ladies who are looking for jobs?'

'Large ladies?' said Lineham.

She laughed. 'I still need a couple of new staff and I make it a policy never to employ anyone below a size sixteen. It wouldn't do the egos of my customers much good to be served by young slips of girls with sylph-like figures.'

Sound psychology, thought Thanet. He was right, she was pretty acute, and he was hopeful that this augured well for the coming interview. 'If we think of anyone we'll let you know. Do you always come in on Sundays yourself?'

'Yes, to catch up with the paperwork. I never seem to find time during the week. But that's enough of my business. What about yours? Do sit down. I've made some coffee,' she went on, making for the counter at the back of the coffee shop. 'It's fun playing with the new equipment and I thought we might as well be comfortable. You will have a cup?'

'Please.' Her earlier reservations about the interview seemed to have disappeared, thought Thanet as he and Lineham settled down in two of the new chairs, which were just as comfortable as they looked. Perhaps it was just that she had really enjoyed showing off her new baby. She was obviously very excited about it. It had been lucky for them that they happened to have caught her at the right moment.

Her next words punctured his complacency. 'I'm not dim, you know,' she said as she handed out the coffee. 'I mean, yesterday the Fairleighs were talking as if it were a foregone conclusion that it was a burglar who finished off the old girl. Oh, don't look so po-faced, Sergeant. I couldn't stand the woman and refuse to be hypocritical about it. Anyway, I gather from this visit that the police have a different view of the matter.'

Thanet took a sip of coffee. It was good, hot and strong. 'Delicious coffee.'

'Good.' But she wasn't going to let him get away without replying. She raised her eyebrows at him over the rim of her cup and waited.

Refusing to respond would annoy her and he wanted her cooperation. 'At the moment we have an open mind on the subject.'

'Really. I'm glad to hear it. All the same. I'll be interested to hear what Hugo has to say when he finds out he's a suspect in a murder case, along with his wife and his aunt.'

'He's no fool, Miss Plowright. He must be aware that we have to consider the possibility.'

'Consider it, maybe, but take it seriously . . . I gather you haven't actually broken the joyful news to him yet?'

'Not in so many words.'

'Would I like to be there when you do! He's going to blow his top!'

Thanet grinned. 'You want me to arrange it?'

She gave a rueful smile. 'Well, it would have been fun.'

He decided to risk a snub. 'It doesn't sound as though you're too fond of Mr Fairleigh.'

She shrugged. 'I make no secret of it. We're civil to each other, no more. I've no time to waste playing social games.'

'But you're obviously fond of his wife.'

Caroline lit a long thin brown cigarette and blew out a plume of smoke. 'We go back a long way. To our schooldays, in fact. You could say that providing moral support for each other has become a habit.'

Thanet sensed that she was beginning to open up. Her expression had softened, her eyes grown reminiscent. This was the moment to keep quiet and hope that she would begin to talk.

She took another pull on her cigarette and put her head back, this time blowing the smoke out dragon-like through her nostrils. 'I suppose you're thinking, why, especially, did you need it? Moral support, I mean.' She grinned and lowered her head to look him in the eye. 'Everybody does, wouldn't you agree, Inspector? If you're lucky you get it first from your parents, then from your friends and then, if you're very lucky indeed, from your husband or wife. Well, Grace and I were out of luck. We missed out on numbers one and three, so number two was particularly important to us. Still is.'

'Neither of you had parents alive when you were young?'

'Oh they were alive all right, but they didn't do us much good. Quite the reverse, in fact. My mother was so unhappy she spent half her life stuffing herself with food and the other half stuffing me. Added to which neither of us was exactly slim to start with.' Caroline held out her wrist. 'Look at that, Inspector. Big-boned, you see? And did you know it's now been proved that a predisposition to fatness is inherited?' She laughed. 'A fat gene, can you imagine it? I wonder if it's bigger and stronger than its fellows? It must be a bully, because it nearly always wins.' She shrugged. 'When I was fifteen I was fifteen stone, can you imagine? School was hell. Girls can be pretty spiteful. If it hadn't been for Grace ... She took me in hand, you see. Slimmed me down as far as possible, built up my ego, made me see that there are far worse things than being oversized. It took a long time but eventually I learned that she was right. So long as you're fit and have a modicum of common sense you can make your way in the world as well as anyone else, whatever your size. And if you can forget the chip on your shoulder other people will forget it too.'

But despite her protestations, Caroline had never quite recovered from those childhood humiliations, thought Thanet. All the more credit to her, then, for having turned her biggest liability into her greatest asset.

'And young Mrs Fairleigh's parents?'

Caroline got up to fetch an ashtray from the counter, tapped off the long thin worm of grey ash which had been in danger of sullying the new carpet. 'Too engrossed in each other, never had time for Grace. She was a late child, her mother was over forty when she was born, and her arrival was rather a shock to them. I don't think they ever wanted children and certainly the only thing they ever wanted from Grace was academic success.' She shrugged. 'Unfortunately, Grace couldn't come up with the goods. Poor kid, she kept on trying and failing, trying and failing until eventually she gave up. And naturally that just made things worse. They couldn't seem to accept that any child of theirs could be anything but brilliant. No, they always made it very clear that they had no time for Grace, that they could get along very well without a child, thank you very much. Grace, of course, was very different and I'm sure that was why . . .' She stopped, as if aware that she was about to stray into matters too private for the ears of policemen.

Thanet could guess what she had been going to say, though. 'Why she was so devastated when her baby died, you mean,' he said gently.

She raised her eyebrows. 'You know about that, then. My, you have been busy, haven't you? But yes, that was what I meant. She absolutely adored that child, despite . . .' She looked at Thanet, read the knowledge in his eyes. 'So you know that it was a Down's syndrome baby, too.'

Thanet nodded.

'Yes, well, most people couldn't understand why she was so attached to it, being mentally handicapped and so on. But I could. Somehow, the very fact that it was handicapped, so much more helpless even than a normal baby, made her feel more protective towards it.'

Caroline leaned forward to stub out her cigarette, took another sip of coffee. 'She told me once that one of the reasons why she so longed for a baby was because she'd then have someone of her very own to love, and love her back. You should have seen them together.'

Caroline shook her head and briefly there was a sheen of tears in her eyes. 'She insisted on breast-feeding, and on looking after the child herself. Hugo wasn't too pleased about that, as you can imagine. It was inconvenient, you see, meant that she wasn't always available to accompany him to functions. In the end she gave in and employed a nanny, and of course that was what she never forgave herself for, when the baby died. She was always convinced that if she'd been looking after it herself, that cot death would never have happened. She and Hugo were away that night, you know, at some function in London. And when she heard . . . I saw her next day.' Caroline compressed her lips and shook her head. 'I thought she'd go out of her mind with grief and guilt. I don't think she's ever got over it. If she'd ever had another child, it might have been different, but she never did.'

'You said, "someone of her very own to love". But she had her husband.'

Caroline's lip curled. 'Her husband. Oh, maybe I'm prejudiced, but I can't help it. He was as much use to Grace when she needed him as an empty water bottle in the desert. To be honest . . .' She gave Thanet a considering look.

He knew what she was thinking. *Shall I tell him what I really think?* This was what was so fascinating about interviewing witnesses. If you were lucky and handled it well you could almost see the invisible barriers going down, one by one. And if they did, people would become progressively more and more confiding, tell you things that they had originally had no intention of revealing. Perhaps it was because they were enjoying the relatively unique and seductive experience of having someone listen to them with complete attention and genuine interest. This applied especially to those who lived alone. Did Caroline? he wondered.

But as far as she was concerned, there was more to it than that. Realising that her friend must be a suspect Thanet thought that Caroline's aim in this interview would be twofold: to present Grace in as favourable a light as possible and Hugo as the potential villain of the piece. This was why she had told him so much about Grace's background and why Thanet suspected that she would now not hold back from launching into a character assassination of Hugo.

And yes, she had made up her mind. He could read the decision in her eyes before she spoke.

'To be honest, I think he was relieved when the baby died. I don't think it would have suited his image, especially as the child grew older and its handicap became more evident.'

Now he could risk a question he would never have dared ask earlier. 'Did young Mrs Fairleigh blame him, especially for their being away the night the baby died?'

'Oh yes, of course she did. With disastrous effect.'

'In what way?'

Caroline rummaged for another cigarette, found one. She took her time in lighting it, then gave a cynical little laugh. 'I always think it's so sad, don't you, when dreams turn to ashes?'

'Dreams?'

'Yes. The irony of it, you see, is that it was always Grace who was keen on Hugo. Even at school . . . Our school and his used to get together for certain events, you see, and of course there was always a lot of excitement about this. Well, you can imagine! We were boy-starved, and Hugo was the one most of us fell for. He was really something in those days—I suppose some people might think he still is. But anyway, Grace thought he was the last word, and worshipped him from afar for ages.'

'He never took any notice of her, then?'

'No. It wasn't until years later that they met again, when he was a practising barrister. It was at a dinner party, at the house of a mutual friend. Grace rang me up the next day. She was so excited, he'd asked her out . . . Anyway, six months later they were married and I'm afraid it was downhill all the way from then on.'

'Why was that?'

She blew out a plume of smoke. 'Basically because there's only one thing that matters to Hugo and that's Hugo. To him, Grace was just a social attribute—she came from a good family, could hold her own in society, was an excellent hostess and as a bonus was highly decorative, as I'm sure you'll agree. She soon found out that there was little more to it than that, and became more and more disillusioned. That was why the baby meant so much to her and why things got so much worse between her and Hugo when the tragedy happened.'

'Did he . . . ?' There was no way to put this tactfully. But it wasn't necessary, she understood at once what he meant.

'Did he play around, you mean?' She looked thoughtful. 'I don't think so. Not for years, anyway. He was too busy making his way in the world. But then . . .'

Thanet waited. Here came another of those barriers. Would this one come down too? He guessed that she was trying to decide whether her loyalty to Grace would be compromised by talking about Hugo.

She gave him another considering look. 'I did say,

didn't I, that if it was dirt you were looking for, I wasn't prepared to play.'

Thanet nodded. There was no point in putting pressure on her. She would make up her own mind and nothing he could say would influence her. But he was willing to bet that she was going to be unable to resist the temptation.

She was silent for a few moments, smoking thoughtfully and gazing out of the window at the street. There were a few more people about now, he noticed.

'Well . . .' she said, then broke off, frowning.

Someone was tapping at the window. A middle-aged couple was peering in, the woman shielding her eyes in order to get a better view of the interior.

Thanet cursed silently. Just the wrong moment for an interruption. He hoped Caroline would pick up where she had left off.

She rose and went across to the window. The woman outside was pointing at their coffee cups and miming drinking movements. Caroline was shaking her head and pointing to the 'OPENING SOON' notice. Eventually the couple gave disappointed shrugs and turned away.

Caroline came back. 'Perhaps I'd better consider Sunday opening, for the coffee shop. There's nowhere else in Sturrenden you can get a decent cup of coffee on a Sunday. Speaking of which, would either of you like some more?'

Thanet and Lineham shook their heads. She picked up her own cup and went to refill it.

Should he wait for her to take up the thread of the conversation again? Thanet wondered. He decided to risk doing so himself. 'You were saying?'

'What?' She gazed at him blankly for a moment, then remembered. 'Ah yes, the dirt. Shall I, shan't I?

Will I, won't I? That's what you want to know, isn't it, Inspector?'

Thanet shrugged. 'It's up to you.'

'What, no strong-arm tactics?' She laughed. 'No, not your style, I can see that. Softly softly catchee monkey, that's more your line. No doubt you've realised that putting pressure on me would merely make me clam up. Now, the question is, do you get a reward for your restraint, or not?'

Thanet said nothing, merely tried to make his expression as non-committal as possible. This, he felt, was the turning point in the interview. If she decided to go on now, they were home and dry. Lineham was aware of this too, he could tell. The sergeant was sitting as still as a statue, almost willing himself into invisibility.

Go on, Thanet urged her silently. *Go on.*

She stubbed out the cigarette and took a leisurely sip of coffee. She was enjoying keeping them in suspense, he could see that.

Eventually she grinned and Thanet glimpsed a spark of malicious satisfaction in her eyes. She was going to enjoy this.

'Well, why not?' she said.

8

Thanet became aware that he had been holding his breath. He released it slowly, unobtrusively, feeling the ache in his lungs subside.

'After all,' said Caroline, 'what do I owe Hugo? Nothing. Less than nothing, in fact, after the way he's treated Grace. And if I don't tell you, someone else is bound to. I imagine all sorts of skeletons fall out once you lot start poking around in cupboards. Can't say I envy you your job, but I can see that it might have a horrible sort of fascination, for those so inclined.'

Was that how she saw him? wondered Thanet. As someone who enjoyed prising out people's grubby little secrets? He had to admit that there was some truth in the accusation. But it wasn't that he enjoyed the 'dirt', as she called it, for its own sake. A murder investigation was a complex business and he remembered Lineham saying once that it was like trying to complete a really difficult jigsaw without ever having seen the picture. To find another piece was to fill in a little more of the picture and if he found enough pieces and managed to put them together then the crime would be solved, it was as simple as that.

Now Caroline was about to hand him one.

'Of course, this is just speculation,' she said. 'I can't give you chapter and verse. And Grace and I have never actually discussed the matter. She wouldn't. Whatever she feels about Hugo she's never been the type to complain about him behind his back. But my guess is that he met someone about a year ago, and the affair is still going on.'

'What grounds have you for suspecting this?'

Caroline shrugged. 'Nothing specific. Just a lot of little things which add up. A change in his attitude towards her, for a start. When he speaks to her, for instance, he never actually looks at her any more. He very rarely asks her to accompany him to functions now, and that's something he's invariably expected of her. It's always been part of his image, you see, to have his charming wife by his side. And then, he has a flat in London and for years he's usually spent two or three nights a week there, but now he hardly ever comes home during the week and quite often he stays up at the weekend, too.'

'You think he might be contemplating a divorce?'

Caroline frowned. 'That's a tricky one. He certainly wouldn't relish the idea of a scandal, however minor. It could damage his reputation in the constituency, Grace is very well liked down here. And it's difficult to imagine Hugo casting all aside for love, he's much too hard-headed for that. I'd say it depends on the woman. If she's happy to remain his little bit on the side, he'd probably be content to go on like that indefinitely. But I could be doing him an injustice, I suppose. If he really is in love with her I imagine it's just conceivable he'd be prepared to throw caution to the winds.'

'How would his wife feel about that, do you think?'

'I don't think she'd make a fuss, if that's what you mean. Personally, I think it would be the best thing that could happen to her. I can't think of a single benefit she gets from being his wife.'

'A comfortable life-style?'

'She has enough money of her own not to worry about that.'

'What about old Mrs Fairleigh? How would she have reacted to the idea of a divorce, d'you think?'

'Ah. I wondered when we'd be getting around to Isobel.' Caroline pursed her lips thoughtfully. 'To be honest, if he was trading Grace in for a younger model, one who'd be able to provide Hugo with an heir, then I'm sure the old bat would have been all in favour of it. In fact, I gather she's even hinted as much, to Hugo, in the past.'

'You didn't like her, either.'

'She and Hugo were my two unfavourite people.' She grinned. 'I wouldn't like you to think I feel like this about everybody, you know. Letty, for instance, is a poppet. No, on the whole I like people, but those two . . . I suppose I've always resented their making Grace so unhappy.'

'She and her mother-in-law didn't get on?'

'I wouldn't put it quite like that. It was an interesting relationship, really. On the one hand you had Isobel, who was selfish, egocentric and demanding, and on the other Grace, who was compliant, eager to please. I suppose you could say that each supplied something the other needed. So superficially at least they seemed to get on reasonably well. It's just that I could see it was doing Grace more harm than good. She was never going to begin to feel more positive about herself all the while Isobel was constantly making her feel a failure.'

'In what way, a failure?'

'Well, by producing an heir that was flawed, for a start. And then, after the baby died, failing to produce another one at all. Isobel used to watch Grace like a hawk, you know, for signs of her being pregnant again. And when nothing happened she began dropping subtle hints. Then the hints became less subtle and, eventually, reproaches . . .' Caroline shook her head in disgust. 'It used to make me sick. Mad, too. Why couldn't the old bitch see that Grace longed for more children herself, that she had suffered enough over the baby's death and was still suffering over her failure to conceive again, without making it worse by twisting the knife in the wound?'

Thanet was beginning to wonder if there was such a thing as an altruistic killing. Caroline Plowright obviously cared deeply about her friend. What if she had seen the opportunity to bring this tyranny to an end, and had grabbed it?

'This was still going on?'

'Oh no. Grace is forty now. I think even Isobel could see that the hope of another baby was becoming more and more faint with each passing year.'

'You make her sound a very unpleasant person.'

'Oh she was. Believe me, she was. How Letty put up with her I just don't know. Not that she had much choice, poor woman, with no means of her own and no kind of training for a job. The way Isobel used to boss her around . . . She used to behave as if Letty's one aim in life should be to make her own as comfortable as possible. And she never, ever let her forget that she was dependent on her for the roof over her head.'

'What was she like, as a person?' Caroline's view of Isobel would of course be biased, but it always fascinated Thanet to hear how different people saw the same person. He knew that one's view of anyone must be coloured by one's own character, that one automatically

sees other people through the filter of one's own preju-
dices and attitudes. In his work he always had to make
allowances for this, but found nevertheless that if he
talked to enough people about a murder victim he
could gradually attain quite a profound understanding
of that person's character. And experience had taught
him that in the case of domestic murder such understanding was all-important. After all, barring accidents
and ill health, most people live to a ripe old age. But
somewhere in the character of those who die an unnatural death lies buried deep the reason for it. His mission
was to dig, and keep on digging, until he found it.

'Oh God, I'm not exactly going to give you an un-
prejudiced opinion, am I?' said Caroline, unconsciously
echoing his thoughts. 'All the same, let me see . . . Well,
as you'll have gathered, she was entirely self-centred. I
think she genuinely saw the world as revolving around
her. I'd say she was incapable of seeing anything from
anyone else's point of view—even of conceiving that
there could be another point of view, apart from her
own. She didn't suffer fools gladly—she was very efficient herself, a bit of a perfectionist, and was impatient
with people who couldn't attain the standards she set.
Quiet, diffident people irritated her, I think that was
one of the reasons why she treated Letty so badly. And
she was very single-minded. If she set out to do something, she would do it, no matter how much opposition
there was.'

'Sounds as though she must have put a lot of people's backs up.'

'Oh she did. But don't let me give you the wrong
impression. She could be charming at times, when she
wanted her own way. The gloves would only come off
as a last resort. And she certainly got results, I'll grant
her that.'

'Did she have many friends?'

'Not what I would call friends. There were a few people she played bridge with regularly, but I wouldn't say any of them was close to her. She didn't seem to need other people, not in the way most of us do.' Caroline's forehead wrinkled. 'It was odd, really. I mean, in some respects she didn't care what people thought, so long as she got what she wanted, but at the same time she cared very much about keeping up appearances.'

'In what way?'

'Well, she was very proud. It was important to her, to be a Fairleigh and to live in a house which had come down in the family, like Thaxden Hall. And she was very particular about the way she looked—she was always well groomed, beautifully dressed in expensive clothes, hair immaculate and so on.'

'How did she get on with her son?'

Caroline shrugged. 'As well as she got on with anyone. I wouldn't say that there was any deep affection between them, but there wasn't any open disagreement, either. On the whole Hugo used to go along with what she wanted, he probably found it the easiest thing to do. I think his political career was very important to her—she enjoyed the reflected glory, you see. "My son the MP" and all that.'

Walking back along the High Street, Lineham said, 'Well, that didn't get us very far, did it?'

'Oh I don't know. I thought it was fascinating.'

Lineham's grunt indicated that in his view that didn't stop it being a waste of time. 'Not surprising, by the sound of it, that someone decided to pick up a pillow and finish her off.'

'Maybe not, Mike. But who? And why?' But Thanet was content at the moment not really to give his mind to the subject. He turned up his face to the sun. How he loved the summer! As far as he was concerned this glorious weather could go on for ever. Devotees of the British climate who say that it is good to have variety, that we appreciate the sun more because it doesn't always shine, had got it all wrong, in his opinion. He hadn't heard of those who lived in California complaining.

There were more people about now and a number of cars arriving at All Saints' Church where the bells were pealing out for morning service. The bellringers were improving, thought Thanet, and he counted. Ten bells today, the full complement.

Lineham was being single-minded. 'I wonder if she's right about him having an affair. Because if so . . . No, I suppose not.'

'What?'

'Well, I was thinking. I know an MP earns a decent whack in comparison with us, say, but if you think he's got to keep up that great big house, pay a housekeeper and run a flat in town . . . And if he's got a mistress, he'd no doubt want to wine and dine her, give her presents and so on . . . he could find himself pretty strapped for money. But then I thought, no, I bet he's got a nice fat private income on top of his salary to help out.'

'Not necessarily, I suppose. His father could have left everything to his mother—which could be why she was still living in the house. We really must find out about her will, Mike, go and see the solicitor first thing tomorrow morning.'

By the time they reached Thaxden people were coming out of church. 'The service must start at 10.30 here,' said Thanet.

'Reporters waiting for the Fairleighs, by the look of it.' Lineham nodded at three men and a woman clustered around the lych-gate at the entrance to the churchyard.

Thanet spotted Grace and Hugo Fairleigh talking to another couple as they walked down the path to the

lych-gate. Their clothes were sober but not funereal.
Hugo was wearing a dark suit and discreet tie, Grace a
navy linen suit with a navy and white silk scarf tucked
into the neckline. Although the whole village must be
buzzing with news of the murder Hugo must have decided that the best way to suppress gossip was to meet
it head on, appear in public as if nothing other than the
personal tragedy of losing his mother had happened.
Thanet was surprised, though, that Grace had accompa-
nied him. Her absence would surely have occasioned no
comment—or perhaps it would, in the circumstances.
In any case, he wondered what it was that made her
continue to behave as a loyal wife, if everything Caroline had said were true.

'There are the Fairleighs,' he said to Lineham.

The sergeant slowed down. 'You want me to stop?'

'No. Use your head, Mike. We don't want to talk to
them here. No doubt they'll be coming straight home,
once they've got rid of the reporters.'

'Sorry. Wasn't thinking.'

At the entrance to Thaxden Hall a man up a ladder
was taking down the big sign advertising the fête, and
a lorry half loaded with trestle tables was parked in
front of the house. As they awaited an answer to their
knock two men carrying tea-urns came around the corner of the house and put them on the lorry. Heading
back to the village hall, probably, thought Thanet.

The door opened. This must be the Fairleighs'
housekeeper, he guessed.

The girl was in her early twenties, plump, dark and
cheerful with cheeks as rosy as a ripe Cox and eyes that
sparkled with the buoyancy of youth. She was wearing
tight jeans and a T-shirt. Thanet had come across this
new breed of housekeeper before. Quick to spot the
dearth of high-quality well-trained servants, girls like
this went away to expensive colleges to be thoroughly

grounded in all the arts of running a house of any shape or size. Then, flourishing their Cordon Bleu certificates, they sailed into the lucrative waters of high-class domestic employment and commanded substantial salaries, along with fringe benefits such as rent-free accommodation, free food and often a car for their own use too. As in this case it seemed a harmonious arrangement, the employers feeling they got value for money, the housekeeper effortlessly blending in with a background often so like her own.

'Miss Young?' he said. He introduced himself and Lineham.

She looked slightly surprised that he knew her name. 'Yes,' she said. She smiled. 'But everyone calls me Sam.'

'We'd like a word with Mr Fairleigh.'

She glanced at her watch. 'He's gone to church, but he should be back any minute now. Will you wait?' Her accent confirmed her middle-class origins.

'Thank you.' They followed her into the drawing room where this morning, with the curtains drawn back, the room was filled with light, the greens and turquoises blending with the backdrop of sky, lawns and trees visible through the tall windows.

'Would you like some coffee while you're waiting?'

Thanet smiled to soften his refusal. 'But if we could just have a word,' he added quickly as she turned to go.

'Sure.' She perched on the arm of a chair. 'Any way I can help. This whole business, it's awful.' She shook her head. 'I still can't believe it's happened. I mean, it seems unreal.'

But she was showing no sign of grief, Thanet noted. Was there anyone who genuinely mourned Isobel Fairleigh's passing? he wondered.

'Look, sit down, won't you?' She waved a hospitable hand.

Thanet gave Lineham an almost imperceptible nod. *You do this one.*

'We understand that you were around most of yesterday,' said the sergeant, choosing the most business-like armchair he could find, a Victorian piece with scrolled wooden arms and heavily carved legs.

Thanet chose to wander in a leisurely manner around the room.

Sam rolled her eyes. 'Around is the word. It was, to put it mildly, somewhat hectic.'

'You were helping with the fête?'

'Amongst other things, yes.'

'Would you mind running quickly through your day for us?'

She put up her hand, scrunched up a handful of dark curls and tugged at them, as if to activate her memories of the previous day, then launched into a summary of her activities. In between her normal duties she had helped in the morning with setting up the arrangements for the teas and generally lending a hand wherever she was needed. In the afternoon she had run one of the sideshows.

On a table near the window were several photographs in ornate silver frames. Thanet bent to study them, his attention focusing on one of Grace Fairleigh and the baby. It was taken in profile, Grace looking up at the child she was holding in raised arms in front of her, mother and baby smiling at each other with such love and tenderness that Thanet saw at once what Caroline had meant. They seemed to be encircled in an almost visible nimbus of radiant happiness. From this angle the child looked perfectly normal. Thanet wondered that the photograph was still on display, here in the drawing room where Grace Fairleigh would see it every day of her life. He would have thought it would be too painful a reminder of what she had lost.

Lineham was still questioning Sam. 'Did you come into the house at all in the afternoon?'

She shook her head.

'Or see anyone else come in?'

Another shake. 'I was on the lawn at the side of the house. I couldn't see either the front or the back door from there.'

Lineham glanced at Thanet. *Anything else?*

'The post, yesterday, Miss Young . . .'

'Sam, please.'

'All right, Sam. Do you happen to remember how many letters there were?'

She thought for a moment, screwing up her eyes. 'There were some letters, yes, but I couldn't tell you how many. I was in rather a hurry, so I just picked them up, glanced through them to see if there were any for me, and put them on the table in the hall, as usual.'

'Do you remember who they were for?'

'Sorry, no. I never sort them out. There's usually quite a lot of mail, most of it for Hugo—Mr Fairleigh—so he always does that, if he's here. Or Grace, if he's not. I know there were some for him, though, because I saw him go off to the study with them later.'

'We know that Mrs Fairleigh senior received at least one letter yesterday. Did you happen to notice how many letters were left on the table in the hall after Mr Fairleigh had taken his?'

Sam shook her head again. 'No, sorry.'

'And you say you didn't notice who any of them were for, when you were looking to see if there were any for you?'

'No. Why should I? The Fairleighs' mail is their own affair, not mine.' The colour in her cheeks intensified. 'I'm not interested in snooping.'

'I'm sure you're not,' said Thanet, smiling and

meaning what he said. 'You have better things to do. All the same, if you do happen to remember, perhaps you could give us a ring.'

The front door opened and closed, and footsteps crossed the hall. Samantha jumped up and ran to open the drawing-room door, relieved no doubt at the excuse to break off the interview. 'Hugo?'

Fairleigh appeared. 'Bloody reporters. They're a pain in the neck.' He must have walked back from church, and his fair skin was flushed, his forehead beaded with sweat. He took out a handkerchief and dabbed at his face. 'Ah, good morning, Inspector. Phew, it's a scorcher today, isn't it? Sam, if we could have some iced lemonade?'

'It's ready in the fridge.' She lifted her eyebrows at Thanet. 'If you've finished with me, Inspector?'

Fairleigh laughed. 'Been giving Sam the third degree have you, Thanet?'

Thanet smiled. Despite the brush with reporters Fairleigh seemed in a good mood today. Thanet wondered how long the MP's affability would last when he realised that the investigation was focusing on the family. 'By all means go and get the lemonade, Sam.'

Fairleigh crossed to the window and raised the sash higher, fanning himself with his handkerchief. He did not take his jacket off, Thanet noted. Strictly schooled in the rules of polite behaviour, no doubt he would consider it incorrect to remove the jacket of a suit in the presence of a third person, even in his own house.

Fairleigh put his handkerchief away. 'So,' he said, turning. 'Have you any news yet?'

Thanet side-stepped the question. 'We'd be grateful if you'd have a look at this, sir, see if any of the names rings a bell. It's a list of everyone who was at the fête yesterday.' It occurred to him belatedly that he should have shown the list to Caroline.

Fairleigh took the typewritten sheets, put on some

gold-rimmed half-moon spectacles and half turned to catch the light from the window. He ran his fingers down the pages at considerable speed, rather as one does when looking for a particular name in a telephone directory. Thanet supposed that Fairleigh was practised at skimming quickly through documents, but all the same it seemed to him that there could be more to it than that, that the MP was specifically checking to see if a certain name was on the list. If so, whose could it be?

He watched with interest as Fairleigh reached the end of the list, turned back to the beginning and went through it again more slowly. This time it seemed to Thanet that he paused over a name on the last page. But finally he handed the paper back, shaking his head. Was there relief in his eyes?

'Sorry. I know a lot of these people, of course, many of them are local and my constituents, but no one there has any special significance in connection with my mother. So where do we go from here?'

'There are one or two further questions I'd like to put to you.'

'Go ahead.' Fairleigh sat down on one of the sofas. 'Do sit down, Inspector.'

Sam returned carrying a silver tray bearing three tall glasses and a crystal jug clinking with ice-cubes and filled with a pale, opaque liquid. Fresh lemonade, Thanet was willing to bet. No synthetic bottled stuff for Fairleigh.

She poured a glass for her employer, handed it to him, then looked at Thanet. 'I know you said you didn't want coffee, Inspector, but I thought some fresh lemonade . . . ?' She raised her eyebrows, jug poised over a second glass.

Thanet shook his head, catching the flicker of disappointment in Lineham's eyes as he followed suit. He would have loved a glass himself and his mouth watered as he imagined the refreshing tingle of the cool, slightly acid liquid passing over his tongue and down his throat. But he suspected that all too soon now Fairleigh was going to cotton on to the direction Thanet's questions were taking, and an explosion would almost certainly follow. In which case Thanet wanted to avoid anything resembling the atmosphere of a social occasion.

Sam gave a little shrug, refilled the glass which Fairleigh had drunk straight off, and left.

Fairleigh took another long swallow. 'Unwise decision, Inspector. This is delicious. You don't know what you're missing.' He put the glass down, lit one of his low-tar cigarettes and inhaled greedily. 'Well, fire away.' He flicked a quick glance at Lineham, who was opening his notebook and taking out a pen.

'Can you think of anyone your mother knew whose name begins with the letter B?'

Fairleigh looked surprised, then his eyes narrowed. 'Christian name or surname?'

'I'm not sure.'

'Why do you ask?' Fairleigh's tone was cool, his affability rapidly fading.

'Because we've been looking through your mother's diary and . . .'

'You've been *what*?'

'Looking through your mother's diary, sir.' Thanet tried to keep his tone as matter-of-fact as possible.

'For what purpose?' Fairleigh's tone was now positively glacial, his eyes like chips of blue ice.

Here we go, thought Thanet. Out of the corner of his eye he could see Lineham sitting very still. Bracing himself, no doubt.

9

The lines of Fairleigh's face had sharpened, as if the flesh had melted away from the bones. His eyes sparked with anger and his mouth was a thin, hard line, his prominent nose more beak-like than ever.

He looked, Thanet thought, like an eagle about to swoop upon its prey. But he himself had weathered far worse storms than the one about to break and now that it had arrived he was glad. It would clear the air.

It was important, though, to get in first, before Fairleigh had launched into a tirade he might later regret.

'Mr Fairleigh,' he said calmly, 'I think it would be sensible, at this point, to face certain facts.'

'What facts?' The words were as staccato as machine-gun bullets. But the long years in politics had taught the MP the value of self-control and he was containing his anger, just, until he knew whether it would be prudent to unleash it.

Thanet was crisp, formal. 'One: that this is a murder

investigation. Two: that in such an investigation nothing is sacrosanct. Three: that every avenue must be explored, no matter where it leads. Four: that innocent people are bound to be hurt by what seems to them unnecessary scrutiny. And five: that as there is as yet no evidence whatsoever of an intruder, we would be failing in our duty if we did not investigate the possibility that your mother was killed by someone she knew.' He did not add, *Six: and that someone could be one of your family.* This was self-evident.

Fairleigh stubbed out his cigarette with unnecessary force and stood up, once again betraying his tension by thrusting his hands in his pockets and jingling keys and coins. He crossed to stand looking out the window.

Thanet and Lineham raised their eyebrows at each other behind his back. Was it possible that Thanet had managed to defuse the situation? He tried to think himself into the MP's position. If Fairleigh were guilty, it wouldn't help to antagonise the police. If the MP were innocent, he would naturally be upset and angry at the prospective invasion of his privacy. Anyone would, after all. But as a public figure Fairleigh had much more to lose. It would be very much in his interest to keep on good terms with the police, try to persuade them to keep the investigation as low-key as possible. So he might, he just might damp down the fires of resentment and present a cooperative face.

He watched the MP's rigid back for the first sign of capitulation and yes, there it was, a slight sagging of the shoulders. Fairleigh sighed and turned.

'Very well, Thanet, I take your point. The important thing is to get this matter cleared up as quickly as possible. Though how you can imagine . . .' He shook his head apparently more in sorrow than in anger, and returned to his seat. 'So. You were saying?'

'That we've been looking through your mother's diary and it seems that on the first day of every month she met someone with the initial B.' Thanet fished the diary out of his pocket. 'Look.'

Fairleigh took the diary and riffled through it, pausing from time to time. 'Yes, I see.' He shook his head again. 'I'm sorry, I can't help you there. I've no idea who it could be.'

'But if you do think of anyone, you'll . . .'

'Yes, of course. I'll let you know at once.'

'And you have no idea where she might have been going, on those dates?'

'I'm a busy man, Inspector. During the week I'm rarely here. Perhaps my wife or my aunt might be able to help you.'

'I'll ask them, of course.'

'Was there anything else?'

'One minor point. I understand that a number of letters were delivered here yesterday.'

Fairleigh looked surprised. 'Yes, that's true. But what . . . ?'

'Most of them were for you, I suppose.'

'I do get an enormous amount of mail, as you can imagine. Mostly constituency business. And yes, most of yesterday's letters were for me.'

'And the others?'

Fairleigh shrugged. 'I've no idea. I don't think my aunt receives many letters, so I imagine they were either for my wife or my mother. And as they both have the same surname, I wouldn't notice unless I actually looked at the initial. I just took all the ones addressed to me and left the rest on the hall table.'

'Can you remember how many there were?'

Another shrug. 'Three or four, I think. I really can't remember.'

Thanet rose. 'Thank you, sir. I think that's about it, for the moment.'

'Inspector . . .'

'Yes?'

'That list . . . Could I have another look at it?'

'By all means.' Thanet handed it over.

Fairleigh turned to the last page—the page where, Thanet remembered, the MP had paused during his second perusal and where all those who had helped at the fête were listed.

Fairleigh put his finger on a name. 'I did just wonder . . . but I didn't mention it, because the man's still in prison.'

Thanet sat down again. 'What?' Was the MP casting around for something, anything, to direct Thanet's attention away from the family?

'I didn't say anything before because I felt . . . But I do realise, now, that one simply can't afford to allow sympathy to get in the way, not when it's a matter as serious as this, and my own mother was . . . She's a widow, you see.'

'Who?'

'Well, this Mrs Tanner, who was helping with the teas . . . You remember you asked me yesterday if there was anyone who might have a grudge against my mother?'

Thanet nodded.

'Wayne Tanner, her son . . . He's her only child and it was my mother's evidence that helped put him behind bars. I know Mrs Tanner is pretty bitter about it still.'

'I'm surprised, in that case, that she was helping here yesterday.'

'Her father's dying of cancer. She's been involved in working for the hospice appeal for some time. I know she helps in the hospice shop in Sturrenden, for example. That's probably why she agreed to lend a hand.'

'What happened with her son?'

Apparently, one night in early autumn last year there had been a serious fire at the village school. Old Mrs Fairleigh, driving home from one of her bridge evenings, had seen two youths climbing over the wall at the side of the school playground. She knew most of the local lads by sight and had recognised them. Wayne Tanner, aged eighteen, was one. As soon as she heard that the school was ablaze she rang the police and told them what she had seen.

It was generally known in the village that Tanner was a trouble-maker. There had been various minor offences—stealing from the village shop, windows broken in an empty house, vandalism in gardens—none of which had been reported to the police because people felt sorry for his mother, whose husband was disabled. But the consensus of opinion was that sooner or later Wayne would find himself in serious trouble and no one was surprised when after the fire he was arrested. The evidence against him was conclusive: his clothes still stank of paraffin, and his fingerprints were all over a door which had survived the fire relatively undamaged. Although it was a first offence it was a serious one. Thaxden Primary School was large, serving several of the surrounding villages, and there had been around sixty thousand pounds' worth of damage. Tanner had been convicted and got twelve months.

Mrs Tanner, by now a widow, had made her bitterness against Mrs Fairleigh plain, causing an unpleasant scene outside the Court. The old lady had endured the encounter with dignity, but Hugo knew that it had upset her. She told him later, however, that she had no regrets about identifying Wayne. In her view, if action had been taken against him earlier over some of his minor misdemeanours, he might have been given a sufficient shock to prevent him from graduating later to more serious crime. Mrs Tanner, in her view, had only herself to blame. She had been too soft with the boy.

It sounded to Thanet unlikely in the extreme that Mrs Tanner should, nine months later, take it into her head to resort to murder in order to take revenge for her son's prison sentence, but one never knew. Stranger things had happened, and if the woman were mentally unstable . . .

He took down Mrs Tanner's address and thanked Fairleigh for the information. 'We'll certainly look into it.'

There was a knock at the door and Sam came in. 'Sorry to interrupt, Hugo, but there's a TV crew at the door. They want an interview with you.'

Fairleigh groaned. 'I suppose I'll have to have a word with them, or they'll never go away.' He stood up. 'If we've finished, then, Thanet?'

'Just one other point, sir. Could I have the name of your mother's solicitor?'

Fairleigh frowned, then shrugged. 'It's Oliver Bassett, of Wylie, Bassett and Protheroe.'

'Thank you.' Good, a local firm. That should help.

At the door the MP hesitated. 'Er, Thanet . . .'

'Yes, sir?'

'I can rely upon your discretion, can't I? I mean, the press are going to be after you too . . . Nothing too sensational, eh?'

'I'm always discreet, sir.' Fairleigh would have to be satisfied with that, thought Thanet. He wasn't going to tie himself down with promises, false or otherwise. Occasionally the help of the media was invaluable, and one never knew when it might be needed. All the same, he was going to do his best to keep out of their way. He hated public exposure, unless it was essential. 'If I could have a word with Miss Ransome now?'

Fairleigh nodded. 'Sam will take you up.'

'No, it's all right. We can find our own way.'

'Through there, then.' Fairleigh pointed to a door at the back of the hall and without waiting went out, closing the front door behind him.

Thanet and Lineham were halfway across the hall when Grace Fairleigh emerged from a door on the right. She hesitated when she saw the two policemen and Thanet stopped. 'Mrs Fairleigh . . .'

Having heard so much about her from Caroline he was curious to talk to her again, and as an excuse to do so there was one small point that he could raise with her, even if he didn't think there was much point in doing so.

In the past, whenever he had seen her at public functions, he had been struck by her elegance, her poise, her air of dignity and remoteness. She must, he had thought, have always been a naturally reserved person. She and Caroline were a classic example of the attraction of opposites and it was obvious that both had gained much from mutual support and encouragement.

According to Caroline the birth of the baby had transformed Grace and after seeing that photograph in the drawing room Thanet could believe it. The Grace Fairleigh who stood before them now was hardly recognisable as the same woman. How much of that warmth still survived beneath that cool, well-groomed façade? Signs of strain were evident in the bruised flesh beneath her eyes but apart from that there was nothing in her manner or appearance to indicate that anything in the household was amiss.

The carefully plucked eyebrows arched in polite inquiry. 'Yes, Inspector?'

'There was something I wanted to ask you.'

She said nothing, merely tilted her head a little, expectantly.

'When I was talking to you and Miss Ransome yesterday, I had the impression that you were surprised when she said she hadn't been upstairs during the afternoon.'

There was a moment's silence, during which her expression did not change. Then, with a hint of disdain, she said, 'Then you were mistaken, Inspector. And now, if you'll excuse me . . .' She turned away and began to climb the stairs, head held high and back ramrod-straight.

The corners of Thanet's mouth tugged down ruefully. 'Ouch. I suppose I asked for that, didn't I?'

'You didn't really expect her to admit she thought Miss Ransome was lying, did you?'

'How right you are. Mike. No, I didn't. Come on.'

Pushing open the door which Fairleigh had indicated they found themselves in the downstairs corridor of Isobel Fairleigh's flat, near the bottom of the staircase. In the kitchen something sizzled in the oven and one end of the scrubbed wooden table was neatly laid for a solitary lunch, with white tablecloth embroidered with forget-me-nots, knife, fork, spoon and table-napkin in a silver ring.

'Odd lot, aren't they?' said Lineham. 'You'd think they'd have asked her around for dinner next door, in the circumstances.'

'Quite.'

Calling Miss Ransome's name in order not to alarm her by their sudden appearance, they climbed the stairs and tried the sitting room: empty. The bathroom was also empty, its door ajar. Apart from Isobel Fairleigh's bedroom, which was still sealed, the only other upstairs room was along the corridor to the right of the staircase. This must be Letty Ransome's bedroom. They knocked and waited before opening the door to glance inside. It was simply furnished, with narrow brass bedstead, crocheted white bedspread and white curtains sprigged with rosebuds. The few items of furnishing were, Thanet guessed, rejects from the rest of the house: a narrow oak wardrobe with a spotted mirror, a rickety bedside table, a worn Persian rug beside the bed. There was no telephone extension in here, Thanet noticed. The contrast with the other rooms in the flat shouted aloud Letty's position as a dependant. Just how much had she resented that position? Thanet wondered.

On the bed lay a shabby black handbag and a black straw hat which had seen better days.

'Looks as though she went to church too,' said Lineham. 'I wonder where she is.'

'Outside, perhaps?'

They tracked her down dead-heading the roses, trug on the ground beside her. She was wearing a broad-brimmed straw hat fraying at the edges, leather gardening gloves and a heavy-duty canvas apron over her black dress. She straightened up, flustered, as she saw them approaching. Despite the hat she looked hot, cheeks and forehead flushed with the exertion.

'Oh, Inspector . . .' She laid the secateurs in the trug on top of the rose clippings, took off one of the gloves and tucked behind her ear a strand of hair which had fallen across her face. 'I hope you don't think I'm . . . But it was so quiet indoors, without Isobel . . . I had to *do* something, you see.'

She was apologising in case they thought she was being disrespectful to the dead. 'Life has to go on,' Thanet said gravely, aware that in situations like this people find clichés comforting.

She looked relieved. 'Oh, yes. Yes, it does, doesn't it?'

'Could you spare us a few minutes?'

'Of course.' She dropped both gloves into the trug then took a wisp of handkerchief from the pocket of her apron, removed her hat and dabbed delicately at her forehead and upper lip. 'It's so hot today, isn't it?'

'Perhaps we could sit in the shade, over there.' Thanet pointed to a slatted wooden bench under a beech tree.

Letty Ransome nodded agreement, tucked her hat under her arm and removed her apron as they walked, folding it neatly and laying it on her lap when she sat down. Evidently she did not think it proper to be interviewed by the police informally attired.

Thanet sat down beside her and Lineham leaned against the tree.

What was she like, Thanet wondered, beneath that spinsterly façade?

At first it seemed that she had nothing new to tell them. Interestingly enough, she read the list of names in much the same way as Hugo: a swift glance through and then a second, more careful perusal. Had they both been looking for the same name? Thanet wondered.

She dismissed out of hand the idea that Mrs Tanner could have had anything to do with the murder and then, frowning over Isobel's diary, said that to her knowledge Isobel knew no one whose name began with B; the regular entries were a mystery to her. She knew nothing about the previous day's mail, said that it was usually Grace who brought Isobel's letters up and read them to her. 'Such a sweet girl. She used to come up every morning and every evening to read to Isobel. In the morning it would be the newspapers and in the evening *The Forsyte Saga*. Isobel was very fond of *The Forsyte Saga*. I used to come and listen too. Grace reads so beautifully, you know, and she'd just reached the place where Soames and Irene . . . I'm sorry, you won't want to hear all this. But it upset her to see Isobel so helpless—well, it upset us all. Isobel was always so independent.'

'What was she like, as a person, your sister?'

A shadow flitted across Letty Ransome's brow, but she said firmly, 'She was very kind to me. She took me in, you know, gave me a home when Father died. Otherwise I'd have . . . Well, I don't know what would have become of me.' She flushed and said somewhat defiantly, 'Oh, I know people thought she made use of me, but I didn't mind. I felt it was the least I could do, to make life as comfortable as possible for her, in the circumstances. In any case, I think most people misunderstood her.'

'In what way?'

'Well, people thought she was bossy, you know, and overbearing. And it was true, I suppose. But it wasn't her fault she was like that, it was Father's.' She smiled and shook her head indulgently. 'Dear Father, he never really got over his disappointment, you see. He so wanted a son. And when, after me, he was told that Mother couldn't have any more children, he decided that Isobel would have to be the next best thing. I was always too timid, but Isobel, well, she was a bold, headstrong child, and he encouraged her. She was to be strong, determined, even ruthless, if necessary, if she believed herself to be in the right. He disapproved of women in politics—in many ways he was a conventional man—otherwise I'm sure he'd have encouraged her to try for Parliament herself. As it was he told her that she must be ambitious in her choice of a husband, and of course she was. Everyone thought Humphrey was heading for great things.' She sighed. 'We never know what fate has in store for us, do we?'

'I suppose she must have been very pleased when her son became a member of parliament?'

'Oh yes. Delighted. It was what she always wanted for him. And Grace, of course, was the perfect wife. Not

like . . .' She stopped dead, as if she had suddenly come
up against a brick wall.

Thanet's interest quickened. 'Not like . . . ?'

'Oh, just a girl Hugo brought home from Oxford
once. But she wasn't suitable.'

So why this reluctance? Because she didn't wish to
discuss family matters which she felt did not concern
him? No, there was more to it than that, he was sure.
He would have to be careful, avoid direct questions, or
she would clam up altogether.

'I suppose your sister would have had very strong
views about that.'

'Yes, she did.' Letty Ransome's fingers had suddenly
become very busy, rolling and unrolling a corner of the
gardening apron on her lap.

'It's important for an MP's wife to have the right
background.'

'Yes, it is.' She was frowning, scarcely listening to
him. Trying to make up her mind about something?
Her head was bent and she gave him a quick sideways
glance. He could almost see her thinking, *Shall I tell
him?*

Tell him what?

He glanced at Lineham who raised his eyebrows and
lifted his shoulders.

He decided to use silence. Most people find it uncomfortable, and few can withstand the pressure it puts
upon them. Letty Ransome, he guessed, would not be
one of them.

Although she kept her eyes down, looking apparently at her fingers which were still busy with the corner of the apron, he knew that she was aware of his
steady gaze, and could feel her tension mounting.

'I . . .' she said, and gave him another of those fleeting, sideways glances.

He said nothing.

'Yesterday . . .' she began again. And stopped.

He waited.

She put her hand up to her forehead as if her dilemma were causing her physical pain. Which perhaps it was.

'Oh dear. I don't know what to do, I really don't.' She cast a frantic glance around the garden as if looking for help from an unknown source.

'Why don't you tell me what's worrying you?' he said gently. 'You'll feel much better if you get it off your chest.'

'You think so?' She looked full at him now, as if seeking verification of his sincerity.

'I do.' He was firm, authoritative. He meant it. Whatever was worrying her would continue to worry her until she had unburdened herself.

Her restless fingers relinquished the apron and she folded her hands together in her lap. She had come to a decision. 'It's about Pamela.'

Thanet's eyebrows lifted. 'Pamela?'

'The girl I was talking about. The one Hugo brought home from Oxford. I . . .' She lifted her chin. 'I saw her here, yesterday.'

'At the fête?'

'Yes. I'm sure it was her.'

'You've seen her often, since the time your nephew brought her home?'

'No! That's the point! Never! That's why I was so surprised to see her. Here, in Thaxden. I'd forgotten all about her, but she really hadn't changed much. She looked older, of course, and she'd put on a little weight. But apart from that . . . I recognised her at once. It was quite a shock.'

'What was she doing?'

'Oh, just wandering around the stalls, like everybody else.'

'By herself?'

'Yes.'

Thanet was remembering that expression he had caught on Hugo Fairleigh's face yesterday afternoon. Fairleigh had looked disconcerted, had been watching someone or something intently, and Thanet had been sufficiently intrigued to try to see who or what it was. Could it have been this Pamela? If so, why had he looked put out? He might have been surprised to see a woman he had been fond of twenty odd years ago, but discomposed? Surely not—unless . . . Several pieces of the jigsaw suddenly clicked together in Thanet's brain. His mind raced. Was it possible that this two and two really did make four?

He betrayed none of his excitement, but Lineham knew him too well. The sergeant had stiffened. Or perhaps he had come to the same interesting conclusion himself.

'What does she look like?'

'Well, she's an inch or two taller than me, and I'm five feet four, with dark curly hair.'

'What was she wearing?'

Letty Ransome frowned. Thanet guessed that she wasn't very interested in clothes and didn't pay much attention to them. But on this occasion she would have been sufficiently intrigued to notice, surely?

Her eyes lit up in triumphant recollection. 'I remember now. A navy dress with little white flowers on it. And long sleeves.'

So in one respect at least he had guessed correctly. This was the woman that Mrs Kerk, Isobel's housekeeper, had seen walking along the passage to the back door from the direction of the stairs, only a little while before Fairleigh and Doc Mallard had come hurrying in. Lineham had made the connection too. The sergeant's eyes were alert with speculation. He looked, Thanet thought with amusement, like a hunting dog which had just caught the scent of the fox.

Now to see if another of those pieces fitted. 'Tell me, Miss Ransome, I couldn't help noticing that when you looked through this list just now, it was almost as if you were looking for a particular name. Was it this Pamela's?'

Letty blushed. 'Oh, you noticed. Yes. But it wasn't there. But then, it wouldn't be, would it—or at least, I wouldn't recognise it, if she's married, that is. And I should think she would be, she's such a pretty girl.'

Hardly the word to describe a woman of forty-odd, thought Thanet. But then Letty Ransome was in her late sixties, so perhaps it was understandable. 'What was her maiden name?'

'Grice.' Letty's forehead wrinkled. 'That was one of the things Isobel didn't like about her. She said it was such a common name, and just showed what sort of background the girl came from.'

'Your nephew was serious about her?'

'Oh yes. They actually got engaged. Pamela came here several times, to stay, and Isobel was charming to her. Gave dinner parties for her, took her about and introduced her to friends ... I was surprised she took so much trouble over her, considering how much she disapproved of the match.'

Interesting, thought Thanet. He found it surprising too, from what he'd learned of Isobel. He'd have to think about that later.

'So what went wrong?'

'Pamela called it off. Hugo was heartbroken, he really was so fond of her. But she wouldn't change her mind.'

'Did she give any reason?'

A delicate shrug. 'Only that she didn't think they were suited. Isobel was very relieved. And of course, it all worked out for the best in the end, when Grace came along.'

Though perhaps not so well in the long run, thought Thanet, watching the shadow flit across Letty's face as she no doubt thought precisely the same thing. 'Did your nephew know she was here yesterday?'

Letty shook her head. 'I don't know. I've hardly seen him since, and in any case it's not really the sort of thing I'd be likely to mention.'

'You didn't see him speak to her at all?'

Another shake of the head. 'No. Er, Inspector . . .'

'Yes?'

'I don't know whether it's worth mentioning . . .'

'What, Miss Ransome?'

'It's just that, well . . .' She shook her head. 'No, I don't want to waste your time.'

'I'm sure you wouldn't be. What is it?'

'Well, it was a little odd . . .'

This time Thanet just waited.

She looked at him timidly. 'It's just that while Isobel was ill, there were a couple of phone calls.'

'What sort of phone calls?'

'Someone wanting to speak to her.'

'A man, or a woman?'

'I'm not sure. The voice wasn't very clear, a bit sort of muffled.'

'When was this?'

'Well, the first one was during the week after she had her stroke.'

'That would be the week before last?'

'Yes. And the second was a few days ago.'

Both calls had been very brief, apparently. On the first occasion the caller had asked to speak to Isobel, had been told that she was ill and had rung off. The second call had come on the morning when for the first time the fingers on Isobel's paralysed hand had moved a little, and Letty, still excited by this, had told the caller that her sister was much better, though still in bed. Once again, the connection had been cut. On neither occasion had the caller given his/her name. Letty was positive that this person had never rung before, and had had no idea who it could be.

'Of course, Isobel was involved in so many things . . . People were always ringing up and half the time I had no idea who they were or what they wanted. That's why I hesitated to mention it.'

Thanet reassured her that she had done the right thing. Every scrap of information helped, he said, no matter how trivial it seemed. Now, there was just one other question he wanted to ask. 'Miss Ransome, I understand that yesterday, just before you came into the house, a man who works here—I believe his name is Ernie—came to speak to you, at your stall.'

He watched with interest as this time the blush crept up her neck in an ugly red tide which left her cheeks and face glowing. Why the embarrassment? Surely there couldn't be any question of romance between them. Letty Ransome was hardly the type for a liaison with the gardener.

The fingers were at work again, this time plucking at the fraying straw around the brim of her hat. 'Yes, that's right. But I don't see . . .'

'What did he want to speak to you about?'

She shook her head in confusion. 'I can't remember. Something trivial, I'm sure.' Her forehead creased in an apparent effort to remember.

But she did remember, Thanet was sure of it. She was not a good liar.

'I'm sorry. I expect it was something to do with the fête. He was busy with various odd jobs all day.'

Whatever it was, it was sufficiently important for her to stick to her guns. And of course, it might have nothing whatsoever to do with the murder. Thanet decided to leave it at that for the moment. 'Does Ernie live on the premises?'

'Yes. He has a little flat over the stables.'

And although she was relieved that he hadn't pressed the matter she hadn't liked the implications of that question, he noted. He thanked her for her help and they left her sitting on the bench in the shade.

'V-e-r-y interesting,' said Lineham, when they were out of earshot.

'I agree. Very. We'll discuss it later. Meanwhile I want you to nip along to the stables, tackle Ernie himself before she gets to him, try and find out what all that was about. I'm going to see what Mr Fairleigh has to say about this Pamela business. Join me as soon as you can.'

Thanet headed purposefully back towards the house.

10

As he neared the house Thanet's pace slowed. It had just dawned on him that he had been so engrossed in what Letty Ransome was telling him that he had forgotten to query her account of her visit to the house around the time of the murder. Was she perhaps much cleverer than he had given her credit for, deliberately manoeuvring him away from looking too closely at her own movements by telling him about Pamela Grice—if that was still her surname—and about the strange phone calls? He didn't think so, but his judgement was far from infallible. Should he go back?

He hovered near the back door, undecided. It had also occurred to him that perhaps he was being too precipitate, rushing off to tackle Hugo like this. It might be better to discuss the implications of the Pamela/Hugo business with Lineham first. After all, he could hardly come straight out with the questions he really wanted to ask: *Is Pamela née Grice your mistress, and did she murder your mother?*

Besides, it might be better not to let Fairleigh know that they knew about Pamela—if there was anything to know, that is. Her presence here yesterday could have been purely coincidental. Perhaps she happened to be in the area and had simply been satisfying a natural curiosity to see again the house of which she could have been mistress and the man she might have married.

No, he couldn't believe that, in view of the fact that she had been seen near the scene of the murder around the time when it had been committed. And he was still convinced that Fairleigh had been lying in his account of that trip indoors at 3.30.

So, to go back and talk to Letty again, or to alert Fairleigh, or neither? Thanet hesitated. Standing still he became aware of the murmur of voices somewhere over to his left. Straining his ears, he listened. Yes, that was Fairleigh, surely. And then Sam's voice, higher-pitched. They must be out in the garden.

The sounds tugged at him like a magnet. He made up his mind. No, he really couldn't leave without trying to find out if Fairleigh was involved with this woman. But he would have to tread warily, it was a sensitive subject.

Thanet cut diagonally across the courtyard towards the voices.

Fairleigh, his wife and Sam were having pre-lunch drinks in the Victorian conservatory which had been built on to the far side of the house. The glazed doors were hooked back to their fullest extent and at this time of day, when the sun had not yet come around, it was a pleasant place to sit, with cool tiled floor, comfortable white wicker chairs and a wealth of exotic plants in huge terracotta pots. Along the back was a narrow brick-edged border planted with climbers trained against the house wall and along the roof struts, trailing down in brilliant swathes of blue, white and magenta, their scent filling the warm, moist air.

It was a picture of gracious living and Thanet knew what Lineham would have said. *It's all right for some!*

Fairleigh was lounging on one of the broad window seats, smiling at Sam, glass in hand. No one would have believed from his appearance or demeanour that his mother had been murdered yesterday, thought Thanet. And then reproached himself for being unfair. A spurious gaiety often sprang up in such circumstances. It was a way of escaping from grim reality. Who knew what Fairleigh was really thinking or feeling?

Grace was gazing down at her glass with an air of abstraction. She glanced up, startled, as Thanet appeared.

Fairleigh stood up, smile fading.

'Oh really . . . Is there no peace? Not more questions, surely, Inspector.'

'If I could just have a word with you, sir . . .'

'Oh, very well.' Fairleigh drained off his glass and thumped it down irritably on the white wicker table nearby. 'Lunch in ten minutes, you said, Sam?'

'Yes. But . . .'

'Ten minutes,' said Fairleigh emphatically. 'We'll go to my study, Thanet.'

He headed for the door without waiting to see if Thanet was following.

In the study he crossed to look out of the window. 'More bloody reporters arriving, by the look of it. If this goes on we'll be in a state of siege. Can't you do something about it?'

'I'll see what I can do. The trouble is, all the while you're clearing up after the fête the open gates are an invitation for them to come in.'

'That's the last lorry-load out there. As soon as it's gone I'll get Ernie to close them.'

Fairleigh sat down behind his desk as if to ensure that Thanet knew who was in charge around here.

It was a pleasant, masculine room, with book-lined walls, comfortable well-worn leather armchairs and an antique desk as big as a small billiard table, its surface covered with piles of neatly stacked files and papers.

'Well?' said Fairleigh impatiently, lighting a cigarette. 'What is it this time?'

Suddenly, Thanet was fed up with being treated as an inferior being.

When Draco first arrived to take over Divisional Headquarters he was always pontificating about the importance of maintaining good relations with the public. An ambitious man before Angharad's illness, he still went through the motions of insisting that important people in the area should be treated with kid gloves.

Well, in deference to his superior, Thanet had taken care to be polite to this man, and much good had it done him. He had no intention of allowing himself to be manoeuvred into losing his temper, because that would be unprofessional, but he didn't see why he should be hamstrung by an irrational need to be conciliatory, just because Fairleigh was a member of parliament. The man was a suspect, and that was that.

'Your aunt tells me that she saw an old friend of yours at the fête yesterday.'

'Oh?' said Fairleigh, warily.

'A Pamela Grice.' He was watching the MP carefully and yes, although the man's self-control was excellent, there was a fraction of a second in which he froze. 'Did you see her?'

'Yes, I did, as a matter of fact.'

'You spoke to her?'

Fairleigh hesitated.

Thanet could understand his dilemma. If the MP had spoken to Pamela, he must realise that someone could have seen them talking, and he wouldn't want to risk being caught out in a lie.

'Yes. Briefly. I was very busy, as you know.'

'You haven't lost touch, then.'

A lorry engine roared into life outside and Fairleigh half rose to peer over his shoulder out of the window. 'Good, it's going.' He sank back into his chair again.

Thanet wasn't letting him off the hook. He waited, his expression making it clear that he expected an answer.

Fairleigh frowned. 'I really can't see what relevance this has to your inquiries, Thanet. But if you must know, last summer I met her for the first time in many years when I went to present the prizes at the Speech Day of the school in London where she teaches.'

'Do you know why she came yesterday?'

Fairleigh's patience was wearing thin. 'How on earth should I know? Why did anybody come? Why did you?'

'The odd thing is, her name doesn't appear on this list.' Thanet lifted the sheaf of papers he was still carrying.

'Perhaps she left before the list was made.'

'Perhaps.' The thought had occurred to Thanet. The question was, why? Because she knew what had happened, had even had a hand in it, and wanted to get away quickly before the storm broke? 'Or perhaps because she married. Grice was her maiden name, I understand.'

Fairleigh said nothing.

'Did she marry, do you know?'

'Her married name is Raven, I believe.' Fairleigh had attempted a casual tone, but it was obvious that he had been reluctant to give the information.

Thanet experienced a little spurt of elation. Now they had a starting point. He glanced quickly through the list of names. It wasn't there. Should he risk asking for her address? No, it would be best to leave Fairleigh in a state of uncertainty as to whether the police were going to follow this up. It shouldn't be difficult to trace her.

Suddenly Fairleigh leaped out of his chair. 'Oh, my God, look at that!'

A cameraman was trying to take a photograph of the MP through the window.

Fairleigh swept the curtains together, plunging the room into semi-darkness. 'That's it, I've had enough!' He stamped across the room to the door. 'Get rid of them, Thanet,' he snapped. 'I'll get Ernie to close the gates. And for God's sake *do* something about this harassment.'

In the hall Thanet ran into Lineham. 'I was just coming to look for you, sir.'

'Come on,' said Thanet grimly. He could understand Fairleigh's anger and sympathised with it, but he resented being ordered about without so much as token politeness.

He opened the front door and was at once showered with questions, a microphone thrust in his face. A brief statement was unavoidable and he gave it, then told the reporters that Fairleigh would not be coming out to speak to them again and that they were to leave the premises. With much grumbling they began piling into their cars and vans. Thanet and Lineham hurried to their car and followed the convoy down the drive. Ahead, Thanet saw two more cars pulling up. He'd have to arrange for a patrol car to keep an eye on the place, make sure the family wasn't plagued by the press, or he'd have Draco on his back.

Looking over his shoulder Thanet saw a small, elderly man hurrying along behind them.

'Ernie,' said Lineham, with a glance in the mirror.

Outside, the latest arrivals tumbled out of their cars and converged on the police car, waving notebooks.

Thanet wound down his window and shook his head at them. 'Sorry, you've missed the boat. I've already made a statement and there'll be no more at the moment.' But there'd be no peace until they were satisfied. On the spur of the moment he made up his mind. 'Press conference tomorrow morning at nine a.m.'

He wound up the window and Lineham, steering his way determinedly through the crowd, accelerated away.

Thanet put in his request for the patrol car and then settled back into his seat. They drove in silence for a while and then he said, 'So, how did you get on with Ernie?'

Lineham shrugged. 'Got nowhere, I'm afraid.' He assumed a rustic accent. 'Oi were running about here and there all day like a cat with a scalded tail, with messages for this one and that one. Do this, Ernie, do that, Ernie. Proper madhouse it were. How do you expect me to remember whether Oi went to talk to Miss Ransome at her stall?'

Thanet laughed. 'Very good, Mike. You've got hidden talents, I see.'

Lineham gave a sheepish grin. 'He's a bit of a character, sir. Like something out of the nineteenth century.'

'So why d'you think Miss Ransome was so embarrassed when I asked her about him?'

'Search me.' Lineham grinned. 'Perhaps he's her secret lover.'

'Ha ha. Very funny.'

'What about this Mrs Tanner? Think there's anything in it?'

'We can't dismiss it out of hand, of course, but I doubt it.'

OXFORD BOOK STORES

Peachtree Battle
2345 Peachtree Rd
Atlanta, GA 30305
OXFORD AT PEACHTREE BATTLE
OPEN 365 DAYS A YEAR

**** S A L E ****

1-9780553562521
WAKE THE DEAD   4.99 A S
SUBTOTAL   4.99
Sales tax   0.30
TOTAL   5.29
1-PAYMENT
CASH   6.00 N P
CHANGE DUE   0.71

89/812   3   10/07/93 10:51:17 1184

REFUNDS WITHIN 30
DAYS. RECEIPT REQUIRED.

'Unless she's a nut-case. Dear little Wayne the pyro-maniac is her only ewe lamb, isn't he?'

There were overtones of bitterness in Lineham's voice. He himself had suffered much in the past from being the only child of a possessive mother.

'Quite. We'd better check that he's still inside. You never know, with remission for good behaviour he could be out again by now.'

'We'll go and see Mrs Tanner?'

'No, we'll send Bentley, I think. He's good with older women.'

'And we aren't?'

'I have other plans for us.'

'Ah. Pamela Grice?'

'Pamela Raven now.' Thanet gave a brief account of his interview with Fairleigh.

Lineham listened eagerly. 'So d'you think she's the one he's having the affair with?'

'If he's having an affair at all. We've only got Caroline Plowright's word for it.'

'She seemed pretty certain.'

'But it was sheer speculation, remember. All the same . . .'

'It's pretty fishy, though, isn't it? That she was seen coming from the direction of the staircase to the old lady's bedroom around the time of the murder.'

'We are jumping to a lot of conclusions, remember, Mike.'

'You're suggesting that there were two women in their early forties, of medium height, plumpish, with dark curly hair and wearing long-sleeved navy dresses covered with little white flowers?'

Thanet laughed. 'I'm just saying we don't actually know that it was the same woman, Mike. I agree, it sounds likely.'

'Pretty well a dead cert, I'd say. Especially as Mr

Fairleigh apparently wasn't too keen to admit he knew her and talked to her yesterday. For my money, they are having an affair and the old lady found out and didn't like it.'

'No reason to murder her, though, Mike. Unless . . .'

The same thought occurred to them both simultaneously.

'Yes!' said Lineham. They were back at Headquarters and he pulled up with a flourish. 'She threatened to cut him out of her will!'

'If so, the solicitor might know something about it. I don't know though, Mike. It's a bit far-fetched, isn't it? After all, according to Miss Ransome, Mrs Fairleigh senior made the girl very welcome when Fairleigh brought her home, and it was Pamela who called it off.'

'I thought that was most peculiar, didn't you? That she should have gone out of her way to make Pamela feel at home when she was so much against the engagement?'

'I agree.' Thanet was remembering what his mother-in-law had said about Isobel Fairleigh. *She was very manipulative. I've seen her persuade people into doing things they didn't want to do without their ever realising how she'd managed it.* Was this what had happened with Pamela? If so, he couldn't quite see how.

'All the same, say we're right. Say it is Pamela he's having an affair with. Say she's the love of his life and when he met her last year it all started up again. His marriage has been a great disappointment to him and he decides he'll get a divorce and marry Pamela, and this time nothing will stop him. Say he tells his mother . . .'

'Before his wife?'

'We don't know he hasn't told her, do we?'

'True.'

'So say he tells his mother and she's dead against it.

She never did like Pamela, she's not his class, and she's getting on a bit to produce any children. Say Mrs Fairleigh threatens to cut him out of her will, like we said . . . You have to admit it would give him a very good motive.'

'You're right. We have to consider it a serious possibility.'

'Did you tell him Pamela had been seen in the house around the time of the murder?'

'No. I thought we'd keep that one up our sleeve. I'd like to tackle her about it first.'

'Which is why we're going to see her?'

'One of the reasons, yes. If we can find her. Come on, Mike.' Thanet opened the door and got out of the car. 'You'd better get to work, see if you can track her down. I'd like to see her today, if possible.'

'Where does she live?'

'London, I imagine. That's where she works, anyway. She's a teacher.'

'If they are in it together Mr Fairleigh is sure to have rung her to warn her we've been asking questions about her.'

'I know. That's why I want to follow through straight away.'

'Put the wind up them, you mean.'

'Yes.'

'If I find her, do I make an appointment, or is it to be a surprise visit?'

'An appointment. If we're right, she'll have been warned that a visit is on the cards, and we don't want to drive all the way to London only to find she's out. It is a Sunday, after all. She could be anywhere.'

They were back in the office now. The room was hot and stuffy and Thanet made straight for the window, flung it open.

Lineham headed for the row of telephone directories. 'You never know, we might be lucky and she'll be in the phone book.'

'Right, I'll leave you to it, then. I'll go and find Bentley, send him off to interview Mrs Tanner. I'll also get someone to check if Tanner's still inside. And I think I'll get Carson to go and see Jill Cochrane. She opened the fête yesterday and Fairleigh was with her most of the afternoon. She may have seen him talking to Pamela, might even have heard something of what they said.'

They were in luck. By the time Thanet had returned and had checked through the reports on his desk, Lineham had found their quarry. He put down the phone, beaming. 'Four o'clock, sir.'

'So I heard. Well done.' Thanet glanced at his watch. Two-thirty. 'Better make a courtesy call to the Met., let them know we're coming up, then we'll be on our way.'

11

At this time of the afternoon traffic on the London-bound carriageway of the M20 was light and they made good time. Later, of course, it would be nose-to-tail with day-trippers returning from the coast.

Pamela Raven lived in a pleasant tree-lined cul-de-sac of Victorian terraced houses. Thanet knew from Bridget's tentative inquiries that such houses have now become fashionable and command high prices. In many cases even the smallest have been divided into flats too expensive for youngsters like her to buy. For the moment she had had to settle for sharing a rented flat with three other girls and he thought that the prospect of her ever being able to afford to buy a place of her own in London remote in the extreme. He and Joan had often teased her, saying that her only hope was to marry a rich man with a house of his own. Now he hoped that that man would not be Alexander.

As Lineham backed the car into a tight parking

space Thanet said, 'Did she ask why we wanted to see her?'

'Yes. I was deliberately vague, just said it was about an incident at the fête yesterday.'

'Good. Of course, you do realise we've been taking it for granted that she lives alone?'

'It was P. E. Raven in the phone book,' said Lineham, edging the front nearside wing in past the rear offside wing of the car in front with only a hairsbreadth to spare.

'Her husband's name could begin with a P too.'

'Well, we'll soon find out, won't we, sir?' The sergeant, who prided himself on his driving skill, gave a triumphant smile as with no further manoeuvring the car slipped neatly into the space, coming to rest an inch or two away from the kerb and precisely parallel with it.

Thanet, who invariably found himself toing and froing to achieve such perfect alignment, said enviously, 'Why can't I ever do that?'

Pamela Raven greeted them with a nervous smile and led them through a narrow hall into a sitting room which ran the full depth of the house. Thanet guessed that two small rooms had been knocked into one. French doors at the far end led out into a small courtyard garden furnished with white wrought-iron chairs and table. They accepted her offer of tea and Thanet looked around while they waited.

The room had that comfortable lived-in air that makes visitors feel instantly at home. There was a green fitted carpet and curtains and chair-covers in cream linen with a stylised floral design. The floor to ceiling recesses on either side of the tiled Victorian grate were filled with books and there was a small unit stacked with tapes and records next to the hi-fi system. A bundle of knitting lay on one of the chairs and the desk in front of the window was covered with what looked like end-of-term exam papers. Pamela Raven had evidently been spending her Sunday afternoon hard at work.

Thanet stopped to look more closely at a couple of photographs on the mantelpiece: one of a teenaged girl sitting alone on a wall overlooking the beach—Pamela's daughter, Thanet guessed by the resemblance, and another of a younger version of the same girl with Pamela and a man. Mr Raven, Thanet presumed. If so, was he still around?

'Here we are.' She came back into the room carrying a tray of tea and biscuits. Balancing it on one hand she pushed some of the papers aside and set it down on the desk.

'Your husband and daughter, Mrs Raven?' said Thanet, nodding at the photograph.

'Ex-husband. We were divorced five years ago. And yes, that's Gwen, my daughter.'

Thanet watched as she poured the tea. She was informally dressed in a bright pink T-shirt and navy cotton trousers splashed with pink flowers, and certainly matched the description given to them by both Mrs Kerk, the old lady's housekeeper, and by Letty Ransome: early forties, medium height and build, dark curly hair.

They had already arranged that Lineham should conduct the interview and Thanet settled back to watch and listen. The sergeant began by saying that they understood Mrs Raven had attended the fête at Thaxden Hall the previous day.

She smiled. 'Yes, that's right.'

'May I ask why?'

She waved her hand at the window and the suburban street outside. 'Surely it's obvious. It's lovely to get out of London at weekends. I was born and brought up in the country and I miss it.'

Thanet had already guessed as much from her accent, a slow, country burr. This, presumably, was what Mrs Kerk had meant when she had said that the woman she had seen in the corridor was 'not a lady'. He personally found it most attractive. In fact, she was a very attractive woman. Her face was lively, expressive, and what she lacked in conventional beauty she made up for in warmth of personality. Thanet thought she would find it difficult to lie. Certainly his first impression was that he and Lineham had got it all wrong. He really could not see this woman plotting to murder a helpless old lady.

But appearances can be deceptive, as he had sometimes learned to his cost. It would depend, perhaps, on how much influence Hugo Fairleigh had over her—always assuming, of course, that it was indeed Pamela Raven with whom he was having an affair. If he were, Thanet could understand why: Grace Fairleigh would appear cold and unappealing by comparison.

'But what made you decide to attend this particular event?'

She shrugged. 'Someone I know happened to mention it.'

'Mr Fairleigh?'

She met his gaze squarely, almost defiantly. 'Yes.'

Interesting. So she and Fairleigh had decided that there was no point in attempting to conceal that there was a relationship of a kind between them.

'It was such a lovely day, and I knew I'd have to spend all day today marking exam papers. I thought it would be fun to go to a real village fête again, that's all.'

'And there must have been a certain natural curiosity, too, I imagine,' said Lineham.

She frowned. 'Curiosity?'

'I understand you stayed at Thaxden Hall a number of times in the past.'

'That was *years* ago.'

'Still, no doubt you wondered if it had changed at all.'

She grinned. 'You're right, of course. The temptation proved irresistible.'

'I mean, if things had turned out differently, it could have been your own home. We understand you were engaged to Mr Fairleigh, once.'

Her smile faded. 'Yes, that's true.'

'May we ask what went wrong?'

Thanet flinched inwardly. *Too soon, Mike. Too soon.* Everything had been going so well—too well, perhaps. Encouraged by the way Mrs Raven was responding Lineham had gone too far too fast. Perhaps he should have conducted this interview himself. But then Mike was perfectly capable, and how was he ever to gain experience in the more delicate interviews like this one if Thanet never gave him the chance to improve his skills?

Pamela Raven flushed with anger. 'No you may not! I really don't see that it's any of your business.' And she glanced at Thanet as if to say, *Tell him he's gone too far.*

Thanet felt bound to defend Lineham. 'I know that some of our questions must seem impertinent, Mrs Raven, but I assure you we wouldn't ask them if it weren't necessary.'

She was still angry. 'I can't see how something that happened twenty years ago can possibly be relevant to what happened yesterday. And incidentally, you still haven't told me what that was, or how I can possibly be concerned with it in any way.'

This was tricky. As yet they were only guessing that there was anything more than a casual relationship between Pamela and Fairleigh. If there were no close link between them Thanet really did not think that Hugo would have been in touch with her since yesterday and Pamela would be genuinely bewildered by this visit, especially as the story was only just breaking in the media. He wondered if the item had yet been on TV. News broadcasts were less regular on Sundays and if Pamela had been working hard all day she might not yet have heard.

On the other hand, if she and Fairleigh were lovers, he would probably have rung last night to tell her what had happened and she would know that Mrs Fairleigh had been murdered. And he would no doubt have rung again today, to let her know that the police knew she had been seen at the fête.

So, was her apparent ignorance feigned or genuine?

The time had come to tell her about the murder and see how she reacted.

He glanced at the papers on the table. 'You've been working all day?'

She frowned. 'Yes. Why?'

'And you obviously haven't watched television, or listened to the radio?'

'No. Look, what is this all about?'

'Then you won't have heard that Mrs Fairleigh senior was found dead in bed yesterday afternoon. Or that it has become evident that she was murdered.'

She drew in a sharp breath and her eyes opened wide in apparent shock. 'Murdered!'

Had he detected a false note there? He couldn't be sure. 'I'm afraid so.'

'Naturally, I'm appalled! But I still don't understand what it has to do with me. And I certainly can't see why you are asking a lot of questions about matters that are ancient history.'

Was this the moment to tell her she'd been seen in the house at the time of the murder? No, not yet, he decided. He shrugged. 'Where murder is involved we simply gather together as much information as possible and hope that in the end it will become evident what is relevant and what is not.'

'Sounds a bit hit and miss.'

'Perhaps. But it usually works, in the end.'

'Still, I don't have to answer, if I don't want to, do I?'

'No. That is your right.'

She stood up. 'Then I shall exercise it.'

Lineham cast an anxious glance at Thanet. He obviously felt that he had mishandled things badly. But he was evidently also determined to try and salvage what he could. 'Mrs Raven, I apologise. I didn't mean to offend you.'

'There are one or two questions we really have to ask you,' said Thanet gently. 'If not today, then another day . . .'

She hesitated and walked across to the desk, stood for a few moments with her back to them.

Lineham watched her with a worried frown.

Eventually she sighed and returned to her chair.

Thanet could see her thinking, *Better to get it over with, I suppose.*

'Very well, then. If you must.'

'Presumably, from what you say, you've kept in touch with Mr Fairleigh.' Lineham was being careful now, feeling his way.

'Not exactly. We hadn't seen each other for years, until last summer. He came to present the prizes at the school where I teach. Since then we've met occasionally for lunch, usually during the school holidays.'

It was obvious that this was the story she and Fairleigh had decided to stick to, equally obvious that there was no point in pursuing the matter at the moment. Thanet waited anxiously to see if Lineham realised this.

He had. 'I see. And on one of these occasions he happened to mention the fête.'

'That's right, yes.'

'When was this?'

She frowned. 'It must have been at half-term.'

'In June, then?'

'Yes.'

'And you've met since then?'

'Look, Sergeant, what, exactly, is the point of these questions?'

This, Thanet felt, was the moment for Lineham to bring up the fact that she had been seen inside the house. He caught the sergeant's eye. *Now.*

'Mrs Raven, at the fête yesterday you went into the house. Would you mind telling us why?'

If she was disconcerted she didn't show it. She must have been prepared for the possibility that the woman who had seen her might have mentioned the fact to the police. She smiled. 'To answer a call of nature, why else?'

'Toilets had been set up for the public in the car-park field.'

'My feet were hurting, Sergeant. Unwisely I had chosen to wear high heels. It was a long way back to the car park and there were women going in and out of the back door all the time. I thought I would be able to slip into the house unnoticed.'

True or false? At the moment Pamela Raven was wearing trainers, and at school it would be quite in order for her to wear flat shoes. There was no rule, unspoken or otherwise, that said schoolteachers had to look elegant—quite the reverse, judging by the clothes Thanet had seen some of them wearing. And everyone knew that women did suffer from wearing high heels if they weren't used to them.

At the beginning of the interview he had thought

she would make a bad liar. Now, he wasn't so sure. Or perhaps she was just being economical with the truth.

'You were seen coming from the direction of the stairs, and there's a toilet just inside the back door,' said Lineham.

She shrugged. 'I thought I could remember the geography of the house. I was mistaken.'

'Did you go upstairs?'

'That would have been impertinent, don't you think?'

'Did you?' Now that he had put all the questions they had arranged to ask Lineham was prepared to press a little harder and risk her anger.

'Look, I don't know what you're getting at, Sergeant, but whatever it is you're way off beam. I wanted to go to the loo and thought I knew where to find one. I was wrong. And that's it, all right?'

It was obvious that she wasn't going to budge and that they weren't going to get anything more out of her at the moment.

They were in the hall on the way out when there was the sound of a key in the lock of the front door. Pamela swung it open. 'Oh, Gwen. You're early.'

She sounded put out. No doubt she had hoped they would be gone before her daughter got home, Thanet thought.

The resemblance between them was still striking. Gwen was around eighteen, Thanet guessed, her dark hair in a fashionably tousled curly mop. She was wearing jeans and a T-shirt with 'I LOVE THE WORLD' emblazoned across her chest. A scarlet mini-rucksack was slung over one shoulder. She glanced questioningly from her mother to the two policemen.

'Goodbye, Inspector,' said Pamela firmly, standing aside.

There was very little space in the hall and Gwen

stepped back, outside, to let them pass. Thanet wondered how Pamela was going to explain away their visit. Had she told her daughter that she had been to the fête yesterday? If Pamela was having an affair with Hugo, Gwen must surely know about it. How did the girl feel about Fairleigh? he wondered.

As they walked to the car Lineham said, 'Cleverclogs, isn't she?'

'Well, we knew that, didn't we? Oxford graduate, no less.' Thanet grinned. 'Why d'you think I asked you to take the interview?'

'I really messed it up, though, didn't I?' said Lineham angrily. He slammed the door behind him as he got into the car. This was unusual. Lineham's long-running love affair with cars precluded ill-treatment of any kind. 'You should have done the interview yourself.'

'Nonsense, Mike. As usual, you're overreacting. She was looking for an excuse to get rid of us.'

'Then I shouldn't have given her one, should I?' He stared moodily through the windscreen. 'I know what I did wrong. I rushed it, didn't I? I let the fact that she seemed to have relaxed make me push too hard, too quickly.'

'Yes. So now you've worked out what went wrong, forget about it and write it off to experience.'

'I wonder how many times you've said that before! I know what comes next: "That's how we all learn. By making mistakes." '

'But it's true. We do. What's more, we go on making them, as you well know.'

Lineham was not consoled. He always found it hard to come to terms with avoidable failures. It was, Thanet knew, only because the sergeant cared so much about his work. In any case, he soon bounced back. 'Mike . . . Are we going to sit here all day?'

Lineham manoeuvred the car out of the confined

space as efficiently as he had manoeuvred it in and Thanet opened the A–Z. 'Let's see if I can find the way back.'

'It's OK, sir. I think I can remember it.'

'I don't know how. One suburban street looks just like another suburban street to me.' But Thanet closed the book and put it back on the shelf. It would do Lineham's bruised ego good to demonstrate his superiority in this respect at least.

It wasn't until they were on the motorway that the sergeant spoke again.

'She didn't actually tell a single lie, did you notice? There was nothing that we could come back to her about and say, that wasn't true.'

'I know.'

'She and Fairleigh are a pair.'

'I liked her, myself. After all, if she's in a tight corner it's understandable that she should protect her interests.'

'You're not saying you couldn't blame them for killing off the old lady!'

'Of course not! But that's far from proven yet.'

'I know, I know. Now you're going to tell me I've got to keep an open mind!'

Thanet laughed. 'No need, is there, when you're obviously aware of it yourself. Come on, it'll do us good to forget about the case for a while. How are the children?'

But this wasn't the happiest choice of topics, it seemed.

Lineham grimaced. 'We're a bit worried about Richard, as a matter of fact.'

'Why? What's the matter with him?'

'I wish I knew. I mean, he's a bright lad, wouldn't you agree?'

'Yes, he is.'

'Then why is he always in trouble at school?'

'What sort of trouble?'

'His form teacher can't seem to make up her mind if he's deliberately perverse or just plain lazy. And disorganised! He can't seem to keep track of any of his belongings for more than two minutes together. He's always in trouble for losing things, or forgetting them . . . Louise says the only way she can think of for him to keep his things together would be to tie them to him!'

'You don't think people are expecting too much of him, because he is bright?'

'I don't know.' They were travelling behind a container lorry. 'Look at that! He's doing over seventy!'

'Not our problem, Mike. We can't turn everyone in the country into law-abiding citizens single-handed.'

Lineham pulled out to overtake, glowering up at the lorry driver as they passed the cab.

'So what are you going to do about it?'

'The school has arranged for him to see a child psychologist, tomorrow afternoon.'

'Bit drastic, isn't it?'

'It was their idea. They say if there is a problem we ought to nip it in the bud.'

'Well, he's always seemed a perfectly normal, healthy child to me.'

'You don't have to live with him! We dithered and dithered before agreeing, but in the end we decided it couldn't do him any harm and it might do some good. We can't go on like this indefinitely, it's driving us mad. Did you ever have any problems like this with Ben?'

'We've had problems, of course,' said Thanet, thinking especially of that terrible time when one of Ben's friends had died of glue-sniffing and they had discovered that Ben had also been experimenting with 'solvent inhalation'. 'But nothing quite like what you're describing.'

They drove for a while in silence and then Thanet

said, 'You're right. It'll be a good idea for him to see this chap tomorrow.'

'Woman.'

'All right, woman. If nothing else it'll clear the air, relieve your minds, to feel you're doing something about it.'

'I hope you're right.'

It was late when Thanet got home. Alexander's Porsche had gone, he was relieved to see. Much as he loved Bridget he really didn't feel like socialising to-night. He was tired and his back, which had always been a problem ever since he had injured it some years ago, was aching. He longed to stretch out flat and relax.

He wasn't surprised to find that Joan had already gone to bed. He was thirsty and he took an ice-cold can of lager from the fridge and drank half of it straight off before sitting down at the kitchen table to eat the cold meat and salad she had left for him. Afterwards he went upstairs as quietly as he could, hoping not to disturb her.

As he eased himself into bed she stirred, half woke and then settled into sleep again. He stretched out flat on his back, luxuriating in the relief as tired muscles relaxed into the expensive orthopaedic mattress in which they had decided to invest when it became apparent that this back problem wasn't going to go away.

The windows were open to the summer night and the curtains stirred softly in the breeze. Thanet began to breathe deeply and evenly in the hope that he would quickly drop off to sleep. But he knew that, tired as he was, this was unlikely. Always, at the beginning of a case, there was so much to absorb, so much to assess, that his overactive brain took a long time to unwind.

Thanet believed that, random victims of violence apart, murder victims carried in themselves or in their lives the seeds of their own tragic destiny. Something in

their circumstances, past or present, or something in
their character had finally led to that moment of ulti-
mate violence, and it was his job to find out what it
was.

Isobel Fairleigh's character had, according to her sister,
been largely shaped by her father's thwarted desire for a
son. What had Letty said? *She was a bold, headstrong child,
and he encouraged her to be strong, determined, even ruthless,
if necessary.*

Well, she had certainly been well taught, by all accounts. According to Joan's mother—surely as impartial
a witness as one could hope to find—Isobel had been
bossy, managing, manipulative. Caroline had called her
selfish, egocentric, demanding, proud. Her sister Letty
was the only person who seemed to make excuses for
the old woman's unattractive personality, and Thanet
wasn't sure if Letty wasn't just that little bit too good to
be true. Surely no one treated as she had been could
have been as apparently free of resentment as she was?
What had Caroline Plowright said? *How Letty put up
with her I just don't know. The way Isobel used to boss her
around . . . She used to behave as if Letty's one aim in life
should be to make her own as comfortable as possible. And
she never, ever let her forget she was dependent on her for
the roof over her head.* An image of Letty's sparsely furnished bedroom with its cast-off furniture and spotted
mirror flashed through Thanet's mind.

It had already occurred to Thanet that Isobel had
probably left Letty something in her will, and that Letty
might be aware of this. How much of a temptation
would it be, to know that independence was within her
grasp for the first time in her life? That, and freedom
from a tyranny acknowledged by everyone but herself.

And she had definitely been lying about not having
gone upstairs when she went into the house around the

time of the murder. On that final visit to the old lady Grace had seen Letty, Thanet was sure of it.

Thanet couldn't imagine Letty planning and plotting her sister's death, but with Isobel helpless, who knows how strong the temptation might have become? She could have tried to justify giving in to it by convincing herself that she would be doing Isobel a favour, releasing her from the dependence and indignities she must have hated. It was even possible that she had told Thanet about Pamela in the hope that suspicion would be diverted away from herself. Perhaps he had underestimated her, and her apparent reluctance to confess that she had seen Pamela at the fête yesterday had been carefully calculated to make him eager to know what it was she was apparently withholding.

Still, it had certainly been a valuable piece of information, explaining much that had come before and opening up an important avenue of inquiry. In Thanet's view Hugo was a much more likely suspect.

Fragments of conversation floated through Thanet's mind. Caroline: *My guess is that he met someone about a year ago, and the affair is still going on.* Letty: *Pamela called it off. Hugo was heartbroken.* Hugo: *If you must know, last summer I met her for the first time in many years* . . . Pamela: *I really don't see that it's any of your business.*

Thanet sighed. Ah, but it is, Pamela, he thought as he grew drowsy. It is very much our business.

For if they were having an affair—which seemed more than likely—and if Hugo had told his mother, and if she had objected, and if she had threatened to cut him out of her will . . . If, if, if! Stop it, he told himself sleepily. What is the point in speculating?

But he had to know, and soon.

First thing in the morning, he promised himself. Oliver Bassett, Isobel Fairleigh's solicitor . . .

12

As soon as Thanet walked into the office next morning he could tell that Lineham was on to something. The sergeant was seated at his desk surrounded by neat piles of paper and his face as he looked up was triumphant.

'Just listen to this!'

There was an answering twist of excitement in Thanet's stomach. 'What?'

Lineham picked up one of the bundles of paper. Bank statements, by the look of it. 'On the first day of every month a large cheque was paid out of old Mrs Fairleigh's account.'

'How large?'

'A thousand quid a month, for the last six months. Before that, for the previous six months, it was nine hundred. For the six months before that eight hundred . . .'

'I get the picture.'

'Don't you see, sir?' Lineham was brimming over with excitement. 'B day. Bank day. The first day of the month . . .'

'No need to spell it out, Mike. I'm not an idiot.' And
then, as Lineham looked crestfallen, 'Well done, Mike.
Brilliant, in fact. It was a cheque, you say, not a standing order or direct debit?'

'That's right.'

'When it opens, get on to the bank, make an appointment to go and see them.'

'What d'you think the money was for?' Lineham was
reluctant to let the matter go.

'Waste of time to speculate at the moment. Let's wait
and see what you find out.'

'Then there's this.' Lineham handed Thanet a sheet
of paper in a plastic envelope. 'Anonymous, but sounds
as though it'd be worth following up.'

The letter was written in block capitals on cheap,
lined notepaper.

ASK ABOUT THE ROW WHEN MRS
FAIRLEIGH HAD HER STROKE.

'Envelope?' said Thanet.

Lineham handed over another plastic envelope.
'More block capitals. Addressed to you. Postmarked
Sturrenden. Who do you think wrote it, sir?'

'Assuming the old lady was at home when she had
the stroke, take your pick, Mike. Hugo Fairleigh, Grace
Fairleigh, Letty Ransome, Sam, Mrs Kerk . . .'

'I'd plump for Mrs Kerk, wouldn't you?'

'I agree. Anyway, we'll take the letter with us when
we go out to the house later, see what reactions we get.'
Thanet was pleased. Two leads already this morning.
'Anything else?'

'Confirmation that Tanner is still inside. And reports
from Bentley and Carson, on the interviews with Mrs
Tanner and Jill Cochrane.'

'What do they say?'

'Well, Bentley says Mrs Tanner is a bit weird. And definitely very anti the old lady. Called her, what was it?' Lineham flipped through the report. 'Yes, here it is. An "evil old cow, who went around poking her nose into everyone else's business". Says she swears she never went upstairs, was busy in and out all afternoon, "run off her legs" was how she put it, carrying trays of crockery.'

'So she was actually working in the house, not out in the tent.'

'Apparently, yes.'

'And no one would have noticed if she happened to take a few minutes longer on one of those occasions.'

'So do we take it any further?'

'Not at the moment. But we obviously can't rule her out. If we run into a lot of dead ends elsewhere, we'll follow it up, go and see her ourselves. What did Jill Cochrane have to say?'

'Nothing helpful, I'm afraid. She and Fairleigh weren't together all the time. He kept stopping to talk to people and she was duty bound to go around all the stalls, people expect it of the person who opens the fête.'

'Quite. Pity. So she doesn't actually remember seeing him speak to someone of Pamela Raven's description?'

'No.'

Thanet glanced at his watch. Time for the morning meeting. 'Must go or I'll be late. Ring Wylie, Bassett and Protheroe, make an appointment for this morning, if possible, with Oliver Bassett. And ring the bank.'

Morning meetings these days were subdued affairs, a far cry from when they were first instituted. Then, Superintendent Draco had been like a terrier, snapping at the heels of his staff and making sure that no detail was overlooked. Thanet, Boon and Tody had long since given up regular inquiries after Angharad Draco's progress; it merely depressed Draco even further, and her illness had reached a stage when they were afraid of what they might hear. Today Draco looked exhausted, his face drawn, with dark, bruised circles beneath lacklustre eyes. Even his wiry black hair looked limp and tired, like its owner.

Thanet's report was of necessity the longest. Draco listened carefully, asked a few pertinent questions and then said, 'You'll handle this matter with tact, I'm sure, Thanet. If you run into any problems you know where to find me.'

Gone were the maxims and admonitions which had so irritated Thanet in the past. Now he felt that he would suffer them gladly if only Draco would return to being his former ebullient self. After a brief press conference he returned to his office still feeling depressed on the Superintendent's behalf.

'Mr Bassett will see us at 10.30,' said Lineham, as Thanet walked in.

'Good.'

'And I've arranged an appointment with the bank manager at 11.15.'

'Excellent.'

'Didn't Doc Mallard say he'd managed to fix the PM for first thing this morning?'

'Yes. He should let us have a verbal report later on.'

While they waited Thanet and Lineham went through Mrs Fairleigh's papers again, searching for something to indicate what the large regular payment could be for, but there was no clue. By the time they left for their appointment with Bassett, Lineham was becoming increasingly frustrated. 'There must be something,' he said as they walked along the High Street. 'I can't believe a woman can lay out a thousand pounds a month and there'd not be some reference to it in her papers.'

'Patience, Mike, patience. Perhaps the bank will reveal all.'

Lineham merely grunted.

On this sunny Monday morning Sturrenden was looking its best, preening itself in the sunshine for the benefit of an artist who had set up his easel in a spot which afforded him the best, much painted view of the church. As Thanet and Lineham passed he was covering the bare canvas with a base colour, applying the paint with sweeping enthusiastic strokes. No doubt he couldn't wait to get started on the painting proper.

'All right for some,' said Lineham as they separated to walk around the easel. 'I bet he's glad he doesn't have to spend his time combing through a load of dusty old papers ... That's a thought, sir. Perhaps we missed some. Papers sometimes slip down at the back of drawers.'

'You can look when we go out, later.'

They had arrived. This was not their first visit to the offices of Wylie, Bassett and Protheroe. On the previous occasion, some seven years ago, Oliver Bassett had himself been a suspect in a murder case, when a woman had been strangled on the first night of a visit to Sturrenden after an absence of twenty years. Thanet had of course seen Bassett out and about in the town during the intervening period and he thought once again, as Bassett rose to greet them, how little the man seemed to change. The solicitor was now in his mid-forties, tall and well-built, with a jutting nose rather like that of his dead client. The height of his forehead was emphasised by the fact that his hair was beginning to recede and the small, prim mouth was turned up in a welcoming smile which vanished as soon as the greetings were over.

'A terrible business,' he said, when they were all seated. 'What sort of person could murder a helpless old woman in her bed?'

'That's what we intend to find out.'

'I imagine you want me to tell you about her will.'

'Mrs Fairleigh was a wealthy woman. Someone stands to gain by her death, no doubt.'

'That does not necessarily mean that they are implicated.'

'Not necessarily, no. But it is obviously a possibility that we have to consider.'

Bassett pursed his lips. 'I find myself in a difficult position. This firm has always acted for the Fairleigh family and I therefore represent both the victim and those whom you no doubt regard as suspects. I have to ask myself where my loyalties lie, with the dead or the living.'

'Oh come, Mr Bassett. You're a man of the law. You couldn't possibly condone murder, under any circumstances. And in any case the contents of the will must become public sooner or later.'

'True.' Bassett sighed. 'I guessed you would be coming to see me, of course, and I suppose my duty is plain.'

But he still sounded very uncertain about it. Why? Unless . . . Thanet's scalp prickled with excitement. Suddenly he was sure that there was more to Bassett's reluctance than met the eye. The solicitor knew something, but he felt he shouldn't divulge it.

'Would you like some coffee?'

Delaying tactics now, thought Thanet. But he was willing to play along and he accepted.

Bassett's secretary must have been primed. The coffee arrived almost at once and Bassett dismissed her with a word of thanks and began to fuss with coffee, sugar and cream in a spinsterish manner. Watching him, Thanet wondered whether the secret of Bassett's homosexuality, revealed to the police during the course of the earlier case, had yet leaked out into the community. He rather thought not. If Bassett ever indulged his tastes, he was very discreet indeed. Even now, in a small country town like Sturrenden, skirts would be drawn aside and in Bassett's profession a spotless reputation was of paramount importance.

Once the little ceremony was over the silence stretched out. Thanet was content to wait and so, for a while, it seemed, was Bassett. Finally, the solicitor put down his cup and sat back, steepling his hands beneath his chin as if to emphasise that the decision he had made had been reached only after due and judicious consideration. 'The terms of the will are straightforward. The bulk of Mrs Fairleigh's estate goes, as might be expected, to her son Hugo.'

'How much does that amount to?' Thanet already had some idea, from the broker's statement, but Bassett didn't know that and would be expecting him to ask.

'Something in excess of half a million pounds. Death duties, of course, will be substantial, but fortunately I managed to convince Mrs Fairleigh that it would be a good idea to make the house over to her son some ten years ago, so the house itself will be exempt.' Bassett looked smug, as well he might.

'You said, "the bulk of the estate". Where does the rest go?'

'There's an annuity of ten thousand a year for her sister, Miss Ransome. I'm sure that Mr Fairleigh will be happy for his aunt to continue to live in the flat she shared with his mother, but I suppose the old lady thought it would be nice for her sister to know that she wouldn't have to face a poverty-stricken old age.'

That was uncharacteristically careless of Bassett, thought Thanet, more certain than ever that the solicitor's attention was focused on some personal dilemma. 'So Miss Ransome was aware of this bequest.'

Bassett looked disconcerted, suddenly aware that he

had given away more than he intended to. 'Certainly. Why not?'

'I agree. Why not, indeed. And Mr Fairleigh?'

'Of course,' said Bassett stiffly.

'Were there any other major bequests?'

'No. There's a small sum for Ernest Byre, her gardener, and one or two items of jewellery for her daughter-in-law, nothing of exceptional value. That's all.' He leaned forward. 'Look here, Thanet, it's out of the question, what you're thinking.' But his tone lacked conviction.

How could he get Bassett to open up? Thanet wondered. This man was no fool, to be manipulated into divulging something he wanted to keep secret. Try a direct approach, then?

'Mr Bassett. There's something you're not telling me, isn't there?'

'I don't know what you mean, Thanet.' The solicitor reached for his cup, drank, replaced it carefully in the saucer and put them down on the desk again, each movement as automatic as that of a Victorian mechanical doll. His eyes met Thanet's squarely, almost defiantly.

Thanet guessed that Bassett was being careful in case later on he found himself in the unsavoury position of having to defend one of his clients for murder. His behaviour indicated that he suspected that this could happen. So, what had given rise to those suspicions? It must be something to do with the will. Thanet remembered the anonymous note. Say there had been a row, and the old lady had threatened to change her will. And say she had made an appointment with Bassett, told him why she wanted to see him? If the solicitor refused to talk, as well he might, in the interests of his clients, Thanet could at least infer the truth by seeing which questions he refused to answer.

'I understand that Mrs Fairleigh had her stroke as a result of a row with a member of her family.'

Bingo. Thanet caught the flash of dismay in Bassett's eyes before the solicitor raised his eyebrows and said blandly, 'Did she?'

'Did you know about this row, Mr Bassett?'

'No.' But Bassett was prevaricating, Thanet could tell.

'Did you guess that there had been one, then?'

'Really, Thanet, what is the point of entering the realms of speculation on such a matter?' Bassett was at his most pompous. And avoiding the issue, of course.

'Mrs Fairleigh was going to change her will, wasn't she?'

'You're guessing again, Thanet.'

But coming far too close for comfort. Bassett's prim lips were clamped together as if he were afraid the truth would escape him unawares.

It was time to press a little harder. 'Did Mrs Fairleigh contact you, to tell you she wanted to change her will?'

The telephone rang. Bassett almost snatched it up in his relief at the interruption.

Thanet cursed inwardly and out of the corner of his eye he saw Lineham's biro stab viciously at his notebook as the sergeant gave unobtrusive vent to his feelings.

'It's for you, Thanet.' Bassett handed over the phone.

'Thanet here.'

'Sir? Carson. Sorry to interrupt your interview, but I didn't know where you were going next, and I wanted to catch you . . .'

'Yes, yes . . .' Thanet tried to prevent his irritation showing.

'There's a young girl here, sir. A Miss Raven. Says she wants to see you about the Fairleigh case. She's come down from London especially, she says.'

Gwen Raven, here. Why? Thanet's disappointment of a moment ago vanished. 'Tell her I'll be along shortly. Give her a cup of tea and make her comfortable.'

'Right, sir.' Carson's relief was evident. Thanet's change of tone had not escaped him.

Thanet put the phone down and said, 'Did she, Mr Bassett?'

'Did who what?' Bassett had recovered his composure. He'd had time to work out his answer now.

'Did Mrs Fairleigh contact you to tell you that she wanted to change her will?'

Bassett stood up. 'I can't imagine what gave you that idea, Thanet.' His tone was mocking. 'And now, I'm afraid I have another appointment.'

And so have I, thought Thanet as they took their leave. It was a pity that he hadn't been able to prise any more out of Bassett but he was eager now to hear what had brought Gwen Raven down to Sturrenden to see him.

13

'She was going to, wasn't she?' said Lineham, as soon as they were outside. 'Change her will.'

'Looks like it.'

'Slippery customer, Mr Bassett.'

'He certainly wasn't giving much away.'

'We're beginning to get the picture now, aren't we? That anonymous letter was right on target.'

'Ah, but there's a snag, Mike. The letter implies that she had the stroke during or after the row. And if so, and if it was because of the row that she was going to change her will, how did Bassett know she was going to? She hasn't been able to speak since.'

'Unless she rang him just before she was taken ill. That's it, sir! She's having this row. She's absolutely fuming, so she goes to the phone, rings Bassett up and tells him she wants to change her will. And she has the stroke *while she's speaking to him*. Later, Bassett discovers what had happened and draws his own conclusions.

Only he daren't tell us in case it compromises his client.'

'Sounds feasible. But which client, I wonder?'

'Mr Fairleigh, for my money. I can't see Miss Ransome having a blazing row with her sister, can you? I bet,' said Lineham eagerly, warming to his theme, 'Mr Fairleigh told his mother he was going to get a divorce and marry the woman she was so against him marrying in the first place.'

'According to Miss Ransome, remember. We've only got her word for it that old Mrs Fairleigh was against the match. And, as I said before, even if she had been it looks as though she was prepared to go along with it. She took a lot of trouble to introduce the girl into her own circle, and it was Pamela who called it off, not Hugo.'

'Yes, but as I keep saying, there's another reason why she'd be dead against it now, isn't there? Remember Miss Plowright telling us she thought old Mrs Fairleigh would be all in favour of her son marrying again provided it was someone likely to produce an heir? Pamela Raven is in her forties. Not much chance of an heir there, as I've said before.'

'Women do have babies in their forties, Mike.'

'Yes. And as we've been told often enough, the chances of producing a handicapped child are vastly increased. The old woman wouldn't want to risk that happening again, would she?'

They had arrived at the bank and they stopped. 'I'll see you back at the office, Mike.'

Lineham's eyebrows rose. 'You're not coming in?'

Thanet grinned. 'Other fish to fry. That phone call was Carson, telling me that Gwen Raven is in Headquarters, asking for me. Came down especially, from London.'

'Really?' Lineham's face was alive with speculation. 'I wonder why? Perhaps . . .'

'Enough perhapses, Mike. We'll soon find out.'

Gwen Raven was waiting for him in one of the interview rooms, having been given what amounted to five-star treatment: a couple of women's magazines, some chocolate fingers and tea—in a bone-china cup decorated with tiny roses, Thanet was amused to see. Where on earth had Carson managed to find that? he wondered.

'Miss Raven. I'm sorry to have kept you waiting.'

She shook her head. 'It doesn't matter.'

Once again she was wearing jeans and T-shirt, the ubiquitous uniform of the young. But today she looked apprehensive, and tired, too, with dark shadows beneath her eyes and a dispirited droop to her shoulders.

'How can I help you?'

She ran a hand through her hair. 'I'm not sure I ought to be here, really.'

'But you are here,' said Thanet gently. 'So on balance you must have decided it was the right thing to do.'

'I suppose so.' But she still sounded doubtful.

He had to get her to trust him before she would open up.

He sat back in his chair. 'I have a daughter of my own, of about your age.'

She welcomed the change of subject eagerly. 'Is she at University too?'

'No.' Thanet grinned. 'She's always been mad on cookery. So she took a Cordon Bleu course and now she cooks for a directors' dining room, in the City.'

'So she doesn't live at home?'

'No. She shares a flat with three other girls.'

'That's what I want to do, when I come down.'

Gwen, he learned, was reading French and German

at Durham University. She had hoped to get into either Oxford or Cambridge, but hadn't made it.

As they talked she began to relax, as he had hoped she would. They chatted for a while about her future plans and then he said, 'You don't have to tell me anything you don't want to tell me, you know. And if, at any time, you change your mind and want to call it a day, I promise I won't put any pressure on you. I can't be fairer than that, can I?'

'I suppose not.' But the strained look was back in her eyes again. Then suddenly she said angrily, 'I expect you think I'm stupid, coming down here like this and then holding back.'

'I certainly don't think you're stupid. And I imagine you have good reasons for hesitating.' He waited a moment and then said gently, 'Perhaps you feel you're being disloyal to your mother?'

Her mouth twisted. 'Yes. You're right, of course. How did you guess? Oh, now I *am* being stupid. In your job, you must . . .' She ran a hand through her hair again. 'I'm not thinking straight this morning, I hardly slept all night, trying to make up my mind whether to come.'

'And here you are.'

'Yes. Here I am. So yes, you're right again. I suppose, as you said just now, I wouldn't be here if I hadn't made up my mind. So . . .' She took a deep breath. 'As I expect you've already guessed, it's about my mother and Hugo Fairleigh.'

Thanet nodded and said nothing, hoping that he looked as receptive and sympathetic as he felt. The last thing he wanted to do was make her feel she was being cross-examined. That would simply make her clam up again. In any case he was confident that now she had taken the first step she would go on.

'After you'd gone last night Mum told me what had

happened—to Mr Fairleigh's mother. I couldn't believe it. An old lady like that, and she was pretty helpless, wasn't she, she'd had a stroke?'

'Yes, she had.'

Gwen's face screwed up in disgust. 'It's horrible. Obscene. But what I don't understand is why you came to see Mum. She told me you were interviewing everyone who was there yesterday and knows the Fairleighs. Is that right?'

'More or less, yes.'

'I knew there'd be trouble if she got mixed up with them again!'

Thanet raised his eyebrows. 'What do you mean?'

'After what they did to her the first time . . .'

'Are you talking about when she was engaged to Mr Fairleigh?'

'Yes.'

'But that was getting on for twenty years ago! Before you were born.'

'You have to understand! My mother and I are— were,' she added bitterly, 'very close. Oh, I know they say teenage girls and their mothers don't get on, that they're always fighting about something, but that's not necessarily true. We've had our arguments, of course, but on the whole, well, I suppose we're more like sisters than mother and daughter. Perhaps it's because I'm an only child. Or because she's always talked to me on equal terms, as long as I can remember. Or because my father really didn't want to know, as far as I was concerned . . . Anyway, for whatever reason, that's the way it was. And one of the things she told me about was the time when she was engaged to Hugo. It was when I had a boyfriend who was pretty serious about me. I was only sixteen at the time and I expect she thought I was too young to have just one boyfriend, but she didn't say so. What she really felt strongly about was the fact that his mother was pretty nasty to me. He was an only child too, you see, and his mother was very possessive. To be honest, I think she would have behaved the same towards any girl he brought home, but that wasn't the point. It made me pretty miserable at the time and I talked to Mum about it. And that was when she told me about Mrs Fairleigh.'

'What about her?'

'Well, Mum came from a working-class background, and of course the Fairleighs are upper middle class. I mean, plenty of money, public school, house in the family for generations, that sort of thing. Mum knew straight away that Mrs Fairleigh didn't approve of her.'

'Did Mrs Fairleigh say so?'

'Oh no, she was much too clever for that. And of course, Mum didn't know what was going on at the time. It wasn't until years later, when she was older and knew much more about life, that she really began to understand what had happened.'

'What do you mean?'

'She realised that what Hugo's mother did was systematically set about demonstrating to Mum how unfit she was to be the wife of someone with Hugo's background. She gave elaborate dinner parties for her, with so many knives and forks that Mum went cross-eyed trying to work out what to eat with what. Everyone had plummy voices and talked about things Mum knew nothing about—hunting and farming and charity balls and God knows what else. And of course, Mum's clothes were absolutely unsuitable—she was scraping along on a grant and clothes were the last thing she could afford to buy. Mrs Fairleigh took her on an endless social round, introducing her to families who lived in elegant country houses with tennis courts and ponies in paddocks and gorgeous daughters who'd known Hugo for years, had been to finishing schools in Switzerland and looked as though they stepped straight out of *Harpers & Queen*. Oh, she was clever all right. She never actually said in so many words, *You would never fit into this world*, but everything she showed her shouted it aloud. As I say, Mum had no idea what was going on. All she knew was that she was very unhappy. She felt inadequate all the time, and in fact the experience undermined her self-confidence for years. It was diabolical.'

Diabolical indeed. Fleetingly Thanet thought of Bridget. If she and Alexander became serious about each other, was this what lay in store for her?

'It was soon after she told me all this that she met Hugo again. So you can imagine how I felt, when they started seeing each other regularly. I didn't want her to be hurt!'

'You don't like Hugo Fairleigh.'

'No I do not! He's not right for Mum. And don't think it's just because I feel he's coming between me and her. I'd be only too glad if she found someone who's kind. Someone who'd really care about her, make her happy.'

'Perhaps he does care about her. I understand it was she who broke off the engagement, and that he was very upset about it.'

'Maybe. But that doesn't mean he could make her happy. He's so . . . Oh, God, he's so superficial. And so ambitious. All that really matters to Hugo is Hugo!' she cried, unconsciously echoing Caroline Plowright.

'Are you sure you're not being a little unfair? Maybe his career does matter to him, but perhaps your mother matters more. If, as you seem to be implying, he's serious about her, he's obviously willing to go through a divorce and risk alienating his constituents, who by all accounts are fond of his present wife.'

'That's how he feels at the moment, yes. But what

happens afterwards? What if it did damage his career? It would be my mother he'd blame and what do you think that would do to her?'

'I'm still not sure why you've come to see me.'

'He's a very determined man,' said Gwen, her mouth setting in a stubborn line. 'Takes after his mother, obviously. She was still against him and Mum getting married, you know.'

'What makes you think that?'

She shook her head. 'Just something Mum said, that made me think so.'

So he and Lineham could be right about the reason for the row, thought Thanet. Hugo Fairleigh had obviously broached the subject with his mother.

'What did your mother say exactly?'

'I can't remember. But that was certainly the impression I got.'

'Let me get this straight. Are you trying to say that you think Hugo Fairleigh killed his mother because she was against this marriage?'

'I don't know!' The girl's anxiety and passion drove her from her chair and she stood behind it, gripping the back so hard that her knuckles whitened. 'But someone did. And even the possibility that it could be Hugo . . . that my mother might be thinking of marrying a murderer! Can't you *see*.'

'Yes,' said Thanet gently. 'Of course I do. Come on, sit down again and try to calm yourself.'

He waited until she had settled down again, then said, 'Now, let's try and be rational about this. Have you anything specific to tell me, to back up your suspicions?'

She was silent, thinking, leaning forward in her chair and frowning down at her hands. The nails, Thanet noticed, were bitten down to the quick. Finally she shook her head. 'No,' she said. She sounded exhausted, defeated. 'Nothing specific.' She looked at him squarely, her eyes full of determination. 'But if there is, believe me, I'll be on to you like a shot.'

Thanet escorted her to the main entrance. Lineham was just coming in and together they watched her walk away across the forecourt, shoulders drooping.

'She doesn't look too happy. What did she have to say?'

Thanet told him as they walked together up the stairs.

'So that explains why Mrs Fairleigh apparently took so much trouble to introduce Pamela into her social circle. Talk about devious!'

'Yes. My mother-in-law said that she was very manipulative, that she'd seen Mrs Fairleigh persuade people into doing things they didn't want to do without their ever realising how she'd managed it. Sounds as though this is a classic case in point.'

'Well at least we now know that we were right about Mr Fairleigh wanting a divorce. And it does sound as though we were right about the row, and the stroke, too. So I bet we're also right about the will. And you must admit, sir, that half a million is one hell of a motive.'

'True. Well, we'll have to see. You're looking pleased with yourself, Mike. What did you find out at the bank?'

'Ah, well, listen to this. Those thousand pounds were drawn out *in cash* by Mrs Fairleigh herself, each month.'

'In cash!'

There was a knock at the door and Doctor Mallard came in. He glanced from Thanet to Lineham and said, 'Do I detect a somewhat electric atmosphere in here?'

Thanet grinned. 'Not much escapes you, does it,

Doc? We've just discovered that the old lady has been drawing out a thousand pounds a month in cash.'

The little doctor's mouth pursed in a silent whistle. 'Not exactly chicken feed. What was it for, d'you know?'

'Your guess is as good as ours. The obvious answer is blackmail, of course. The withdrawals go back for—how long, Mike?'

'At least five years. Her bank statements only go back to then.'

'But who? And why?'

'Quite. There doesn't seem to be a clue anywhere in her papers. Though it's just occurred to me—you remember those phone calls Miss Ransome told us about, Mike?' Thanet explained to Mallard.

'Yes!' said Lineham. 'The timing is right, too, if they were from the blackmailer. He'd be wondering what had happened to his money.'

'Or she, Mike.'

'Didn't Miss Ransome say if it was a man or a woman?' said Mallard.

Thanet shook his head. 'She couldn't tell. The voice was muffled.'

'The B could still be an initial, of course,' said Lineham.

'You've lost me,' said Doc Mallard. 'What B?'

Thanet explained. 'It was obviously important to her. She's entered it in her diary on the first day of the month right through the year.'

'Does she know anyone whose name begins with the letter B?'

'Not that we've discovered so far.'

'Intriguing,' said Mallard. He perched on the edge of Thanet's desk and looked thoughtful. 'What else could it stand for? What on earth could an old woman find to spend a thousand a month on?'

'Clothes?' said Thanet, remembering the wardrobe

crammed with expensive coats, suits, dresses. 'No, it's just too much. And always a regular sum.'

'Anyway, she always paid for clothes by cheque,' said Lineham. 'She used to note it down on the cheque stub—you know, hat, dress, skirt and so on.'

'Perhaps she was a secret gambler,' said Mallard, with a mischievous grin. 'B for Betting.'

Thanet and Lineham laughed.

'You may laugh,' said Mallard, 'but she always was keen on the gee-gees, I believe. And a surprising number of these doughty old ladies do get hooked on form.'

'Well, we'll look into it,' said Thanet. 'Drawing the money out on the first day of the month could imply settling up some monthly account. But in cash?'

Mallard shrugged. 'If it was gambling, maybe she wouldn't have wanted the bank to know, by paying by cheque.'

'I can't really see her trotting into Sturrenden Turf Accountants with a thousand pounds in her handbag every month, can you?' said Lineham.

'She could have got someone to do it for her,' said Mallard.

The same thought struck Thanet and Lineham at the same time.

'Ernie!' they chorused.

'The Fairleighs' gardener-cum-handyman,' Thanet explained to Mallard.

'No one would look twice at him going into a betting shop,' said Lineham.

'True.' Thanet frowned. 'But I still think it very unlikely. The sums are too regular. If she were paying off gambling debts I'd have thought they'd vary wildly.'

'Unless she was a very strong-minded type and allowed herself so much a month and no more,' said Lineham.

'Difficult, for a gambler, by the nature of the beast,' said Mallard.

'I still think blackmail's the answer,' said Thanet. 'All the same, send Bentley along to the bookie's, just to make sure. And we'll have a word with Ernie when we go out to Thaxden later.'

'Odd,' said Mallard, 'I feel an almost proprietorial interest in this case.'

'If it hadn't been for you there wouldn't be a case!' said Thanet. 'Talking of which . . . I gather the PM report confirmed your diagnosis?'

Mallard nodded. 'Yes. No surprises at all, in fact. Evidence of stroke as expected, and yes, cause of death was asphyxiation.'

Thanet had not doubted Mallard but he was relieved. He could just imagine the fuss that Fairleigh would have made if the old lady had died a natural death after all.

'So,' said Mallard. 'Have there been any other developments?'

'One or two. Though we still have to confirm a lot of the stuff we've learned.' Thanet filled him in on Fairleigh's intended divorce, the row, the stroke and what they suspected about the proposed change of will.

'Well, well, well. Curiouser and curiouser.' Mallard slid off the desk and straightened his jacket. 'Just goes to confirm once again that skeletons lurk in the cupboards of even the best-ordered families. Keep me posted, won't you, Luke. You'll be getting a written report in due course. Must dash now.'

With the loss of Mallard's brisk presence the room settled back into normality.

'So,' said Lineham. 'What next?'

'About these cash withdrawals,' said Thanet. 'I've been thinking. We'll keep an open mind, of course, but I think we ought to concentrate on the possibility of blackmail. Now, assuming that this was what the money was for, how would it have been paid?'

'In person?'

'Unlikely, don't you think? A secret rendezvous every month. And if it was blackmail, I can't see old Mrs Fairleigh agreeing to regular meetings. I think she'd have wanted to make it as impersonal as possible.'

'By post, then. A parcel, to an accommodation address.'

'A possibility, I agree, though it's a great deal of money to risk sending by mail. And where would she send it from?'

'Different post offices every month.'

Thanet frowned. 'If it were just one payment, or two, perhaps. But as it went on month after month for at least five years . . . Even assuming she used a different post office each time, that's an awful lot of parcels. Village postmasters get to know everybody's business, I shouldn't have thought she'd want to risk it. We'll put a couple of men on to it, just in case, but I would have thought she'd prefer a really anonymous method.'

'But how? The blackmailer wouldn't have wanted to risk having it paid into his—or her—account. Too traceable.'

'I wonder if there is a method of bank payment which couldn't be traced? Give the manager a ring, Mike, and ask.'

It didn't take Lineham long to find out that there was. Apparently, provided that Isobel Fairleigh had the sorting code and account number of the payee, money could be paid into that account at any branch of any bank. Her own anonymity could be preserved either by leaving the 'paid in by' space blank, or by filling in a false name. Provided money was being paid in and not withdrawn no bank was going to bother overmuch with the name of the depositor.

'Neat,' said Thanet. 'I bet that's what she did. Assuming, of course, that we're right about the blackmail. We'll have to do a bit of digging.'

'We're going out to Thaxden now, sir?'

'Yes. And I think we'll pay another visit to Pamela Raven this evening. I'm sure she knows a lot more than she's telling us. Make another appointment, Mike, then we'll grab a sandwich in the canteen before we leave.'

14

The close-cropped green lawns of Thaxden Hall were covered with black spots, as if they had developed melanoma overnight. Ernie, wheelbarrow beside him, was busy filling in with peat and sharp sand the various indentations made by stalls and sideshows at the fête on Saturday. He straightened up as Thanet and Lineham approached.

'You've got quite a job on there,' said Thanet.

Ernie scowled. 'Bloody fête. Same every year.'

He must be in his seventies, Thanet thought, short, thin and wiry with face and stringy forearms tanned to the colour of old leather by constant exposure to the vagaries of the English climate. His sparse brown hair was peppered with grey and there was a large wart on the tip of his bulbous nose.

'You've been with the family a long time, then.'

'Nigh on fifty years.'

'Stone the crows!' said Lineham. 'Fifty years!'

Ernie grinned, revealing a row of blackened stumps

which would have made any self-respecting dentist blench. 'You won't find many people as can say that these days.'

'You certainly won't!' said Thanet. 'You must have seen a lot of changes in that time.'

'Some.'

'And you must have known old Mrs Fairleigh pretty well.'

Ernie looked wary. 'What d'you mean?'

'Simply that you must have had a lot of dealings with her, over the years.'

'Ar.'

Thanet took this archetypally rural monosyllable for assent. 'Fond of horses, was she?'

'Damn good seat, she had. No one to compare, hereabouts.'

'Used to hunt, I suppose?' Thanet could imagine the old lady, back straight as a ramrod, leading the field.

'That she did.'

'And follow form, too, I suppose?'

Ernie squinted up at Thanet suspiciously. 'Form?'

'Well, being fond of horses . . . I suppose she was interested in bloodlines and so on.' If that was the right expression. He wasn't too sure of racing terminology.

'Not so far as I know.'

'Liked a little flutter too occasionally, I expect.'

Something subterranean happened to Ernie's face. The skin rippled and bulged and then he suddenly erupted into a great roar of laughter. He doubled up with mirth, shoulders heaving. He shook his head from side to side and gasped, ' "Flutter"!'

Thanet and Lineham raised eyebrows at each other and waited for the paroxysm to pass.

Finally, leaning on one hand on the wheelbarrow as if the spasm of mirth had depleted his strength, Ernie fished a red-spotted handkerchief out of his trouser pocket and wiped his streaming eyes. A glance at their faces almost set him off again, but he blew his nose instead.

'The idea seems to amuse you,' said Thanet mildly, deliberately understating the effect the suggestion had had upon this odd little gnome of a man.

'If you'd knowed her . . . She were dead against gambling. It was her father, I heard tell. A great gambler, he was, by all accounts.' Ernie shook his head, face splitting once more into a huge grin. ' "Liked a little flutter"!'

But there was something in that grin that Thanet couldn't pin down, something unexpected and disconcerting. What was it?

Ernie picked up his shovel decisively and plunged it into the peaty mixture. 'Well, can't stand here talking all day. Got a lot to do.'

As they walked away they heard a chuckle escape him, like gas bubbling up from underwater. ' "Flutter",' floated after them.

They grinned at each other.

'Looks as though we needn't have bothered to send Bentley to make inquiries at the bookie's,' said Lineham.

'I don't know, Mike. Didn't you think there was something a bit, well, excessive, about his reaction?'

'Not really, no. What are you getting at?'

'I don't know. I'm not sure.' Thanet shook his head. 'Well, I don't suppose it matters.' But the idea niggled away at the back of his mind as they were admitted to the house by Sam.

Hugo Fairleigh, it seemed, was out. 'He's gone to London,' she said. This morning her dark hair was tied up in a ponytail with a red ribbon and she was wearing a crisp red and white striped blouse with her jeans. A wicker shopping basket stood on the hall table beside a tan leather shoulder bag and some car keys. 'And I'm just going out too, I'm afraid.'

'Never mind. We want a word with Miss Ransome, as well, and Mrs Fairleigh.'

'Mrs Fairleigh's not here either. Sorry. She should be back soon, though.'

'Good. Has Mr Fairleigh gone to the House of Commons?'

'I imagine so. I don't know.'

'Will he be back tonight?'

'No. Tomorrow evening, he said.'

Perhaps Fairleigh planned to see Pamela tonight, Thanet thought. It would probably be the first time they had met since Saturday. They would have a lot to discuss, he thought grimly.

'If there's nothing else . . .' said Sam, slinging her bag over one shoulder and picking up the basket and keys.

'Just one point. I understand that just before her stroke old Mrs Fairleigh had an argument with someone here in the house.'

'Oh?'

This was news to her, Thanet was sure of it. Her eyes were without guile as she frowned.

'You don't know anything about it?'

She shook her head. 'Sorry.'

'Were you here, that day?'

'No. I was out, shopping. I heard about Mrs Fairleigh's stroke when I got back.' She glanced at her watch. 'I'm sorry, I really must go.'

'Miss Ransome's here, at any rate?'

'So far as I know, yes.'

'We'll find our own way, then.'

Thanet wanted a word with Mrs Kerk first, to test his theory that it was she who had written the anonymous letter. They found her in the kitchen of Isobel

Fairleigh's flat. She was frying pieces of stewing steak in a Le Creuset casserole dish, familiar to Thanet as Bridget's favourite cookware. On the draining board was a small pile of prepared vegetables: onions, carrots, parsnips. She glanced up apprehensively as they came in but did not stop what she was doing.

'Smells good,' said Thanet with a smile.

'Miss Ransome's supper.' She continued to turn over the pieces of meat with what Thanet considered to be excessive concentration. He decided to broach the matter directly.

'We received an anonymous letter this morning.'

Her hand jerked and fat splashed on to it. She released the wooden spatula and rubbed her hand against her apron. Then she picked the spatula up again.

'If you would just turn off the gas for a moment . . .' said Thanet.

Reluctantly she complied and almost at once the sizzling diminished as the flame went out. She turned to face them but gave him only a fleeting, nervous glance before dropping her eyes. He became more certain than ever that it was she who had sent that letter.

'It mentioned a row that Mrs Fairleigh had with someone and implied that this was why she had the stroke.'

She said nothing, but folded her arms protectively across her chest.

'Which means, of course, that it must have been written by someone present in the house at the time. Were there any visitors, that day?'

She shook her head, reluctantly.

'Which in turn means that it could have been written by only a very few people.'

She was chewing the inside of her lip, fingers nervously pleating the skirt of the old-fashioned crossover apron she was wearing.

'Presumably,' he went on, 'the argument was with a member of her family, and as they are bound to feel a certain loyalty to each other, I think we can assume that none of them was responsible for sending the letter. Which leaves Sam, and you. And Sam was out at the time.'

She was staring at him, as if mesmerised by his logic.

He waited a moment or two for what he had just said to sink in and then said gently, 'Why did you write it? Why didn't you just tell us about it?'

He knew why, of course. She had been hoping to avoid being questioned like this.

'It was Cyril said I ought to send it,' she said. 'My husband. I didn't know what to do.' Her lips tightened and her chin lifted defiantly. 'I know I didn't like her, not many people did, but it upset me, to think ... I mean, she was helpless, wasn't she? Couldn't put up any sort of fight or struggle ... It doesn't bear thinking about ... No one deserves to die like that, whatever they're like. So I talked it over with Cyril and he said look, if it's worrying you, put it in a letter. Then they'll know about it but you won't be getting yourself involved.'

'Yes, I understand,' said Thanet. He smiled reassuringly at her. 'Know what, exactly?'

'I heard them arguing,' she admitted. Then, quickly, 'And don't go thinking I'm the sort who listens behind doors all the time, because I'm not.'

Pity, thought Thanet.

'I was cleaning the stairs, see, and they were in the sitting room.'

'Who?'

She shook her head. 'I'm not sure. I could hear her, all right—Mrs Fairleigh. She had a very, well, penetrating sort of voice. And I could tell she was angry.'

'What was she saying?'

'I couldn't make the words out. They were sort of blurred. This house is built solid, and it was more the way she was speaking than what she said. I thought, Lord, she's going to be in a mood after this, all right. So as soon as I got to the bottom of the stairs I shut myself in the kitchen and turned the radio on. I don't like rows,' she added defensively. 'They upset me.'

Disappointing. Thanet had hoped for more. 'So what happened after that?'

'Nothing, for about half an hour. Then Mr Hugo came and told me that his mother had had a stroke.'

'Did he say anything about how or when it happened?'

She shook her head. 'Just that the ambulance would be arriving soon and that was why.'

'Did you have the impression that it was Mr Fairleigh she'd been arguing with?'

'Yes. At the time. But thinking about it, later, that was only because it was him who came and told me. But she could have had the stroke after the argument, couldn't she, and Miss Letty could have found her. And the first thing she would have done was go to Mr Hugo for help. So I don't know, you see.' Her voice was rising in the effort to convince him. 'I really don't.'

'It's all right, Mrs Kerk. Don't upset yourself. I believe you.'

'Pity,' said Lineham as they went in search of Letty Ransome. 'If only we could have *known* it was him. Perhaps we can get Miss Ransome to tell us.'

'We can try. But I doubt it.'

Letty Ransome was in the sitting room, chewing a pencil and gazing thoughtfully at the folded newspaper on her knee.

Evidently a crossword addict, Thanet thought.

'Oh, Inspector . . .' She bundled the newspaper on

to the seat beside her and stood up, a little stiffly, he noticed. Too much gardening yesterday, probably. She was also, he saw to his surprise, blushing again. Why, this time? Because she was unused to receiving male visitors, official or otherwise? Hardly. She had seemed comfortable enough with Hugo. But perhaps he didn't count, being a relation and therefore familiar to her.

To begin with, it looked as though she had nothing useful to tell them. She denied all knowledge of the row, though Thanet was pretty certain she was lying: that tell-tale blush was much in evidence again. She had been working in the garden, she said, when Hugo came to tell her that Isobel had had a stroke.

Her astonishment when Thanet began to question her about the large sums of money Isobel had been withdrawing each month was evident.

'A thousand pounds? Oh, good gracious me, what a lot of money! Whatever could Isobel have been . . . I just don't know what to say, Inspector. I'm astounded, I really am.'

'You have no idea what the money could have been for?'

'No, not at all. Absolutely not. Such an enormous sum! Oh, but just a moment. On the first of every month, you say? Wasn't that when you said . . . Could it have any connection with the B you were asking about? Oh! I wonder if that's it?' She stared at him, cheeks pink with excitement this time, eyes open so wide that the whites showed clear around the irises.

'What?' said Thanet.

'B day,' she said. 'Bank day! Perhaps that's the expla-nation! Perhaps she put the B in her diary every month to make sure she didn't forget to go to the bank!'

'Possibly. But even if that were true, it still doesn't tell us where the money went.'

'Of course,' said Lineham. 'The B could stand for

something else. An initial, for example, as we suggested yesterday. Or it could be B for Blackmail.'

'Blackmail?' Letty's eyes stretched wide with shock and the very hairs on her head seemed to quiver with indignation as she said, 'What a . . . a preposterous idea. What possible reason could anyone have to black-mail Isobel?'

'We even wondered if those two mysterious phone calls you had, asking for your sister, could have been from the blackmailer.'

'Oh, surely not. They couldn't have been! They could have been from anyone, anyone at all. Isobel was involved with so many organisations, so many commit-tees . . . Forgive my saying so, Sergeant, but you really have no idea what you're talking about. If you'd only known my sister . . . Isobel was such an upright person, she devoted her whole life to the public good. The idea of blackmail is unthinkable.'

'No need to upset yourself, Miss Ransome. We're just exploring possibilities.' Lineham glanced at Thanet. *How d'you think she'll react to our last suggestion, then?* He grinned to take the sting out of his next words. 'We even wondered if it could stand for Betting.'

'Betting!' For some reason this idea seemed to upset her as much or even more than the last. She put her hand up to her throat and the colour in her cheeks in-tensified. She shook her head vehemently. 'Oh no, not Isobel. She was dead against gambling in any shape or form.'

'So we gathered, from Ernie,' said Thanet. 'We sent someone around to the bookie's, of course, to check, but it looks as though we needn't have bothered. Still we have to follow up every . . . Miss Ransome, what's the matter?'

The tide of colour had vanished as quickly as it had

come, leaving her deathly pale. She swayed and put up a hand to her head. 'I feel . . .'

'A glass of water, Sergeant, quickly. Put your head down, Miss Ransome, between your knees.' Thanet steadied her with one hand on her shoulder, hoping she wasn't going to pass out on him.

Lineham was back in less than a minute. He knelt beside her. 'Here, Miss Ransome, drink this.'

She sipped obediently and slowly her skin lost its unnatural pallor. 'I'm sorry . . .'

Thanet shook his head. 'Please, don't apologise.'

She straightened her shoulders and glanced timidly at him. 'Inspector . . . I can see I shall have to tell you.' She paused, evidently plucking up courage.

'I have a confession to make.'

15

Thanet waited. What now?

Letty Ransome, having begun, seemed at a loss for words. She shifted uneasily in her chair and the newspaper crackled. She glanced down at it, picked it up, laid it on her knee and flattened it out. Then to his surprise, still without saying anything, she held it out.

He took it. One glance was enough to explain her confusion when they came in. Crossword, indeed! It was a copy of the *Daily Telegraph*, open at the racing pages. The schedules of runners were heavily marked with underlinings, question marks, exclamation marks. Isobel may have been against gambling because of her father's addiction but Letty had evidently shared it. A number of small pieces of the jigsaw clicked into place in Thanet's mind. Ernie's immoderate laughter, for instance. That, of course, was what had been puzzling about the old man's reaction; Ernie had been enjoying the irony of the police suspecting Isobel of being a secret gambler when he had no doubt been involved in keeping Letty's activities from her.

Thanet handed the paper to Lineham.

He stated the obvious. 'Your sister didn't know about this?'

She shook her head wordlessly.

'And Ernie helps you?'

She nodded.

'Was that what he went to see you about, on Saturday afternoon, at the fête?'

Another nod.

'He had a tip for one of the afternoon's races?'

'The ...' She cleared her throat, tried again. 'The Northumberland Plate.'

Thanet raised his eyebrows.

'It's ... It's a big betting race in the North of England.'

'I've heard of that!' said Lineham. 'A friend of mine comes from up North. Popularly called the Pitmen's Derby, isn't it, because it's held at the time of the miners' annual holiday?'

She nodded, a spark of enthusiasm loosening her tongue. 'Ernie knows someone who works ... who had some inside information. We'd been waiting all day for him to ring.'

'What time was this race?'

'Three-twenty.'

'And it was around 3.15 when Ernie came to speak to you. Didn't leave you much time, did it?'

'No. I came straight up to ring the Turf Accountant.'

'The one in Sturrenden?'

'Yes.'

'You have an account with him?'

'Yes.'

So that's why she was 'confessing'. Bentley's inquiries would have revealed that she was a regular client.

'Did the horse win?'

She smiled for the first time, her face lighting up. 'Yes.'

'Did you make a lot of money?'

'A modest amount. I know what I'm doing, Inspector. I never bet more than five pounds, and always on sensible odds, six to four, something like that.'

'You told me you didn't come upstairs when you came into the house on Saturday afternoon.'

'Yes. I'm sorry.'

'Miss Ransome, I don't want to be unreasonable about this, but you are making our job rather difficult, aren't you? First you say you didn't come indoors at all during the afternoon. Then you say, oh yes, you forgot, you did come in to go to the loo, but you certainly didn't go upstairs. Now you tell me you did go upstairs, to ring the bookie. You must see that I am beginning to wonder what else you haven't told me.'

'Nothing!' she said. 'Well, I did see Grace, coming out of Isobel's room, but you knew about that, she told you herself that she'd been in there around then. And I couldn't say so at the time because you'd have wanted to know what I was doing upstairs and I couldn't think of a good excuse . . . I wasn't sure if she'd seen me or not.'

'The fact still remains that your sister was killed between 3 and 3.45 that afternoon. And by your own admission you were here. Upstairs. In the very next room.' Thanet was polite but implacable. Bullying old ladies was not his style, but it had to be faced: in the circumstances Letty Ransome was a prime suspect.

Letty's lips began to tremble and she put up her hand and pressed it to them. 'I didn't see anyone else, Inspector, really I didn't. I was in a hurry to get back.'

Thanet's humanitarian instincts were urging him to reassure her, to accept what she was saying and leave.

But reason held him back. After seeing Grace come out
of Isobel's room Letty Ransome would have known that
her sister would be unattended. It would have taken
only a matter of minutes to slip along the corridor, pick
up that pillow and guarantee herself independence and
financial security for the rest of her life. Because she
had, all unwittingly, handed the police a further motive
on a plate.

'We have only your word for that, haven't we? And
as I've just pointed out, you have already lied to us a
number of times. Why should we believe you now?'

'Because it's true! It is, really. Oh, what can I do to
make you believe me?'

'Look, Miss Ransome, I think you have to recognise
that you are in a serious position. I repeat, you were
close by when the murder was committed. The means,
the pillow, was to hand, and—'

'Inspector! You don't . . . You *can't* be implying that
I had anything to do with Isobel's murder. Me, personally?' She was aghast, her eyes filled with horror at the
enormity of the idea.

If she were guilty she was a brilliant actress, thought
Thanet. 'I'm not implying anything, I'm afraid, Miss
Ransome. I am stating a fact. In the circumstances we
have to consider you a suspect.'

She stared at him, speechless, for a seemingly inter-
minable length of time. Even a minute's silence can appear endless in an interview like this. Then she said,
'But why? Why should I do something so . . . so dreadful as to . . . to kill my own sister? What possible reason
could I have?'

'Under your sister's will you stand to inherit a substantial annuity. Many people would consider ten thousand a year an extremely powerful motive.'

She was shaking her head. 'I don't believe it. I can't
believe it. I'd willingly give up any prospect of inher-

iting a penny if it would bring Isobel back. People who have never been alone don't realise . . . And as you get older . . . I know Isobel was difficult, but she was all I had.'

Thanet understood what Letty was trying to say. All too often he'd seen the surviving partner of an apparently unhappy marriage go to pieces. This didn't always happen, of course, far from it, but it did seem that some people found it preferable to be downtrodden, abused or even perpetually locked in conflict than to be alone, with no one to care whether they lived or died. Though this wasn't strictly true in Letty's case. 'You have your nephew, and his wife.'

Another shake of the head. 'Not the same, Inspector. Isobel and I . . . How can I explain? We had a shared past. Despite our differences this was the bond between us and we both knew it.'

There was nothing more to be said at the moment.

Lineham waited until they were out of earshot. He had recognised Letty's possible further motive, too. 'That's all very well, but the fact remains that she's really hooked, isn't she? And gambling, well, like any other addiction, it can easily get out of hand. What if she's tired of placing piddling little bets, would like to bet twenty quid instead of five, or even fifty, a hundred . . . And as you say, she did know about the annuity. Ten thousand a year isn't peanuts. And sir!' He stopped as a thought struck him. 'We've only got her word for it that she didn't know about that row. Say she did hear it, or hear some of it, anyway, heard her sister say she was going to change her will . . . Or, even better, say the row was with her! Say her sister found out about the gambling, and that was what the argument was about! And then Isobel threatened to cut her out of her will altogether! That gives her an even better motive.'

'I know.' Thanet was reluctant to believe this. He

liked Letty Ransome. But she obviously had hidden depths. Who would have suspected her of being a secret gambler? And Lineham was right. A passion for gambling can be a deeply destructive force. To feed their obsession men have been known to put the whole future of their family at risk. Letty Ransome had little else to enliven her dreary life of ministering to her difficult sister's moods and needs. If Isobel had found out and threatened perhaps to cut off the meagre allowance she gave her as well as cancelling the promised annuity, might the temptation to ensure that this did not happen have proved too great? People have a tremendous capacity for self-deception, if it serves their ends. And as he had told himself before, in her own mind Letty might even have justified the killing by convincing herself that it was an act of kindness, that dear Isobel must have hated being a helpless dependant, subject to all the indignities which a severe stroke can involve.

He said as much to Lineham.

'Exactly! Anyway, I'll just nip along and check that no papers have fallen down the back of Mrs Fairleigh's desk.'

'Right. I'll wait on the landing in the main house.'

Lineham wasn't long. He shook his head as he joined Thanet. 'Nothing.'

Down below the front door opened to admit Grace Fairleigh. Thanet hurried down the stairs to meet her. 'Mrs Fairleigh, I was hoping for a word . . .'

Apart from that brief and somewhat mortifying encounter yesterday morning, he hadn't spoken to her properly since Saturday afternoon. Somehow other matters had always taken precedence. But of all the people in the house at the time she was the only one known to have been in Isobel Fairleigh's room around the time of the murder. They only had her word for it that the old lady had been alive when she left her around 3.20. She had to be a prime suspect.

She had put her shoulder bag down on the hall table and now she led them into the drawing room and invited them to sit down.

'How are your inquiries going?'

She was evidently inclined to be more cooperative today. Elegant as ever, she was wearing silky black trousers and a loose black and white top in a complicated geometric design, caught in at the waist by a wide belt which accentuated her narrow waist. Her hair had been swept back into an elaborate pleat, accentuating the classic beauty of her bone structure. She would still be beautiful at eighty, Thanet thought, though lacking warmth and animation it was a beauty which did not appeal to him.

'We are making progress, I think.'

'I gather you've found out about my husband's mistress. Or should I call her his fiancée? Can he have a fiancée, while he's still married to me, I wonder?'

'Has he discussed this with you?'

'What, exactly? That he wanted a divorce and was planning to marry her? Or that she was down here on Saturday, viewing her future home? The answer to the first question is yes, and to the second no. I could see that something had upset him after your visit yesterday and when his aunt told me she'd seen this Pamela woman down here at the fête on Saturday and that she felt she'd had to tell you, I realised what it was. Naturally he wouldn't want her involved in all this.'

'You seem remarkably calm about this proposed divorce, Mrs Fairleigh.'

And it was interesting that she hadn't confided in her friend Caroline.

She shrugged. 'Our marriage was over in everything but name long ago, Inspector. To be honest, I'm past caring.' She looked away, out of the window, and he could almost hear her unspoken thought. *About anything, in fact.*

Caroline was right, Thanet thought. Something in Grace Fairleigh had died along with the child that had meant so much to her, and had never come to life again. He had occasionally come across women like this before, women who had never recovered from a miscarriage or an ill-considered abortion, for example, who many years later still grieved as if the loss had happened only yesterday. On the face of it Grace Fairleigh had much that many women hungered for: exceptional beauty, wealth, a successful husband and a beautiful home. But the beauty was an empty shell, the money meant nothing to her, the marriage was a sham and the house a mere stage set for a barren life.

'How did your mother-in-law feel about the divorce?'

'I've no idea. I don't know that my husband ever discussed it with her.'

'I understand that she was a fairly conventional person. She might not have liked the idea. Especially in view of the fact that she didn't approve of the lady first time around.'

'My husband is a grown man, Inspector. He's long past the stage when his mother's approval or disapproval would have affected such a matter.'

Unless it meant being disinherited, thought Thanet.

'I understand that when your mother-in-law had her stroke, it was because of a serious argument with someone here in the house.'

She was either a good actress or this was news to her. The beautifully plucked eyebrows arched in surprise. 'Who told you that?'

'Is it true?'

'I've no idea. Just what are you implying, Inspector?'

'You were here, at the time?'

The brief flicker of curiosity had already died. She didn't pursue the matter. 'When she had the stroke? Yes.'

'In this part of the house?'

'I was in my bedroom changing to go out when my husband came to tell me that she'd been taken ill and he'd rung for an ambulance.'

It was obvious that, true or not, this was her story and she would stick to it. Thanet decided to leave, but at the door he remembered that he had forgotten to ask her about the letters delivered on the day of the murder. She seemed surprised that he should be interested, but said yes, since her mother-in-law's illness she had been in the habit of taking her letters up and reading them to her. She herself had received a couple of letters that morning and there had been one for her mother-in-law, an estimate from a local builder for some decorating. She'd been so busy during the morning that she'd forgotten about it until after lunch.

Mentally Thanet shrugged. One more loose end tied up.

'I was thinking,' said Lineham as they crunched across the gravel towards the car, 'if this was a detective novel it would have to be her.'

'Because she's the most unlikely candidate, you mean? That doesn't necessarily count her out, though, does it?'

'But what motive would she have?'

'The old lady wasn't the easiest of mothers-in-law, by all accounts.'

Ernie was still busy with his shovelfuls of peat. The lawns looked worse than ever. Idly, Thanet wondered how long they would take to recover. Leaning against the car, he took out his pipe and began to fill it.

Lineham frowned.

Thanet grinned. 'Don't worry, Mike, we'll keep the windows wound down.' He lit the tobacco, tamping it down with his forefinger as it flared up. Long habit had deadened the nerves in his fingertip. It took a second match and then a third before it was drawing properly and out of consideration for Lineham only then did he get into the car. There was always far more smoke when he was first lighting up.

'Even so,' said Lineham as they set off down the drive, 'this would hardly be the time to knock the old lady off, would it? It sounds as though she wasn't going to be her mother-in-law much longer.'

'True.'

A few moments later they passed a row of little terraced cottages. A woman was sweeping the concrete path in front of one of them with brief, angry strokes, as if she had a grudge against the world in general and dirt in particular. The words incised in a stone tablet over the centre cottage caught Thanet's eye. 'Webster Cottages 1873.' The name rang a bell.

On impulse he said, 'Stop the car, Mike. Webster Cottages. Isn't that where Mrs Tanner lives—you know, the woman whose son was put away because of old Mrs Fairleigh's evidence?'

Lineham's forehead wrinkled. 'I believe it is.'

'I wonder if that's her.'

Both men turned to look over their shoulders. The woman was walking back up the path to the front door.

'Let's go and see,' said Thanet, getting out of the car.

'I thought you said we wouldn't bother to interview her ourselves unless something turned up to make you change your mind,' said Lineham as they walked back along the narrow pavement.

Thanet shrugged. 'We might as well, as we're passing.'

There were five cottages in all in the row. The gar-

dens of two were a riot of cottage garden flowers—
rosemary, lavender, pinks, alchemilla, hollyhocks and
nepeta. Two more had neat pocket-handkerchief lawns
surrounded by narrow beds containing a mixture of hy-
brid tea and floribunda roses. The fifth, the one in
which the woman had been working, proclaimed a profound dislike of gardening. Apart from a skimpy bed
along the front wall of the house planted with alternate
orange tagetes and scarlet salvias the whole area had
been paved over. There was not a weed to be seen. The
effect was bleak, grudging, as if the owner conceded
that a garden was a place in which plants should be displayed but was determined to show nature who had the
upper hand.

'What makes you think she lives here?' said
Lineham as he knocked at the door.

'Just a hunch.'

The door opened almost at once, as if the woman
had been waiting to pounce on intruders.

'Yes?'

She was in her early forties, short and whipcord
thin, as if the fierce emotion which emanated from her
in waves had burned away all surplus fat. Her brown
hair was short, cut in an uneven line. Thanet could
imagine her cutting it herself, resigned to a necessary
task but not caring about the final effect. She was wearing a cheap nylon overall over a cotton dress.

'What do you want?' The grey-blue eyes, hard as
water-smoothed pebbles, moved from one to the other
with undisguised hostility.

'Mrs Tanner?'

She gave a tight nod.

Thanet introduced himself and Lineham.

'You've been around once already. I've got nothing
more to say.' She turned away, closing the door, but
Lineham put out his hand and held it open.

'D'you mind?' Her glare intensified.

'I'm afraid we do.' Thanet was at his most benign. He glanced to right and left. Next door a lace curtain twitched. 'I see your neighbours are interested. Do you really want to talk here on the doorstep?'

Pushing between the two policemen she took a few steps down the path and shook her fist at the window. 'Why can't you mind your own bloody business?' she shouted. She turned back to Thanet. 'You'd better come in, I suppose.' She glanced at the pipe in his hand. 'And you can put that thing out, for a start. I'm not having smoking in my house.'

Without a word Thanet tapped out the pipe on the heel of his shoe, earning himself another glare as shreds of charred tobacco fell upon the path she had just swept. He checked that it was out and put it in his pocket before following her inside.

They stepped straight into a small square sitting room, which was hot and stuffy, as if fresh air was only ever allowed into it when the door was opened. It was spotless but sparsely furnished with a couple of small tables, two wooden-armed easy chairs upholstered in faded green moquette and a fawn carpet from which the floral pattern had almost been worn away. There was a rental television set in the corner beside the fireplace but no evidence of any other activity whatsoever, not a newspaper, a book, a magazine, a bundle of knitting, anything. What did she do when she wasn't watching television? Thanet wondered. Clean things and brood, by the look of her.

Had she always been like this, simmering with suppressed fury like a kettle about to boil over? he wondered. Perhaps not. Her present attitude to her neighbours would scarcely endear her to them and yet village opinion had apparently been behind her at the time of Wayne's earlier misdemeanours. Even now, difficult as it was to believe after having met her, there was a softer side to her nature, as she apparently did voluntary work for the Hospice fund. A growing bitterness would be understandable, if she had had a difficult time with her disabled husband, and it couldn't have been easy, after Tanner died, to raise a teenage boy alone. Wayne had apparently been her Achilles heel and it must have been his imprisonment which had triggered off the anger which seemed to crackle in the air around her.

Briefly he wondered what it was that made people react so differently to adverse circumstances. He had seen women carry intolerable burdens and yet emerge the stronger, had met people who had survived the most appalling tragedies apparently unscathed by the experience. Was it some genetic factor which imparted inner strength, or a personality which had been nurtured by a secure background and parental love?

Whatever it was, it was clear that it had been lacking in Mrs Tanner's life. And it was ironic that it was through the son upon whom she had squandered her meagre hoard of tenderness that she had suffered the cruellest blow of all.

She walked across to the fireplace and turned to face them, folding her arms across her flat nylon chest. 'This is a complete waste of time. I told you, I've nothing to add to what I said before.' She obviously had no intention of inviting them to sit down.

'We have to be thorough. Murder is a serious matter.'

'I can't see what it's got to do with me.'

'Oh come, Mrs Tanner. You must realise that we have to look very closely at everyone known to have a grudge against Mrs Fairleigh.'

She gave a harsh bark of laughter, an unpleasant

sound. 'You're going to have your work cut out then, aren't you?'

'What do you mean?'

'Always poking her nose in where she wasn't wanted, wasn't she? You'd think she owned the bloody place.'

'Did she seriously upset anyone else in the village, apart from yourself?'

'Ask around, you'll soon find out. Good riddance, I say. Whoever did her in deserves a medal, if you ask me.'

'Do you deserve that medal, Mrs Tanner?' said Thanet softly.

She unclasped her arms as if unleashing her anger and wagged a forefinger at him. 'Oh, no you don't! Don't think you're going to pin that one on me! I've got more sense than to put my head in a noose because of her!'

'You were there, though, weren't you, in the house that day.'

'Like a dozen other people, yes. Why don't you go and bother them?'

'I see you watch television, Mrs Tanner.' Thanet glanced at the set in the corner. 'So I'm sure you must be familiar with the fact that when the police investigate a murder they look for someone with motive, means and opportunity. You had the motive, the means were to hand, and you also had the opportunity.'

She clenched her fists as if she would have liked to fly at him and hammer at his chest. 'When?' she demanded. 'I was run off my feet, like everyone else.'

'But nobody was watching you. You were in and out all the time with trays, collecting crockery from all over the place. It would have taken only a minute or two to slip up the stairs near the kitchen and do what you had to do.'

'Well I didn't!' Her sallow skin had suddenly taken on an unhealthy greyish tinge, as if she had only just become fully aware of the danger of her position. 'And no one can prove otherwise.'

'Not yet, Mrs Tanner. Not yet. Look,' he added more gently, 'we are not in the business of wrongly accusing people, but—'

'But you are, aren't you! You're accusing me!'

He shook his head firmly. 'No. I'm not.'

'But you said—'

'I did not accuse you. I simply said that we have to take a close look at everyone who had a grudge against her. You are one of those people. You also had the means and opportunity. That's all I said.'

'You're twisting words! Oh, it would suit them, wouldn't it, them up at the big house, if one of us was charged, one of the *common* people. What do we matter, after all? They're the ones with the power, aren't they? It's the same old story, one law for the rich and another for the poor. Money can buy anything these days . . .'

'But it can't buy justice,' said Thanet, raising his voice to stop the tirade. 'That is a fact.'

'Tell me another one! You can't open the paper these days without hearing of some policeman who's been taking backhanders!'

Lineham stirred beside him and Thanet hoped the sergeant was not going to lose his temper. He could feel his own anger rising. *Keep calm. Call her bluff.* 'Do you wish to lay charges against me, Mrs Tanner?' A polite inquiry. The message, *You can't get to me like that.*

She backpedalled at once, as he knew she would. 'I didn't say that,' she said sulkily. And then, in a different tone, almost pleading, 'You're not going to arrest me, then?'

'I'm not arresting anyone yet. I just wanted you to understand the seriousness of your position and to tell

you that it might be wise to tone down your attitude towards the old lady a little. She is dead now, after all.'

She stared at him, rubbing her forearms as if, despite the heat of the room, she suddenly felt cold.

'Don't you see?' he said. 'Carrying on like this does
you no good, no good at all.'

'Yes,' she said grudgingly. 'I suppose you're right.
I . . . I'm sorry.' She frowned and clamped her lips together, as if the apology had caused her physical pain.

'You certainly put her in her place, sir,' said
Lineham as they walked back to the car.

'Made a real hash of it, didn't I?' Thanet was depressed. He should have been able to handle the
woman better, without trampling all over her like that.

'I think you were brilliant! I'm glad I wasn't doing
the interview, I can tell you. I'd have lost my temper at
one point.'

'Pity I didn't stick to my original plan. We didn't
learn a single thing we didn't know already.'

'I disagree,' said Lineham stoutly. 'I can just imagine
her sneaking up the stairs and gloating as she put the
pillow over Mrs Fairleigh's head.'

'Perhaps.' Thanet wasn't convinced.

'Finish your pipe, sir.'

Lineham suggesting that he should light up?

Thanet took out his pipe, looked at it, then glanced
at the sergeant and grinned. 'Put my dummy in, you
mean?'

The tension dissolved as they both started to laugh.

16

Bentley had obviously been looking out for their return. He caught them at the door of Thanet's office.

'Sir!' His round, placid face was unusually animated.

Thanet sighed inwardly. In the past he, too, had discovered nuggets of interesting information only to find that his superior was there before him. But it was just one of those disappointments policemen learned to live with.

'Sorry, Bentley, I think I know what you're going to say. It's about Miss Ransome, isn't it?'

Bentley's face fell. 'Yes, sir. She's a regular client at the bookie's. Has been for years.'

'I know. She told us herself. Large sums?'

'Never more than a fiver, sir. She's careful, chooses sensible odds. Wins a bit more than she loses, that's all.'

Thanet nodded. 'Thanks. At least that confirms what she said.'

Lineham waited until Bentley had gone and then

said, 'Sir, d'you mind if I give Louise a ring? She should be back by now.'

Of course. The interview with the child psychologist. Thanet was ashamed that he had forgotten about something so important to Lineham. The sergeant must have been on tenterhooks about it all afternoon and there wouldn't be time for him to go home before they left for London to see Pamela Raven. 'Go ahead.'

He busied himself with papers while Lineham made the phone call, but couldn't help overhearing.

'Louise? How did you get on? *What?* Oh, no.' A long silence while he listened, then, 'I see. Yes . . . Yes. How's Richard? . . . Yes, I suppose so. Oh God . . . Yes, we'll talk about it tonight.'

Lineham put the phone down and sat staring into space. He looked stunned.

'Mike, what is it? What's happened?'

Lineham's eyes focused again. 'Richard is dyslexic.'

'Oh, no. Are they sure?'

Lineham shrugged. 'They seem to be.' He put his head in his hands.

'Mike . . .' Thanet was at a loss for words. He didn't know enough about dyslexia to discuss the subject sensibly. He got up and went to sit on the corner of Lineham's desk. 'Look, it's a blow, yes, and I know it's not much consolation, but at least you now know there's a reason for the way he's been behaving. Do they really think that this would account for it?'

'Apparently. I'll know more later. They've given Louise some stuff to read . . . But it's bound to affect his future. How's he ever going to pass exams if he's got reading problems?'

'It's bound to cause difficulties, yes, there's no point in pretending otherwise. But it doesn't stop people being very successful. You know that series in one of the Sunday magazine supplements, the one about famous people who have something in common? There was one quite recently about people who were dyslexic. Susan Hampshire, for example. And there were lots more.' Thanet wished he had paid more attention to that particular article. Would the magazine have been thrown away, he wondered? He'd have to look.

Lineham shook his head. 'I didn't see it.' But he was looking marginally less miserable.

'Well try not to get into a state about it until you've found out a lot more. So much research has been done into these things nowadays, there's all sorts of help available. Isn't there a Dyslexic Society?'

'I don't know. I expect they'll have told Louise. She said they'd given her a whole pile of literature.'

'How's she taking it?'

'She's upset, of course. But you know Louise. She's a great one for finding out about things and getting things done. And they made all sorts of practical suggestions about helping Richard on a day-to-day basis.'

'Such as?'

'She didn't say.'

'Look, would you prefer to go home? I can take Bentley to London with me instead.'

'I don't know.' Lineham was clearly torn. The sergeant loved his work and jealously guarded the privilege of being Thanet's chosen companion on such excursions. He was silent for a while, thinking, fiddling with a paper clip that he had picked up from his desk. Finally he tossed it into the wastepaper basket. 'I don't suppose a few hours is going to make much difference. And the appointment with Mrs Raven is at seven, we shouldn't be too late getting back.'

'It's up to you. I'll quite understand if you want to opt out.'

But the sergeant's mind was now made up. He shook his head firmly. 'No. I'll come.'

By 5.30 they were on their way. The journey should take only an hour or so, but they had to allow for rush-hour traffic further into London. The other carriageway of the motorway was even more congested than it had been on Sunday, with commuters streaming out of London in an endless nose-to-tail queue, but heading in to the capital the traffic was relatively light until they left the M20. Lineham grew fidgety as the hands of the clock crept nearer and nearer the hour of their appointment. He drummed his fingers on the steering wheel as once again they found themselves creeping along at a snail's pace. 'Come on, come on!' he muttered.

'No point in getting worked up about it, Mike. It won't get us there any more quickly. I don't suppose it'll matter if we're a few minutes late.'

In the event they made it with five minutes to spare. 'I wonder if Fairleigh will be there,' said Thanet as they got out of the car.

He was, looking very much at home, smoking a cigarette and lounging in an armchair. 'Good evening, Inspector. We thought we'd give you a little surprise.'

Thanet wondered where Gwen was, and whether she had told her mother of her visit to Sturrenden to see him. He doubted it.

'No surprise, Mr Fairleigh. When we heard you'd gone to London we rather expected to find you here.'

'We decided to come clean, you see.' Fairleigh smiled and tapped away the long worm of ash on his cigarette.

'Ah, did you.'

'Do sit down, Inspector,' said Pamela Raven, perching on the broad arm of Fairleigh's chair. Tonight she was more formally dressed in a navy pleated skirt and navy and white polka-dot blouse. Unlike Fairleigh she looked tense, nervous.

Fairleigh was obviously aware of this. He gave her a

reassuring smile and took her hand. *Don't worry, everything's under control. I'm here.*

Thanet chose an armchair and Lineham seated himself at the desk near the window, adjusting the angle of his chair so that he could see everyone in the room and pushing aside a pile of exercise books to make room for his notebook.

'It was obvious you were going to find out about us sooner or later, so we thought we might as well get in first. We've nothing to be ashamed of, after all, nothing to hide.'

Pamela was wearing open-toed sandals and, alert for small, betraying signs, Thanet noticed her toes curl up. People could school themselves to control facial expressions but it was much harder to prevent giving themselves away by the movements of feet and hands. So these two did have something to hide. What? he wondered. For the first time he contemplated the possibility that they might have been in it together.

'Good. Then you won't mind answering a few questions.'

Fairleigh waved his cigarette in an expansive gesture before leaning forward to stub it out. 'Not at all,' he said genially. 'Go ahead.'

But Thanet noticed that almost immediately the MP lit up again. So he, too, was nervous, though he was hiding it well.

'Mr Fairleigh. You knew Mrs Raven intended coming to the fête on Saturday?'

'No.' They spoke simultaneously.

Fairleigh twisted his head to smile up at her and nodded. *You first.*

'It was entirely my idea. Hugo knew nothing about it. I told you last time, I was curious.'

'About what, exactly?'

'To see what the place was like. Whether it had changed. And, well ...'

'Perhaps I should make it quite clear, Inspector. Mrs Raven and I intend to marry. Thaxden is her future home. And as, at the moment, it is rather difficult to take her there ...'

With your present wife in residence, supplied Thanet.

'... well, it's understandable that she should have taken this opportunity to look at it.'

That wasn't how you felt on Saturday, thought Thanet, remembering how disconcerted the MP had looked when he spotted her—for by now he was convinced that this was what had caused the look which had aroused his curiosity. And it was that look, he realised, which had probably subconsciously prevented him from considering the conspiracy theory.

'When did you make the decision to go down to Thaxden, Mrs Raven?'

'Well, after Hugo told me about the fête, first of all I toyed with the idea. But as the date came closer it took hold more and more. It was as if ... Oh, it's difficult to describe ... As if something was tugging at me, urging me to go. Perhaps it was sheer curiosity, to see if the place had changed at all, or perhaps because I knew that one day I should be living there, as Hugo says ...' She shook her head. 'Anyway, I'd more or less made up my mind by Saturday, and then when I woke up it was such a lovely day ... The thought of getting out of London into the country was so tempting ... I knew there were always a lot of people at the fête, and I just intended to mingle with the crowd, take a quick look around and then come away. But then I found I was enjoying it so much ... I thought I was quite safe, that no one but Hugo would know me ... But I'd forgotten about his aunt.'

Fairleigh's lips tightened.

'Let me clarify this,' said Thanet. 'I gather, from my conversation with Miss Ransome when she told me she'd seen you, that she is still unaware of the fact that you two are back together again?'

'She was until yesterday,' said Fairleigh, bitterly. 'We saw no point in telling her just yet. She's very fond of my wife and she's also rather strait-laced. She wouldn't have approved of a divorce.'

'But she'd have had to find out eventually.'

'In time, yes. But we didn't feel the right moment had come.'

'But she knows now.'

'My wife told her. I gather she and Letty were talking about the . . . about Saturday, and she mentioned she'd seen Pam at the fête. Then, of course, Grace realised why I wasn't in too good a mood after seeing you yesterday and felt she ought to put Letty in the picture.'

'And how did she react?'

'I haven't seen her since. But I imagine I'm not exactly her blue-eyed boy at the moment.'

Nor she his favourite aunt, Thanet guessed. Fairleigh was no doubt furious with her for having given away Pamela's presence on Saturday and had probably deliberately been avoiding her.

He returned to his questioning.

'You knew old Mrs Fairleigh was ill, of course, Mrs Raven?'

'Yes. Hugo told me.'

'And you knew about the living arrangements of the two households.'

'Yes.'

She could see where his questions were leading, he could see her bracing herself.

'Did you know that the day nurse had failed to turn up on Saturday?'

The question had caught her unprepared. She hesitated and her eyes flickered down at Hugo.

Seated as they were, they were ill placed for silent collusion.

'No, Mrs Raven, there is no need to consult Mr Fairleigh. Surely the question is straightforward enough?'

She sighed. 'Yes. Hugo rang me on Saturday morning.'

'Especially to tell you?'

'Don't be ridiculous, Inspector!' Fairleigh exploded. 'Why on earth should I ring Pamela to tell her something like that? It was merely a . . . well, a social call. I often ring her, as you can well imagine.'

Thanet ignored this outburst and addressed himself to Pamela. 'And did Mr Fairleigh also tell you what arrangements had been made for looking after the old lady during the day?'

'Well, yes . . . I asked him how they were going to manage, as they were all so tied up with the fête, and he told me his wife was going to look in every half an hour or so during the afternoon.'

'Right, that's enough!' Fairleigh was on his feet. 'Pam, you're not to answer any more questions. I'm going to ring my solicitor.'

Thanet was surprised at this reaction. Surely Fairleigh must have realised that Pamela would be questioned along these lines, especially as she must have told him she had been seen in the house. It occurred to him now to wonder why, in fact, Fairleigh had not insisted that this entire interview be conducted in the presence of his legal adviser. Perhaps Fairleigh's natural arrogance had encouraged him to assume that together he and Pamela could pull the wool over the eyes of the police, that they would be able to reveal just what they chose to reveal and no more. Fairleigh was learning a valuable lesson, he thought: never underestimate your opponent. It was surprising that as a politician he hadn't learned it long ago.

'It is 7.30 in the evening, sir. You won't be able to get hold of him now.'

Fairleigh shot Thanet a contemptuous look. *That's what you think.* He took out a pocket diary and began to leaf through it.

Only people like Fairleigh would have the home number of their solicitors in their pockets, thought Thanet resignedly. Ah well, pity, just when they were beginning to get somewhere.

Fairleigh began to dial.

'No, Hugo, stop!' Pamela was tugging at his sleeve. He ignored her, twitching his arm to shake her off. She grabbed it again. 'Hugo, please!'

He turned his head to look at her and a silent battle of wills took place. But Thanet was sure that the argument was not just about whether to ring Bassett or not. There was another issue involved, something they were afraid he would find out if he went on questioning Pamela. He wished he could see their faces properly.

It was Pamela who broke the silence. 'It's no good, Hugo. We'll have to tell them.' Her voice was flat, resigned.

'For God's sake, Pam,' hissed Fairleigh through clenched teeth, soothing a sideways glance at Thanet.

Thanet's face must have told him that it was too late, the damage was done.

'Tell us what, Mrs Raven?' said Thanet softly.

Fairleigh very deliberately replaced the receiver and cast a furious glare at Pamela. *Now look what you've done!*

Pamela was still holding his sleeve. Now she gave it a little tug. 'Don't you see, Hugo. It was bound to come out eventually. Much better that it does. We've done nothing wrong, after all.'

Fairleigh was still glowering at her and now, once again, he shook his arm to cast her off. Then he returned to his chair, slumped down into it and felt in his pocket for his cigarettes.

Pamela remained where she was, watching him with a worried frown, as if awaiting a sign.

Fairleigh lit the cigarette, inhaled deeply and leaned his head back, blowing the smoke out in a long, thin stream. Then he shrugged, glanced at her and patted the arm of his chair.

Gratefully, eagerly, she went.

Like a little dog, thought Thanet, his dislike of Fairleigh intensifying. Despite her stand of a moment ago there was not much doubt about who called the tune in that relationship.

They both looked at him apprehensively.

'You were saying, Inspector?' said Fairleigh, with an attempt at nonchalance.

The man was a fighter, you had to grant him that.

'Tell us what?' repeated Thanet.

Again, they spoke together.

'That it was—' Hugo.

'It was I—' Pamela.

'Let me tell them,' said Pamela. Taking Fairleigh's silence for assent she took a deep breath.

'It was I who discovered that Mrs Fairleigh was dead.'

'I see.' So despite her earlier denials, she *had* been upstairs. 'Perhaps you'd better tell us exactly what happened.'

'I know I shouldn't have gone up to see her, of course. I wish to God I hadn't!'

They heard the front door open and shut.

'Oh no, there's Gwen!'

Hugo frowned. 'I thought you said she was going to be out this evening.'

'She told me she was!'

They all looked at the door.

It swung open. Gwen stopped dead on the threshold. 'Well, well,' she said, 'quite a reception committee.' Her eyes flicked an anxious, interrogatory glance at Thanet. *Have you told her?*

He shook his head imperceptibly.

Fairleigh was sharp. His eyes narrowed. *What's going on here?*

Pamela was too disconcerted by her daughter's appearance to have noticed. 'Gwen . . .' she said weakly. 'I thought you were out for the evening.'

'Yes, I thought you thought that. In fact, you were so keen to establish that I *was* going to be out that I began to wonder why. So I decided to come back, surprise you.'

'Well you've seen why now, Gwen.' Fairleigh was obviously trying to prevent himself sounding too impatient with her, but his irritation came through. 'Your mother and I are talking to the police.'

'I'm not an idiot, Hugo. I can see that. And don't treat me like a child. As whatever you're saying is bound to affect me, I'm sure the police won't object if I sit in on this.' And she walked across to a corner, picked up a pile of books from a low stool and dumped them on the floor. Then she plonked the stool down in front of the fireplace and sat down on it, hugging her knees.

How were her mother and Fairleigh going to deal with this? Thanet wondered.

'Gwen,' Pamela protested, 'I'm sure you don't want to hear all this.'

'Oh but I do, Mum. In fact, I can't wait.' Gwen glanced at Thanet. 'Do carry on, Inspector.'

It was Fairleigh's turn to try. 'Gwen! Surely it's obvious that your mother would prefer you not to be present.'

'Tough!' She hugged her knees more fiercely. 'I'm staying. If it concerns my mother it concerns me. So unless you want to physically throw me out . . .'

Pamela tried pleading. 'Darling, it's true that I really would prefer you not to be here. It's all so difficult, so embarrassing . . .'

'I see. It's all right for Hugo to be present, but not for me!'

'I didn't mean that! At least . . .' seeing that she was unable to justify that statement Pamela tried again. 'It's just that I don't want you upset, that's all.'

'Upset! Mum, try and get it into your head that I'm not a little girl to be protected from all the unpleasant things in life, not any more. I'm quite tough enough to be upset and survive, you know.'

'Yes, I know that. But—'

'No! Sorry, Mum. I'm staying.'

Fairleigh and Pamela both looked at Thanet as if to implore him to exercise his authority. The trouble was, as usual, he could see all sides. Pamela genuinely wanted to save her daughter distress and at the same time did not want to lose face in front of her. Fairleigh merely found the girl's presence an embarrassing irritation. And Gwen herself was, beneath all that bravado, genuinely concerned for her mother. True, she was no doubt partly motivated by a dislike of Hugo, but after all she was, as she said, beyond the age when she should be protected by adults for her own good. How would Bridget feel in the circumstances? he wondered. She, like Gwen, would be desperate to know what was going on. There was nothing worse than uncertainty in a situation like this. If Pamela were innocent Gwen would be relieved and delighted. If not, somehow she would have to come to terms with the fact, learn to live with it. And in either case it would not help her to be treated as a child.

'I think Gwen is sufficiently sensible to stay, if she wishes.'

Gwen smiled and ducked her head at Thanet in gratitude. Hugo scowled and Pamela sighed, her mouth tugging down at the corners.

Still, thought Thanet, the decision really should not be his alone. This particular issue was a family matter. Much as he himself would regret having to cut the interview short at this point, perhaps Pamela ought at least to be given a choice.

'However,' he added, 'there is a possible alternative. If you wish, Mrs Raven, you could come down to Sturrenden with us and make your statement there.'

He sensed Lineham stir in protest, and it was true that this would not be an ideal solution. Much of the impetus of the present interview would be lost. Pamela had obviously not intended to tell them what she had been about to tell them, and would not have prepared her story. If she chose the way out he had offered her she would have plenty of time to rehearse herself on the way down. He hadn't thought of that. He was an idiot to have suggested it.

Fairleigh had obviously come to much the same conclusion. 'Good idea,' he said, rising and putting out his hand to pull Pamela to her feet. 'I'll drive you down.'

But she did not respond. 'No, wait . . .'

They all looked at her expectantly.

After a moment she said reluctantly, 'Gwen's right. She isn't a child any more and all this does concern her.'

'But Pam . . .' said Hugo.

Gwen jumped up and crossed to put an arm around her mother's shoulders. 'Thanks, Mum.'

Fairleigh scowled. 'Pam! I really don't think this is a good idea.'

She looked up at him and shook her head. 'I'd like to get it over with.'

He stared at her in exasperation and glanced irritably at the two policemen.

Thanet was sure that if they hadn't been present the MP would have put pressure on her to change her mind. Time to intervene. 'Right,' he said pleasantly. 'That seems to be decided, then. If you'd just sit down again,' he added, glancing from Fairleigh to Gwen, 'we can proceed.'

Fairleigh hesitated and seemed about to argue further but apparently decided that there was no point. He sat down ungraciously, face set, refusing to look at Pamela who was watching him anxiously.

Gwen shot him a triumphant glance and sat down on the stool again.

When they were settled Thanet said, 'I'll just fill you in, Gwen. Your mother was just telling us that it was she who discovered that old Mrs Fairleigh was dead.'

'What?' Gwen stared incredulously at her mother. 'But how? Why?'

'That is precisely what we were about to find out,' said Thanet. 'And perhaps I could just add one condition to your being present. No interruptions. Understood?'

She gave him a mutinous look but nodded reluctantly.

'Right, then, Mrs Raven. Perhaps you would continue.'

'Well . . . I certainly hadn't planned to see her, or to go into the house at all for that matter. But it was true, what I told you last time. I did want to go to the loo, and I was wearing high heels and my feet were hurting, and I couldn't face trailing all the way back to the car park. I knew there was a loo just inside the back door. Before the house was split up it was the one we all used when we were playing tennis, it was so convenient. So I thought there'd be no harm in using that. But when I got inside, although I could hear voices in the kitchen there was no one about and I knew the stairs were only just along the corridor ... It was just one of those things you do on impulse ... Oh, it was so stupid of me! It's just that I was curious to see what Hugo's mother looked like after all these years, and to find out how ill she really was.'

Gwen stirred and opened her mouth but Thanet shot her a warning glance and she subsided again.

Pamela looked nervously at her daughter and said defensively, 'If she was going to be my mother-in-law I felt ... Well, I suppose I felt I had the right. If she was severely incapacitated I might well have to take my turn in looking after her ... I just wanted to see for myself, that's all.'

She glanced down at Fairleigh, who by now had apparently decided that it would be politic to make the best of the situation. He gave her an encouraging nod. 'Perfectly understandable.'

'Crazy, if you ask me,' muttered Gwen.

'I thought we agreed no interruptions,' said Thanet.

'Oh, I see! *He* can say whatever he likes, but I'm not allowed to say a word!'

'Precisely!' said Thanet. 'I am interviewing your mother and Mr Fairleigh. He is entitled—indeed, I wish him to make any comments he chooses to make. But if you want to stay you *will* remain silent. Understood?'

She gave a sulky nod.

'Please go on, Mrs Raven.'

'There's not much more to tell. When I went into

the room I thought at first she was asleep. Then I realised she wasn't breathing, that . . . that she was dead.' Pamela stopped, her face reflecting what she had felt at that moment: shock, disbelief.

'Did you touch her?'

'No! I just . . . Well, I panicked, I suppose. I went straight off to find Hugo. That was when I ran into the woman who must have told you she'd seen me, in the downstairs corridor.'

'Pam came to me in the garden,' said Hugo. 'She was upset, naturally, and I told her I thought she ought to go home. At that point, of course, I didn't know that there was anything . . . unnatural about my mother's death, I just assumed she'd had another stroke. I hurried up to her room to check, then I remembered seeing Doctor Mallard only a few minutes before and thought I'd better get him to take a look at her, just in case there was anything to be done. One hears of these cases when one assumes someone's dead and they're not . . .'

'Did you touch your mother?'

'Just felt for her pulse, that's all.'

'Or anything else?'

'I told you. No. On the way back in with Doctor Mallard we met my wife and told her what had happened. She came with us. Well, the rest you know, you've heard it all before.'

'And you, Mrs Raven, left immediately after speaking to Mr Fairleigh?'

'Yes.'

Which explained why her name had not been on the list compiled at the gate.

'I understand that your mother wasn't too pleased about your proposed divorce and remarriage, Mr Fairleigh.' This was a gamble, but a gamble worth taking. There was still no confirmation that that row had been with Fairleigh and, if it had, what it had been about. It would be interesting and possibly revealing to see his reaction.

'I really don't think that that's any business of yours, Inspector.'

'Don't you? You and she had a row about it, didn't you.' It was a statement, not a question.

Fairleigh stared at him and Thanet could see him trying to make up his mind: was Thanet guessing? Had someone overheard? Would it be best to deny it, and risk being proved a liar, or to admit it and find himself having to answer further questions?

Pamela frowned. 'Is that true, Hugo?'

Fairleigh's shoulders twitched in irritation. It was obvious that, used to getting his own way, he resented being forced into replying against his will.

She took his silence for assent. 'Why didn't you tell me?'

'I didn't want to upset you.'

So it was true. Thanet decided to press his luck a little further. 'It was because of that row that she had her stroke, I understand.'

'Hugo!' Pamela was on her feet, staring down at him. Either this was all news to her or she was a very good actress.

It was too much for Gwen. She too jumped up, and confronted her mother. 'You see?' she shouted. 'I told you Hugo would bring you nothing but trouble, but you wouldn't listen! That wretched old woman! She made you suffer last time and now it's happening all over again!'

'Oh, for God's sake keep out of this!' said Fairleigh, standing up and pushing his way between the two women.

Gwen tried to elbow him aside. 'Why should I?' she

shouted. 'She's my mother, isn't she? Why should I just stand by and see her hurt?'

'Gwen . . .' said Pamela. 'Hugo . . .'

'That's enough!' said Thanet. 'I will not have this interview reduced to a family brawl.'

'Don't worry!' Gwen flung at him. 'I've heard enough, thank you. But believe me,' she said to Fairleigh, 'I'll have plenty more to say in the future!' And she marched out, slamming the door behind her.

They heard her run upstairs, another door slam.

'See what you've done?' said Fairleigh, turning on Thanet. 'If you hadn't allowed her to stay . . .'

'Sit down, Mr Fairleigh,' said Thanet quietly.

'It was obviously a ridiculous idea . . .'

Thanet raised his voice a little. 'Mr Fairleigh. Sit down, please.'

'It's all your fault!'

'Is it?' said Thanet coldly. 'I think not. And I repeat. Please sit down. Or are you going to flounce out of the room too?'

His deliberate choice of verb achieved the desired effect. Fairleigh could not now leave without feeling that he had been made to look ridiculous. He shot a furious glance at Thanet before seating himself again.

'Mrs Raven?'

Thanet was interested to see that this time she did not return to the arm of Fairleigh's chair but sat on the stool which Gwen had vacated.

'Now,' said Thanet. 'I believe we're getting somewhere. It would of course have been a great deal easier on everyone if you had both volunteered all this information instead of having to have it dragged out of you. And it does, naturally, make me wonder if there are still things you haven't told me.' He noted the flicker in Fairleigh's eyes. No doubt the MP was thinking of his mother's threat to change her will. Was this the right moment to bring that up? No, he decided, he would keep that card up his sleeve for future use. Pamela's expression remained unchanged. Fairleigh obviously hadn't told her about that, either.

'What, for instance?' said Fairleigh, already regaining his aplomb.

'You tell me,' said Thanet.

Fairleigh shook his head. 'No, there's nothing else. It should give you great satisfaction, Thanet, to know that you have succeeded in dragging, as you put it, everything out of us. You can return home knowing that your work is well and truly done.'

'For the moment, perhaps. But I'm sure you understand that you are both in a somewhat difficult situation.'

'Oh come, Inspector! You are surely not suggesting that I killed my own mother just because she was against my proposed remarriage!'

Thanet rose. 'Your suggestion, not mine, Mr Fairleigh. But murder has been done for much less.' *And for much, much less than half a million pounds.* 'I would ask that neither of you makes plans to go away in the immediate future.'

Fairleigh jumped up. 'But that's ridiculous! My work takes me all over the place.'

'I see no reason why your work should not continue as normal, provided that you notify us of your whereabouts—and provided that you don't leave the country, of course.'

For once Fairleigh was speechless.

17

'Luke, what on earth are you doing?'

Thanet was on his knees in the hall, surrounded by piles of newspapers. When he arrived home he had been disappointed to find that Joan was out. He'd forgotten that it was the second Monday in the month, Victim Support Group night. He'd eaten the supper which she had left for him and then dived into the cupboard under the stairs, where they kept discarded newspapers until the Scouts collected them for charity.

He sat back on his heels. 'You remember that article in one of the Sunday supplements? On famous dyslexics?'

'Yes. Why?'

'It's Richard, Mike's son. They've been having a lot of problems with him. Louise took him to see a child psychologist today, and he's been diagnosed as dyslexic.'

'Oh, no. What a shame. He's such a bright lad.'

'I know. Mike's feeling pretty low about it, as you can imagine. I tried to cheer him up, but I don't really know enough about it to be of any help. Anyway, I remembered that article and thought I'd try and look it out.'

'It was some time ago, I think. I'm afraid it'll have gone.'

'Looks like it. I've nearly finished going through these.'

Joan was feeling the soil in the pot of Alexander's hydrangea. 'This is a bit dry. I must remember to water it in the morning. I'll make some coffee. Or would you prefer tea?'

'Tea, please. I won't be long.'

But the magazine was not there. Thanet rose stiffly, careful of his aching back, and put the newspapers away before joining Joan in the kitchen.

'I remember Susan Hampshire was in it. She wrote a book about dyslexia, didn't she?'

'Yes.' Joan frowned, thinking. 'Let me see, who else was mentioned? There was Jackie Stewart . . .'

'The racing driver?'

'Yes. And Christopher Timothy. And Beryl Reid . . . Oh, and Richard Rogers, the architect. I can't remember any more, I'm afraid. But there's a lot of help available now, from the Dyslexic Association.'

'So I gather. They gave Louise stacks of information at the clinic. Thanks.' Thanet took the cup Joan handed to him and followed her into the sitting room. He lit his pipe and relaxed, easing his stiff back muscles into a comfortable position. They went on talking for a while about Richard and then Thanet gave Joan a brief résumé of his day's activities.

'We're not getting very far, I'm afraid. The trouble is they were all there, in the house, at around the time of the murder. So they all had the opportunity. And the means, of course, was to hand.'

'And most of them had motives, too, by the sound

of it. Hugo Fairleigh and his aunt because they both knew they'd benefit under her will . . .'

'Yes. And Hugo an even more powerful motive if the old lady was threatening to cut him out of it.'

'You don't really know that yet though, do you?'

'No. But I'm pretty certain of it, judging by Bassett's behaviour when we talked to him.'

'What about the woman he's in love with, Pamela Raven? Could she have done it, d'you think?'

'Well, there again she had the means and the opportunity, and if Hugo had told her that the old lady was against the marriage . . . I'm pretty certain, judging by her reaction, that she didn't know they'd actually had a row about it and certainly she was pretty shocked when she heard that it was that argument which had caused the old lady's stroke, but even so Hugo might have told her that his mother was threatening to disinherit him . . . Pamela might have thought this would make Hugo call the whole thing off, and could have seen his mother as the sole obstacle to their marriage all over again. Oh, I forgot to tell you. Her daughter came to see me this morning.'

Briefly, Thanet recounted what Gwen had told him of the subtle way old Mrs Fairleigh had gone about undermining Pamela's confidence in her ability to cope with Hugo's life-style.

Joan frowned. 'Nasty. And it worked, apparently. It was Pamela who broke it off, you say?'

'According to Gwen. Took her mother years to get over it, she said.'

'So you think Pamela might still bear a grudge?'

Thanet shrugged. 'I don't know. She seems a nice woman, I liked her. But you can never tell, can you? Old wounds go deep, as we both know, we've seen it often enough in our work. And she did know that the old lady would be unattended, except for Grace's half-hourly visits; Hugo told her. So she'd only have had to watch out for Grace coming back out of the house into the garden and she'd have known the coast was clear. But if she did do it, I wouldn't think she planned it. Maybe, as she says, she just wanted to have a look at old Mrs Fairleigh out of sheer curiosity. And then, when she saw her lying there, the temptation was too great . . .' Thanet shook his head, raised his hands helplessly. 'I just don't know,' he repeated. 'It even crossed my mind that they might have been in it together, but I think that's a bit of a non-starter. I really don't think I can see Pamela Raven sitting down and plotting it all with Hugo. And I'm pretty certain he was telling the truth when he said he had no idea she was coming to the fête.'

'What about this Mrs Tanner? She sounds pretty unbalanced to me.'

'I agree. And I certainly don't think we can rule her out. She was there, on the spot, and of all the people I've met in the case she's the one who is most outspoken about her hatred of the old woman.'

'Isn't that a good reason for thinking she must be innocent? I mean, if she'd done it, surely she'd keep quiet about how she felt?'

Thanet frowned. 'I'm not sure. She's not very bright.'

'And what about Grace Fairleigh? You haven't mentioned her yet.'

Thanet grinned. 'Ah yes. Grace. Mike suggests she's bound to have done it, on the grounds that according to the rules of detective fiction she's the most unlikely person!'

But Joan took the suggestion seriously. 'Not so unlikely, surely. It sounds to me as though anyone having to put up with Isobel Fairleigh as a mother-in-law might be tempted to finish her off if the opportunity to do so presented itself. And Grace is the only person who actually admits to being there in the room around the time of the murder.'

'I know. But I just can't see it, somehow. She doesn't seem to care enough about anything to commit murder for it. And if she's managed to put up with the old lady all these years, why kill her now, when it's pretty obvious she'd never be the same again, after such a severe stroke? And in any case Grace wouldn't have had to put up with her much longer, in view of the proposed divorce. No, it just doesn't add up.'

Suddenly Thanet was sick of talking about the case. 'Anyway, that's enough about me. What about you? What have you been doing today?'

Joan grimaced. 'Well I'm not getting very far either. Not with Michele, anyway.'

The battered girlfriend again, the one whose father had walked out in her teens, who was convinced that it was her bad behaviour that had driven him away and had been trying to punish herself ever since.

'Ah, yes. You said her mother had died a couple of weeks ago and she'd heard from her father again. He wanted to see her and she was trying to make up her mind whether to agree.'

'That's right. Well she did. See him, I mean. Yesterday. And it's had an absolutely devastating effect on her.'

'Why?'

'She's discovered that it wasn't her father's fault the marriage broke up, it was her mother's. He didn't abandon them, it was her mother who more or less threw him out. When Michele asked him why, in that case, he had just walked out like that, without telling her he was going and why, he said he couldn't bring himself to do it, he was afraid he would break down. And that he'd left her mother and her in their flat so that she, Michele, wouldn't suffer too much from the break-up by losing her home as well as her father.'

'It sounds as though he did care about her, then. But if so, why didn't he keep in touch?'

'Said he thought it was best to make a clean break, that it would be easier for her to adjust.'

'So how did she take all this?'

'Well that's the point. As I say, she's devastated. She's spent all these years blaming herself for the break-up—and I must say, her behaviour at the time does sound pretty extreme, enough to drive any parent up the wall—and now she finds she's been looking at the whole thing the wrong way around. She's completely disorientated.'

'But she'll adjust, surely. It's a very positive thing, to have discovered for certain that she wasn't to blame. As we said when we were talking about her the other day, this could be the breakthrough you were hoping for.'

'True. No doubt, in time, it's bound to be all for the good, especially if she and her father now keep in touch.'

'Does he want to?'

'Apparently. But the thing she's finding so hard to deal with is her anger with her mother. She and her mother got on reasonably well. I wouldn't say they were close, but at least her mother was always there. But now Michele simply can't forgive her for allowing her to think all those years that her father just walked out on them. And the awful thing is, her mother's dead, she can't have it out with her, so this anger is going to stay unresolved.'

'You can only hope she'll come to terms with it eventually.'

'I know. It would help if she didn't spend all her time thinking about it, if she had something positive to focus on, a job for instance. But with her record of un-employment . . .'

'What about the drinking?'

Joan shook her head. 'That was never a problem, really. I know she was drunk when they picked her and her boyfriend up joy-riding, but I really do think she was just unlucky there. He's a bad influence on her. I'm sure she'd never have stolen a car on her own account and she's not an alcoholic, never has been.' Joan sighed. 'If only I could get her to smarten herself up and lose some weight she'd be quite presentable. She eats to compensate, you see, and I think she feels there's no point in dieting, no one will ever give her a job anyway.'

Thanet had an idea. 'Is she grossly overweight?'

Joan's eyebrows rose. 'Not grossly, no. Not really. Why?'

Thanet told her about Caroline's coffee bar and her policy of employing no one under size sixteen. 'She's recruiting staff now. In fact, she actually asked us if we knew of anyone suitable.'

Joan was enthusiastic. 'D'you think Caroline Plowright is the type to employ someone like Michele?'

'Quite possible, I should think. She's had her own problems and she might well be sympathetic. And it's not as though Michele is a thief or a con-artist.'

'I'll mention it to Michele, then, and if she's interested, go and have a word with your Caroline, see if she'd be prepared to consider taking her on. Thanks, darling, that's a brilliant idea.' Joan yawned and stretched. 'Well, I think I'm about ready to go up, are you?'

'Yes.' Thanet knocked out his pipe on the stout ashtray kept for that purpose, and stood up. 'Ben isn't in yet, though. Where is he?'

Joan glanced at the clock. 'He's been to the cinema with Chris and Mike, and then they were going to have a pizza. He should be back any minute now.'

As if on cue the front door banged and a moment later Ben came in.

'Hi!'

'Good time?' said Thanet.

'Great.' Ben grinned. 'I still can't believe it. No more exams! And the summer holidays ahead!'

Thanet smiled. It was good to see Ben looking so carefree. 'Enjoy it!' he said. 'We're just going up. You coming?'

'No, there's something I want to watch on the box.'

Thanet refrained from saying, 'At this hour?' At the moment parental restraint was definitely not the order of the day. 'Don't forget to unplug the set.' An oft-repeated maxim in the Thanet household ever since some friends of theirs had had a serious fire through omitting to do just that.

Ben grinned. 'Yes, Daddy,' he said in a little-boy voice.

In bed, Joan said, 'Odd, isn't it, how misconceptions and distorted memories can influence personality and behaviour for years, when they have no basis in reality.'

'Darling, give it a rest, will you? Switch off. We go to bed to sleep, remember?'

'Amongst other things,' said Joan teasingly, rolling over and putting her arms around him.

Thanet wasn't going to argue about that.

Next morning Lineham was late and still hadn't arrived by 8.45, the time of the morning meeting. This was so unusual that Thanet couldn't help feeling concerned. But there was no message, so presumably the sergeant wasn't ill.

The meeting was not a success from Thanet's point of view. A lack-lustre Draco listened in silence to Thanet's report, asked a few pertinent questions and then said, 'So you haven't got a single lead at the moment?'

'No, sir.'

'Has forensic come up with anything yet?'

Thanet shook his head. 'The trouble is that three of our suspects, Fairleigh, his aunt and his wife, were all in and out of that room regularly, so we're unlikely to come up with anything useful as far as they're concerned. And the same applies to Mrs Raven, who admits to being in the room even though she claims that the old lady was dead by then. Of course, if there were any evidence to prove that Mrs Tanner had been in there, that would be a different matter.'

Draco frowned. 'Better try and hurry forensic up, then, hadn't you. Sure you're not barking up the wrong tree altogether, Thanet?'

'What do you mean, sir?'

'Concentrating on the family. Oh, I know, I know,' and Draco held up his hand as Thanet opened his mouth to protest, 'it usually does turn out to be one of the nearest and dearest in a case like this. But we mustn't ignore the fact that there were a couple of thousand other people around at the time, and by your own admission it would have been relatively easy for any one of them to sneak in unseen. What have you been doing about them?'

'As soon as the list of names and addresses was typed up I put a couple of men on to it, and they've been working their way through it systematically. I've been keeping an eye on the reports they've been putting in each day, but there's been nothing of interest so I haven't bothered to mention it.'

Draco scowled. 'Sounds to me as though you're going around in circles. We really do want to get this one cleared up, or before we know where we are we'll have Fairleigh complaining of police harassment. Get on with it, Thanet, get on with it.'

All very well, thought Thanet gloomily as he

climbed the stairs back up to his office. But what was there to get on with at the moment?

Lineham still hadn't turned up. Where was he?

Thanet put his head into the main CID room. 'Any message from Mike?'

Apparently not. Thanet returned to his office and sat down, still smarting from Draco's rebuke. He rang the forensic science laboratory and was told that they were doing their best. They weren't miracle men and his wasn't the only case they had to deal with. Thanet put the phone down and felt for his pipe. As Lineham wasn't here he would console himself with a smoke, put off the unwelcome moment which was, reluctant as he was to admit it, upon him.

When a case ground to a standstill, as this one apparently had, there was only one thing for it, to settle down and go conscientiously through every scrap of information which had come in and make absolutely certain that every lead had been followed up. He had learned from past experience that this could be an invaluable exercise. When you were deeply immersed in a case it often became impossible to see the wood for the trees and during a report-reading session sometimes an unexpected overall picture emerged, obscured until then by the day-to-day trickle of information. Connections hitherto missed could be spotted, new angles become evident.

His pipe was burning steadily now and with a sigh he took out the first file and opened it.

He was coming to the end of the report on the interview with Caroline Plowright when feet pounded up the stairs and Lineham came in with a rush.

'Sorry, sir. I thought I'd never get here! I had to take Richard to school and go in to see his teacher, explain to her what the psychologist had said. Louise was going to do it, but her car wouldn't start. I didn't think it would take so long, or I'd have rung in.' Lineham coughed and glanced reproachfully at Thanet's pipe.

Thanet laid it down in the ashtray. 'I know, I know. Open the window wide and leave the door ajar for a few minutes, the smoke'll soon clear.'

Lineham flung the window open and watched the coils of smoke drift out. He grinned. 'Let's hope they don't call out the fire brigade.'

'You sound a little more cheerful this morning, Mike. Tell me what Louise had to say about Richard.'

Lineham perched on the corner of Thanet's desk. 'Well, dyslexia is apparently a sort of umbrella term covering problems with visual and auditory memory, and the sequencing of sounds, letters, numbers and so on. They gave Louise a lot of tips on how to cope with the everyday aspect of it. It all sounds pretty intimidating, I must say. Apparently dyslexics find it very difficult to be organised so we have to try to make it easier for Richard by, for instance, marking every single item he takes to school. All his shoes have to be marked with an R and an L, so that he knows which foot they go on. And we have to check every morning that he has everything he needs to take with him and every evening that he's brought it all home again, whether there are any letters from the school in his pockets or lunchbox. When we ask him to do things we've got to be specific. It's no good saying, "Tidy your room", we have to say, "Pick up all the books and put them on the shelves, pick up your toys and put them in the cupboard"—that sort of thing.'

'What about learning difficulties?'

'Hard to generalise, apparently. They vary from one dyslexic to another. Some cope pretty well. We just have to wait and see. But it should be easier for Richard now that the school knows he's not just being lazy or bloody-minded.'

Lineham stood up and began to wander restlessly around, picking things up and putting them down without really seeing them. 'There's no point in denying we're worried, especially about his future. And it's going to involve a pretty big adjustment all round. It's funny, there you are, going along as normal and then something happens which shakes you rigid. And the extraordinary thing is, the situation existed all the time. It hasn't changed, but your perception of it has, and you feel, well . . .' Lineham paused, groping for words. 'It's as if there's been a minor earthquake in your life. You look around and everything's the same but different.' He shook his head. 'I'm not explaining this very well. It's a hell of a shock.' He glanced at Thanet. 'What's the matter, sir?'

Thanet shook his head. 'Sorry, Mike. I am listening, and I do understand what you're trying to say, but I've just got to think for a minute . . .' He put his elbows on the desk and closed his eyes, lowering his head and clasping his hands over the top of it to contain his excitement. Without warning, tumblers were clicking over in his brain. He had experienced this sensation before, a surge of exhilaration and a sense of dawning enlightenment which was virtually indescribable. He waited, scarcely daring to breathe, for the turmoil in his mind to ease and then suddenly, with a kind of sweet inevitability, that elusive last piece of the jigsaw fell into place and he had it, the whole picture, clear and true. Was it possible? His mind raced, testing, checking, and yes, he was certain now. He raised his head. Lineham was staring at him. 'Mike, you're brilliant!'

'I am?'

Galvanised, Thanet jumped up, unable to contain his excitement. 'Yes! What you just said!'

'What did I just say?'

'Listen!' Thanet began to explain, watching the

dawning understanding on Lineham's face, the begin-
nings of enthusiasm and finally an excitement which
matched Thanet's own. Almost. 'There's an awful lot of
assumptions there, sir.'

'Maybe. But you must admit, it fits. Everything fits.
Doesn't it?'

'Well, yes . . .'

'I'm right, I know it, you'll see. Meanwhile, there are
things to do.' Thanet shoved away the stack of files with
an impatient hand and grabbed a piece of paper. 'I'll
make a list.'

18

Thanet's mood had changed. On the two-hour drive back to Sturrenden he had had plenty of time to think and his initial exhilaration, boosted further by the interview just conducted, had dwindled to a mere spark as they approached the next stage in the inquiry.

During the course of a murder investigation he was always obsessed by one question: who had committed the crime? Every thought, every effort was directed to this end, and it was as if, beyond this point, the future did not exist. It was only when he had found the answer that he began to think ahead and ask himself, what now? What effect would the arrest have upon the other people involved in the case and, worse, had the murder even perhaps been understandable? Not forgivable, no. In Thanet's book murder could never be justified. Often, of course, there was no problem. If the crime had been particularly brutal, if mindless violence or sadistic enjoyment had been involved, his feelings of triumph were unalloyed and he would find nothing but fulfilment and satisfaction in bringing the criminal to justice. But he did sometimes find, as in this case, that dangerous compassion for the murderer could creep in and he could even ask himself, if I had found myself in that position, would I have behaved as he or she did? He knew that he should not, could not allow such thoughts to influence his behaviour, but there was no point in denying that they didn't help him to be as single-minded as he ought to be.

No, he was not looking forward to the coming confrontation; confrontation and, with any luck, arrest.

For there was no doubt about it, luck would be needed. As Lineham had pointed out, they had no shred of evidence that would stand up in court. If they failed to extract a confession then that would be that. Even feeling as he did, he refused to allow himself to consider the possibility that this might happen.

So as the now-familiar gates of Thaxden Hall loomed ahead his stomach clenched. He wanted to get this over with. What if the suspect were out? He glanced at his watch. The various inquiries they had had to make during the day had taken longer than he hoped, but perhaps this would now work to his advantage. At 6.30 in the evening most people were at home.

Lineham, too, looked tense, his hands gripping the steering wheel more tightly than usual. They entered the drive and gravel crunched beneath their wheels.

As they stepped out of the car silence enfolded them and Thanet became aware that it was a perfect summer evening. All day he had been so wrapped up in their various activities that he hadn't even noticed the weather, but now, despite his preoccupation, the peace and beauty of the old house and grounds claimed his attention. The mellow rose-red brick glowed in the early evening sunlight and as they approached the front door Thanet noticed for the first time that the borders along the front of the house were planted exclusively with white and silver plants. The mingled scents of white roses, white phlox, night-scented stocks and nicotiana drifted to meet them.

Lineham seized his arm as they waited for the door to open. He pointed at the sky. 'Look!'

They moved out beyond the shelter of the portico for a better view. High above the trees over to their left a huge bird was circling. Thanet had never seen anything like it before.

'What d'you think it is, sir?'

'No idea.' He turned as Sam opened the door, beckoned and pointed. 'What's that?'

She moved out to join them. 'That's Carvic.'

'Carvic?'

'He's a heron. There's a big pond over in the trees, he often comes there to fish.'

'Strange name.'

She laughed. 'It's a private joke.' She was more formally dressed tonight, a Laura Ashley frock by the look of it, thought Thanet, knowledgeable about such things by now after years of a teenage daughter.

The heron swooped down, disappearing into the trees, and Thanet turned reluctantly away. 'We've come to see Mrs Fairleigh.'

She glanced at him sharply. Something in his tone had made her uneasy. She frowned and led the way into the house. 'She may be changing for dinner. Would you wait here, please, while I go and see?'

Thanet wondered whether Grace Fairleigh changed for dinner every evening, even when she dined alone. But Fairleigh had said that Sam always ate with the family. Perhaps that was why she was wearing a dress.

'Just a moment, Sam, before you go. One small point . . . Could you tell me if there have been any letters for old Mrs Fairleigh either today or yesterday?'

She shook her head firmly. 'No.'

'You're sure? Only when I last spoke to you about the letters you said you never bothered to look at who they were for, once you'd checked that there were none for you.'

'I know, but yesterday and today I did, perhaps because you'd been asking questions about them. There were definitely none for Hugo's mother.'

Thanet nodded his satisfaction. Just as he expected.

He and Lineham were silent while they waited, both preoccupied with thoughts of the coming interview. Thanet had already decided to play it by ear, but now he ran over in his mind the various points that he must bring up.

Sam appeared on the landing and leaned over the balustrade. 'You can come up.'

She led them to a door at the far end of the right-hand corridor and opened it. They went in and she closed it behind them. In the silence Thanet could hear her soft footfalls receding along the landing.

It was a small sitting room with windows on two sides on the front corner of the house—small by the standards of Thaxden Hall, that is, but still larger than Thanet's sitting room at home. Evening sunshine poured in through the tall sash window facing him, momentarily dazzling him. He blinked a couple of times to clear his vision.

Grace Fairleigh was standing by one of the windows on the left. 'Did you see it?' she said. 'The heron?'

'Yes. I'd never seen one before.'

'I watch out for him every evening. He doesn't always come.' She turned away from the window. 'What can I do for you, Inspector, Sergeant? Sit down, won't you.'

It was an attractive room, graceful, feminine, with a green and cream colour scheme which seemed to merge

with the tranquil rural views through the windows. On
a wing chair near one of these lay a tapestry frame with
a half-worked design stretched on it. On the floor
nearby was an open workbag with a jumble of wools
spilling out. There were books on the shelves in the
fireplace alcoves, a television set and a compact disc
player. This, evidently, was the room Grace Fairleigh
used in preference to the formal drawing room downstairs and interestingly enough it reminded Thanet to
some extent of the sitting room of Pamela Raven's flat in
London. Perhaps, underneath, the two women were not
so different after all. He looked at Grace more closely,
noting that as ever she was immaculately groomed, hair
in a smooth chignon, make-up perfectly applied. She
was wearing a short-sleeved sheath dress in pale blue
linen, its elegant simplicity proclaiming its cost more
clearly than any label. She looked as beautiful, unattain-
able and unreal as the models who float down the cat-
walk of the international fashion shows. And there, of
course, lay the difference between the two women.
Thanet thought now, as he had thought the first time he
met Pamela Raven, that he could understand why
Fairleigh had turned from his wife to his mistress. Who
would not prefer a living, breathing woman to an
empty shell, however beautiful?

She was watching him expectantly and he sighed inwardly. Better get on with it. 'Mrs Fairleigh, there is no
point in pretending that this interview is going to be
pleasant.'

Her perfectly plucked eyebrows arched slightly.

'We know, you see, what happened on Saturday afternoon.'

'Really?' She sounded no more moved or interested
than if they had been discussing the weather.

'We have just returned from a visit to your former

nanny, Rita Symes. She's Rita Kenny now, and lives in Suffolk. But of course you know that, don't you?'

Her composure did not falter and she made no response, but for the first time a hint of some emotion showed in her eyes. What was it? Not fear, nor apprehension. But comprehension, yes, and a touch of resignation, perhaps?

It had taken some hours of intense activity to track the woman down and find out her present whereabouts. When, finally, they had succeeded, there had followed some tense moments while they waited for her to answer the telephone. Would she be out? Away on holiday and inaccessible? But she was neither, and a triumphant Lineham had finally put the phone down and said, 'Three o'clock this afternoon!'

They hadn't known what to expect but the substantial four-bedroomed detached house on a new housing estate had come as no surprise. Rita Kenny, after all, had enjoyed a substantial private income. A new Metro was parked in the driveway.

'She has a very comfortable life-style, as you can imagine. But I can't say that she was exactly pleased to see us.'

An understatement. After fourteen years Rita must until recently have felt that she was safe for ever. She had armoured herself in hair-spray and heavy make-up, but her close-set eyes had been reluctant to meet his and her mouth was pinched with anxiety.

They had had no proof of what he suspected, of course. Thanet could only hope that the bluff he had planned would be successful.

He began formally. 'You are Rita Kenny, formerly Rita Symes, employed in 1978 as nanny to the infant son of Mr and Mrs Hugo Fairleigh of Thaxden Hall, Thaxden, in Kent?'

As he had hoped, this approach, with its formal

overtones of courtroom procedure, intimidated her. He saw her throat move in an involuntary swallow of fear.

She glanced from one to the other. 'Yes.'

'You probably know, from reports in the newspapers and on television, that Mr Fairleigh's mother, Mrs Isobel Fairleigh, was found dead last Saturday, and that she had been murdered. Naturally the police were called in and during the course of our investigation we found this.'

He took an envelope from his pocket. This was an enormous gamble. He didn't know if it was the right colour or even the right shape. Guessing that she would have wanted it to be as inconspicuous as possible they had finally chosen a white envelope of standard size and quality. He held it up briefly, careful to allow her no more than the briefest glimpse of the printed capitals on the front—even more of a gamble, then tapped it from time to time on the palm of his left hand to emphasise the points he was making. He shook his head. 'Very careless of you, I'm afraid, Mrs Kenny. Blackmailers should never commit themselves to paper. Especially when what they say implicates them in a much more serious crime.'

She managed to summon up some bravado. 'I don't know what you're talking about.' But her fear was growing. He saw the sheen of perspiration on her forehead and could tell that the palms of her hands were sweating too: she was rubbing them on her thighs, forward and back in unconscious self-betrayal. And she had said nothing about the envelope. They must have guessed correctly. The bluff was working.

'Oh, I think you do, Mrs Kenny. And if you don't now, you certainly will when you're standing in the dock accused of being an accessory to murder and the jury read this letter to prove it.'

She abandoned her pose of incomprehension and

jumped up, back of hand to mouth. 'That's not true! I didn't do a thing!'

'Ah, but you did, Mrs Kenny, didn't you? You committed a criminal act, and compounded it by following up with another. You stood by and did nothing, knowing that an innocent child in your care had been murdered, and then for years you profited from that knowledge by blackmailing the murderer. You call that nothing?'

That was the point at which she had broken down and he knew that they had won. It took some time but in between the bursts of self-justification and hysteria they had eventually managed to get the whole story from her.

Grace was staring at him as if mesmerised, waiting for him to continue. He braced himself, knowing that he must go on, knowing too that what he had to say next would sound brutal. Trying to cushion the blow he spoke gently. 'She told us what happened, the night your baby died.'

She flinched as if he had struck her and her eyes filled with a pain which had not diminished with the passage of the years.

'It was a terrible thing to happen. Please believe me when I say I'm sorry, I'm very sorry to . . .'

'What did happen?' she interrupted, her voice harsh, almost unrecognisable. 'I want to know.'

'Mrs Fairleigh . . .'

'I want to *know*! Can't you see? I have to *know*!' Her voice broke and tears spilled over and began to roll down her cheeks. She brushed them away with a fierce, impatient gesture.

'Mrs Fairleigh, I really don't think . . .'

'I must!' She stood up, as if impelled by an invisible force, and took two rapid steps towards the window before turning. 'All these years, I thought . . . And then to find out . . . I can't bear it! I've thought of nothing else since Saturday, lying awake at night imagining . . . Please, Inspector, tell me!' She sat down again, on the very edge of her chair, leaning forward and fixing him with an imploring look which pierced him with dread and compassion.

Beside him Lineham cleared his throat and shifted uncomfortably. The sergeant was finding this as harrowing as he was.

'Very well. If you're sure.'

'I am.'

Slowly, choosing his words with care, Thanet told her what they had learned. She listened in silence, and then, when he had finished, buried her face in her hands, struggling but failing to keep back the tears. Thanet longed to go to her, to put his arm around her shoulders and comfort her, but Lineham's presence inhibited him and besides his task was not yet done. He felt a monster, contemplating what he had to do next. He took a clean handkerchief from his pocket and laid it on her lap.

She fumbled it up, began to wipe her face, shook her head. 'I'm sorry . . .'

'Please, don't worry about it.' An inadequate response, but what else could he say?

She was drying her eyes, wiping her face again, more thoroughly. Finally she blew her nose and gave a shaky little laugh. 'I'll have to buy you a new handkerchief, Inspector.'

The unexpected touch of humour broke the tension and Thanet heard Lineham give a little sigh of relief. Surely the next stage of the interview couldn't possibly be worse than the last?

Her composure was returning and now she sat back and gave a wry smile. 'I assure you I don't make a habit of airing my feelings in public like this.' There were still streaks of mascara on her face. The mask of perfection which she had always presented to the world had gone and she was different, more approachable, more human.

'I know that.'

'And thank you. I appreciate that it couldn't have been easy for you to tell me. But I can't tell you what a relief it is, to know, at last.' She gave him an assessing look. 'I suppose you now want to talk about what happened on Saturday.'

He nodded.

'Well, I'm not going to be difficult. I'm not going to protest my innocence, stand on my rights or call a solicitor. To be honest, it'll be a relief to get it over with. I'm not cut out for this sort of thing and I don't think my conscience would have allowed me to go on lying in my teeth much longer . . . Aren't you going to charge me, first?'

He could hardly believe it. Was she going to confess, with no further ado? It scarcely seemed possible.

'Caution you, yes.' He nodded at Lineham and the sergeant delivered the familiar words.

Then he sat back to listen.

19

Joan fastened her seatbelt with a little sigh of contentment. 'I'm looking forward to this.'

'So am I.'

They were going to dinner with Doc Mallard and his wife, and Helen's meals were always memorable. Thanet had accepted the invitation with alacrity.

'Helen's bursting with curiosity about the Fairleigh case, you see,' Mallard had said. 'So she thought she'd bribe you with good food.'

'Helen can bribe me with her cooking any time she likes!' said Thanet.

'I've never known her to be quite so interested before,' said Mallard. 'It's because she was there at the beginning of it, I think. She's felt more involved.'

By then, of course, everyone knew that Grace Fairleigh had confessed and had been charged with the murder of her mother-in-law.

'You know what women are like,' Mallard went on. 'They need to know the ins and outs of everything.' He grinned. 'And I don't mind admitting that I'd like to hear the whole story myself.'

Thanet didn't talk about his work to outsiders, never had and never would, but the Mallards were different. Doc Mallard was one of the team and Helen's discretion could be relied upon. When Thanet told Joan about the invitation she had said that she would wait until Saturday too, to hear the details. Thanet had in any case been very busy dealing with all the administration attendant upon the winding up of a murder inquiry and there had been no opportunity to talk at length.

He glanced at his wife, cool and summery in a deep blue cotton dress splashed with white flowers. Her face and arms were tanned and she looked fit and relaxed. He took his hand from the steering wheel and laid it briefly over hers. 'Did I tell you how gorgeous you look?'

Joan gave him a teasing smile. 'No, but I knew you'd get around to it sooner or later.'

'Don't be smug!'

It was another lovely evening and Doc Mallard led them through to the conservatory which he and Helen had built on to the back of their bungalow a couple of years ago and which the Mallards used as a summer dining room.

Joan exclaimed with delight. 'Isn't this beautiful!'

It was a miniature version of the conservatory at Thaxden Hall. Exotic plants in massive Chinese ceramic pots stood about on the floor of terracotta tiles, climbing plants in bloom where trained up the walls and across the roof-struts, and the delicately arched windows framed views of the garden. Beyond, the evening sky was flushed with turquoise, rose and amber. Birdsong drifted in through the open double doors, together with the mingled scents of roses and of the herbs which Helen grew in pots on the patio outside.

Helen was pleased. 'We love this room. I spend most of my free time out here.'

They had a leisurely drink and then moved across to the table. The first course was iced cream of watercress soup, served with hot, crusty home-made garlic rolls.

They all tasted it. 'Delicious!'

They had agreed that they would not discuss the case until after dinner and Helen began by asking again after Bridget. She was very fond of her and had got to know her well because of their shared interest in cookery. Bridget had spent many a holiday afternoon at the Mallards' bungalow helping Helen to experiment with new recipes she was devising for her books. 'At the fête you were just going to tell us why you didn't like this new boyfriend of hers, when James was called away by Mr Fairleigh.'

'Ah, yes, Alexander.' Thanet pulled a face. 'Well, perhaps I'm being unfair, but he just doesn't seem Bridget's type.'

'Why not?'

'He's obviously very well off, drives a Porsche . . .'

'A Porsche!' said Mallard, eyebrows going up.

'Ben was most impressed,' said Joan.

Mallard grinned. 'I can imagine.'

Joan laughed. 'Alexander took him out for a short drive in it on Sunday morning. Ben was hoping his friends would see him, but no luck, I'm afraid.'

'Right,' said Mallard. 'So he's got plenty of money and drives an expensive motorcar. Is that a bad thing?'

'Not necessarily,' said Thanet. 'But it's his background, too.' He thought of the problems that Pamela Raven had had with Hugo's life-style. 'His parents are obviously very well off. Alexander went to public school and seems to have been everywhere and done everything. Travelled half around the world, it seems.'

'So have a lot of young people these days,' said Mallard. 'It's very much the done thing.'

'And then, he's so much older than her, about twenty-seven, twenty-eight, I should say.'

'One foot in the grave!' said Helen.

Thanet gave a shamefaced laugh.

'Isn't a certain amount of experience a good thing?' said Mallard. 'It means he's that much better equipped to deal with the nasty little shocks life throws at us from time to time. And a lot of people would be delighted that he would be able to provide for their daughter in an even better style than that to which she is accustomed. No, come on, Luke, so far you haven't given us one good reason to disapprove of him. All right, so they come from different backgrounds. But Bridget's an intelligent girl and a sensible one. She could adapt, if necessary.'

Helen was nodding.

'I don't know why we're all talking as if this is necessarily going to be a permanent relationship,' said Joan. 'Bridget's always changing boyfriends. And some of them have been a good deal less acceptable than Alexander. Remember the one with the hair, the black leather jacket covered with studs and the great big motorbike? I nearly had a heart attack every time he roared off with Bridget on the pillion!'

'True.'

'And you haven't told us yet what he's like as a person,' said Helen.

'Well, the evening they came down Joan had cooked a special meal to celebrate the end of Ben's O levels. They were supposed to arrive between seven and eight and it was nearly ten by the time they got here. Alexander had been held up at work, some crisis or another, and it was 8.30 before he even bothered to ring Bridget to explain.'

'But he might genuinely have been unable to get away to make a private phone call until then,' said Joan. 'And he did apologise profusely. And they didn't know I'd prepared a special meal for them, did they?'

'No . . .'

'He even apologised to Ben, for spoiling his celebration dinner. In fact, he went out of his way to be nice to Ben, as I've said.'

'Yes . . .'

'And he bought me a gorgeous present, the most lovely hydrangea—*and* wrote a thank-you note, afterwards. It's the first time any boyfriend of Bridget's has done that.'

'And what was his attitude to Bridget?' said Helen.

Thanet glanced at Joan. 'You'd know more about that. I hardly saw him after that first evening, because of the case.'

'He seemed thoughtful and considerate. Consulted her wishes and so on.'

'So in fact,' said Mallard. 'You really can't find a single thing to say against him.'

'Yet!' said Thanet, reluctant to admit that he had perhaps been wrong. He realised that he'd been so engrossed in the conversation that his soup was gone almost without his having tasted it. He watched regretfully as Helen stood up and began collecting the soup plates.

Mallard rose too. 'I'll give you a hand.' He picked up the soup tureen then gave Thanet a penetrating look over his half-moon spectacles. 'Honestly, Luke, it sounds to me as though you're being prejudiced for no good reason. Maybe you won't like me saying so, but perhaps you ought to ask yourself if you'd feel the same about any boyfriend Bridget brought home.'

Mallard was one of the very few people from whom Thanet would take such personal criticism. He was upset, however. He had always been proud of the way he and Joan had managed to nurture Bridget and Ben towards independence. But it was true that he and Bridget had always been very close. Was he, in the last resort, unable to let go?

'I've never had any children of my own, of course,' Mallard went on, 'so it's easy for me to say, but it seems to me that most parents feel that no one is ever quite good enough for their son or daughter. They want the perfect mate for them, but the truth is, as you know only too well, Luke, no one is perfect.' And with this pronouncement Mallard bore the tureen off into the kitchen.

There was an uncomfortable silence. Thanet glanced at Joan, but she was avoiding his eye, staring at a piece of roll which she was crumbling between her fingers.

'You agree with him, don't you?' he said in a low voice.

She looked at him now, uneasily. 'Don't you?'

Thanet sighed. 'Perhaps.' But he knew it was true. For Bridget he wanted a paragon, and Mallard was right, paragons did not exist. There was the difference in background, yes, but again he had to agree with Mallard. Bridget was intelligent, sensible, adaptable. She would learn to cope, if necessary. And apart from that he really couldn't think of any way in which Alexander fell short. The boy couldn't help having been born into a solid middle-class background. Could it be that Alexander, with his public-school education and traveller's tales, had made him, Thanet, feel inadequate and therefore prejudiced? It was an uncomfortable thought.

'Maybe I have been unfair.'

Joan smiled and reached out to squeeze his hand. 'A little, perhaps.'

Helen came in ceremonially bearing a long oval platter. On it was an exquisitely presented cold salmon on a bed of frilled green lettuce leaves, decorated along its entire length with slices of cucumber so thin as to be almost transparent.

'That looks wonderful!' said Thanet, abandoning his unpalatable insight with relief.

'Seems a pity to spoil it by cutting it up,' said Joan, as Helen began deftly to dissect the fish.

Mallard was depositing vegetable dishes on the table: tiny new potatoes steamed in their jackets, buttered and sprinkled with finely chopped parsley; crunchy mangetout peas; and the *pièce de résistance*, a *confit* of baby vegetables braised, as Helen told them later, in a sealed pot with chicken stock, butter and rosemary and served in little nests of lightly cooked spinach.

This was followed by a *mélange* of fresh raspberries and strawberries steeped in Cointreau.

'A perfect meal for a summer evening,' sighed Joan as she laid down her dessert spoon.

'What I'd like to know,' said Thanet to Doc Mallard, 'is how you manage to stay so slim on Helen's cooking.'

'Ah, well she secretly starves me most of the time, you know.' Mallard gave Helen an affectionate glance. 'All this is just to throw people off the scent.'

Helen laughed. 'Coffee, everybody?'

Mallard stood up. 'No, from now on you're not moving from your chair. I'll do it.'

When at last coffee and liqueur chocolates had been distributed and they were settled the Mallards looked expectantly at Thanet.

'Now,' said Mallard. 'As our transatlantic cousins put it, shoot!'

'Where d'you want me to begin?'

Joan waved a hand. 'At the beginning, where else?'

20

Thanet sipped his coffee, marshalling his thoughts. Then, for Helen's benefit, he filled in the background to the case, sketching each of the personalities involved and the complexities of their relationships, past and present.

'So the problem was, you see, as I said to Joan the other night, all the suspects had the opportunity, and the pillow was there to hand. It would have taken only a few minutes for any of them to slip along to Isobel Fairleigh's room, commit the crime and return to whatever they were doing without having been away long enough for anyone to have noticed their absence. And they all, except apparently for Grace Fairleigh, had a motive. It was, of course, the first murder which led to the second, but we didn't know that at the time.'

'That's what I want to know,' said Mallard. 'What on earth put you on to that?'

This was usually the difficult part: how to get people to understand that final intuitive leap which led him to the solution? Thanet sighed. 'I'll try to explain. It began, of course, as it always does in a murder of this type, with trying to understand the people involved, and especially the character of the victim. Isobel Fairleigh was, as I've already said, a difficult woman. That was obvious from the start. But gradually a fuller picture emerged. She was ruthless, for a start, and saw the world as existing to serve her needs, always a dangerous combination. So I had to ask myself what those needs were. What had she wanted most out of life? Her father was much to blame, according to her sister Letty. He encouraged her to believe that she could get or do anything she wanted, and what she wanted at first was vicarious power, through her husband, who was a promising politician. But her ambition was thwarted when he died relatively young, and so she transferred her hopes to her son. She was determined to ensure that Hugo would achieve what his father had failed to, and she worked very hard on his behalf in the constituency. She managed to avert an undesirable early marriage by some particularly unpleasant manipulation, and approved wholeheartedly when he married a more suitable girl, of his own class and admirably equipped to be the wife of a successful politician.

'The first thing that went wrong was that Grace, instead of providing Hugo with a healthy heir, produced a Down's syndrome child. This didn't suit Isobel at all. A lolling idiot, as she saw the baby, would as he grew up increasingly become an embarrassment to Hugo in his public career, would be incapable of handling the family home and fortune which he would inherit or of fathering suitable future heirs and, worse, would constantly reflect adversely upon Isobel herself. Self-image was very important to her and the thought of having to parade a mongol grandson didn't appeal to her one little bit. She was a perfectionist herself and had to have the perfect son, the perfect family, the perfect home. She must almost at once have decided what she was going to do when the opportunity arose, and hid the revulsion she must have felt towards the child. I don't think she saw him as a human being at all, but simply as an obstacle to be removed. I imagine that as she saw it, this particular brand of lightning rarely strikes twice. Grace would soon get over losing the baby and produce other, healthy children. Unfortunately this never happened. As I said, Grace was passionately devoted to the baby and never really recovered from its death.'

Helen shivered. 'It's horrible. How could Isobel Fairleigh do such a thing? A helpless little baby . . .'

'She could and she did. Her determination must have been strengthened when, having acquitted himself well on a tough Labour by-election, a few months after the baby was born Hugo was selected as Conservative candidate for Sturrenden on the death of the current MP, Arnold Bates. It was what Isobel had always hoped for. Sturrenden was a safe seat and there was little doubt that Hugo would get in. So she bided her time, watching for her opportunity. It came halfway through the by-election campaign, when the baby was about six months old. He had a cold and both Grace and Hugo were to be away for the night. But she hadn't taken Grace's concern for the child sufficiently into account. Grace was very reluctant to leave the baby as it wasn't well, and at first said she wouldn't accompany Hugo to the function in London as planned. But Hugo was angry and kicked up a fuss, so eventually Grace did agree to go, but only after making the nanny, Rita Symes, promise to look in on the baby a couple of times during the night. Isobel, of course, didn't know any of this. The baby had for some time been sleeping right through the night and she knew that Rita wouldn't normally go into the nursery until around seven, by which time the baby would have been long dead.'

'I don't know whether I can bear to listen to this,' said Joan. 'Can we skip the details?'

Helen nodded. 'I agree.'

But those details were engraved on Thanet's mind.

Rita had dutifully set her alarm for two o'clock, when the baby had been all right. He had been snuffling, but there had been nothing that she could do to make him more comfortable and, leaving his door ajar, she had gone back to bed, setting her alarm for five.

This time she entered the nursery to find Isobel Fairleigh turning away from the cot, holding a small pillow in both hands. One glance told Rita that the child had stopped breathing. She had thrust the older woman aside and administered the kiss of life, but her efforts were in vain. Isobel had stood by, watching, until Rita had finally straightened up.

The nanny had turned on her.

'You monster! How could you! I'm going to ring the police.'

Isobel had caught her by the arm as she turned towards the door. 'Wait! I don't think you've thought this through.'

'What is there to think about?'

She had attempted to shake her arm free, but Isobel's grip had been like iron, her face implacable.

Thanet became aware that the others were waiting for him to go on. 'Let's just say that, having been caught in the act, Isobel set out to convince Rita that it would be in her own best interests to keep quiet. First of all she threatened that if Rita insisted on going to the police she would blame the nanny for the child's death.'

'If there's an investigation, it would be your word against mine, wouldn't it?'

'What do you mean?'

'I could say that I was worried about my grandson because he had a cold, that I came in to find you holding a pillow over his face . . .'

'You wouldn't! You couldn't!'

'Try me! And who do you think they'd believe? Me, a respected pillar of the community, or you, a nobody from nowhere?'

Appalled, Rita had stopped struggling to free herself from Isobel's grip and stared at the old woman. Isobel meant every word she said, she could see that. What was she to do?

'And then,' said Thanet, 'Isobel threw in an added inducement. Money. Substantial amounts of it.'

She had swooped in for the kill. 'Besides, this could all turn out to be to your advantage.'

'Advantage? How?' Rita had renewed her efforts to tug herself free. 'You're out of your mind, d'you know that? Crazy.'

'Advantage. Yes. Do you really enjoy this work, Rita? Wiping the bottoms of other people's babies, being at the beck and call of your employers day and night? Just think, you need never work again.'

'What do you mean?'

Rita had begun to waver and Isobel was swift to recognise the fact. Taking her to another room she had begun to talk, persuasively. The baby had been handicapped, its quality of life would have been poor, Isobel had positively done it a favour by putting it out of its misery. Its death would benefit everybody. Hugo would not have to endure the humiliation of parading a mongol child in public and Grace was young, she would soon get over this and have other, healthy children. No one would ever suspect what had happened. Cot deaths were common, the child had a cold, everyone knew that Down's syndrome babies were especially vulnerable to infections. She, Isobel, was quite prepared to carry out her threat of blaming Rita if Rita insisted on dragging the police into it. She would argue that Rita herself had called the police in order to give credence to her story and cast suspicion away from herself. But she really would prefer to avoid any unpleasant and unnecessary fuss, and if Rita agreed she was prepared to make it worth her while. She, Isobel, was wealthy, and could see her way to making Rita a generous allowance, far more than she could ever hope to earn as a nanny.

'An initial payment of five thousand pounds, to be precise,' said Thanet, 'a lot of money in those days, followed by regular monthly payments which would increase along with inflation. The temptation was too much and Rita gave in. Isobel told her what her story should be. Rita would say that her second visit to the child had been at 4.30, not 5, and that the child had still been alive. The next time she checked, at 6.30, he was dead. She had attempted resuscitation through the kiss of life, but without success. She had then rung the doctor and gone to wake up Isobel, tell her what had happened.'

'But how could she hope to get away with it?' said Joan. 'There's always a post mortem in cases of cot death, isn't there?'

They all looked at Mallard, who shook his head sadly. 'I'm afraid that unless there is reason for suspicion, the PM of a cot death is very much a formality. The pathologist would look for bruises, broken bones— reasons to suspect child abuse, in fact—and also do a routine examination of heart, lungs, tissue, brain and so on for obvious medical causes for the death. But if, as in this case, there had been no abuse and the baby had been snuffly or a bit chesty, and especially in the case of a Down's syndrome child who is very susceptible to infections, well, I don't think he'd look any further. Sad, but true. I think they'd get away with it all right—well, they did, didn't they?'

'They certainly did,' said Thanet grimly. He had read the reports of the inquest. 'There's no doubt about it, if it hadn't been for Rita's untimely arrival Isobel would have been home and dry.'

'It's appalling,' said Helen.

'But surely,' said Mallard, 'it's extraordinary that a woman like Isobel Fairleigh, if she was as ruthless as you say, should have been content to go on paying out large sums of money to someone like that year after year without a murmur?'

'Yes,' said Helen. 'What could the girl have done, if Isobel had simply stopped paying up?'

'Quite,' said Joan. 'She couldn't have given Isobel away to the police without incriminating herself.'

'I know. She knew that too, and so did Isobel, I'm sure. But she also knew Isobel,' said Thanet. Just as I do, he thought. After only a few days he felt he knew the arrogant, self-centred old lady as well, perhaps better, than had her own family. 'She knew Isobel would never risk it. Isobel was a proud woman, proud of her son, proud of her family name and above all proud of herself. Her self-image really mattered to her, more than almost anything, I would say.'

'In that case, I'm surprised she didn't take the other way out,' said Mallard. 'Don't they say that murder is easier the second time around? Frankly, I find it surprising that the nanny is still with us.'

'Ah, there's a simple explanation for that. Rita Symes is no fool. She was well aware of the threat to her own safety, so she long ago took the precaution of depositing with her solicitor a letter setting out all the facts, to be opened only in the case of her own death by anything other than natural causes. And of course she made sure that Isobel knew about it.'

'They really were a delightful pair, weren't they!' said Helen, with a grimace of distaste.

'Anyway, you still haven't explained how you got on to all this,' said Mallard.

'Well, it was chiefly something that Joan said, together with a remark that Lineham made, next day.'

'You didn't tell me that,' said Joan. 'Something I said? What?'

'As I recall, I more or less told you to shut up at the time . . .'

'Tut tut,' said Mallard. 'Disharmony in the Thanet household? I don't believe it!'

'It was when we were in bed, after we'd been talking about Michele. Remember?'

Joan was shaking her head, looking blank.

'You said, as nearly as I can recall, that it was odd how misconceptions and distorted memories can influence personality and behaviour for years, when they have no basis in reality.'

'Good grief!' said Mallard. 'Is that the kind of pillow talk you indulge in? I wonder the marriage has lasted so long! We're much less intellectual, aren't we, Helen?'

He and Helen smiled at each other. 'Oh yes, much!' she said.

'All right,' said Thanet. 'Forget the double act. Do you want to hear this or not?'

Mallard pulled an exaggeratedly contrite face. 'Sorry. Of course we do. Would you mind repeating that deep thought of Joan's again?'

Thanet did so.

'Yes,' said Mallard. 'Now that I've had a chance to absorb it, very profound.' He held up his hand as Thanet opened his mouth to protest again. 'I'm serious,

Luke. It is. But what I still don't understand is how it advanced your thinking on the case.'

'Well as I say, it didn't click at the time, but then next day . . . You know Richard Lineham has been diagnosed as dyslexic?'

They nodded, their faces solemn now.

'Lineham's very upset about it, naturally, and when we were talking about it next morning he said that discovering something like that really shakes you rigid. The extraordinary thing, he said, is that the situation existed all the time, that *it* hadn't changed but *your perception of it had* and that this is what is so shattering.'

'That's exactly what happened to Michele—my client,' Joan explained to the others.

Thanet nodded. 'Yes. I suppose my subconscious had been chewing away on that all night, so when Lineham said much the same thing, suddenly I knew at once that this had some relevance to the case.'

'But how?' said Helen. 'I just can't see how. That's what's so fascinating.'

Thanet frowned. How to explain? 'Well, let's put it on a personal level. You know how, sometimes, when someone makes a remark, or perhaps when you read something in a book, you relate it to yourself and you think, Yes! That applies to me and I never realised it before!'

They were nodding.

'It's a moment of revelation, of insight, when you perceive a truth which had been there all the time, waiting to be discovered. The point is, you know in a flash that it's true. Well, there often comes a point in a case when this happens to me.'

'The famous policeman's intuition,' said Mallard with a grin.

Thanet shrugged. 'Whatever you like to call it, it happens.'

'It is fascinating, I agree,' said Joan. 'And we've often talked about it, haven't we, Luke? I see it as similar to the process that takes place in the mind of anyone who is seeking to solve a problem, whether it's a mathematician, or a scientist, or even a creative person such as a writer.'

'That's right,' said Thanet. 'I think that what happens is that all the time we are operating on two levels. The conscious mind is busy collecting together all the information needed to solve the problem and all along the subconscious is assimilating, sifting, considering, seeking to make sense of it all. And then someone says something, or something happens and suddenly, deep down, the connection is made. It's a very exciting moment because my conscious mind knows it's happening. It's an actual physical sensation, as if something is trying to push itself up through the layers of consciousness. And I know that if only I stay quite still and allow it to happen it will surface. And then, when it does, it really is like a revelation and everything slots into place, click, click, click. And I just know that I'm right, that this is true. Perhaps I'm not explaining this very well.'

But the others were nodding.

'So go on,' said Mallard. 'What you're saying is that you suddenly realised that what Lineham was saying could apply to one of your suspects.'

Thanet was nodding. 'I got that sensation I've just described in my head. A certain situation had existed all along, some event had occurred which had been radically misunderstood by the murderer, an event which had had a profound effect upon him—or her, of course. Then something had happened which had in a flash changed his perception of it, revealed the truth. And the experience had been so shattering, so mind-blowing, that he had committed murder.

'Well, there was one suspect who *had* experienced a

traumatic event from which she had never recovered.
Grace Fairleigh. Everyone had told me how she had
doted on that baby, what a profound effect its death had
had upon her. But how could this relate to Isobel? Unless . . . Unless Isobel had murdered the baby and
Grace had somehow found out.'

Thanet paused. His listeners were spellbound.

'And that was when everything fell into place. If this
were true, it would explain everything—why Isobel was
being blackmailed, and by whom, and how Grace had
discovered the truth. I knew, you see, that Isobel couldn't
have paid the latest blackmail instalment because she always drew the money out on the first of the month and
she had her stroke on 30 June. So by the time the murder was committed ten days later the blackmailer was no
doubt becoming impatient. I strongly suspected that two
strange phone calls asking for Isobel which Letty
Ransome had answered were from the blackmailer.'
Thanet glanced at Mallard. 'If you remember, I mentioned
them to you the other day, when we were discussing the
case with Mike Lineham. So I now surmised that having
failed to get through to Isobel by telephone, the blackmailer had decided instead to write. If I was right, of
course, the blackmailer could only be one person, the baby's nanny, Rita Symes. I also knew that it was Grace who
usually took Isobel's letters up and read them to her, and
that she had done so that day. It all fitted, you see.'

'But if Rita knew that Isobel had had a stroke . . .'
said Helen.

Thanet was shaking his head. 'That was the point.
She didn't. Both those phone calls were very brief. On
the first occasion the caller had rung off immediately
when Letty Ransome said that her sister was ill, and on
the second occasion Letty, excited by the fact that Isobel
had that morning for the first time shown some signs of

being able to move the fingers on her paralysed side, had simply said that her sister was much better, though still in bed. So the caller would have had no idea that it was a stroke Isobel had suffered. So Rita assumed that Isobel would read the letter herself.'

'But surely she wouldn't have risked giving herself away in a letter?' said Mallard.

'It was stupid, I agree. But she wanted that money. If you're used to a thousand a month coming in and it suddenly stops, you miss it! What she didn't know, of course, was that the postman was in the habit of delivering the letters for both households to the main house, but even so she took the precaution of printing the envelope, just in case Grace saw it lying around and by any remote chance remembered what Rita's handwriting looked like. But she didn't do the same with the letter.'

'So that was it!' said Joan. 'Grace recognised the handwriting! After all those years?'

'Well, she didn't recognise it immediately. But you must remember that for Grace, everything to do with the baby has remained engraved upon her mind. As soon as she started reading the letter she realised who it was from.'

'What did it say? Have you seen it?'

Thanet shook his head. 'Grace destroyed it. And no, I don't know precisely what it said. I'm sure Rita wasn't foolish enough to spell out what she and Isobel had done. But whatever she said, it was enough to cause Grace to realise the truth.'

Grace's account of what had happened had been painful to listen to.

'At first I couldn't take it in. I was sitting by Isobel's bed, reading the letter aloud. Then, as it dawned on me who the letter was from and what the implications were, it was as if I was suddenly outside myself, and it was someone else's voice I was listening to. I looked at

Isobel lying there. She couldn't speak, as you know, but she could understand all right and she could see that I knew what she had done. Her eyes . . . She was in a panic, I could tell. She put out her good hand towards me in an imploring gesture, but I ignored it. All I could think of was what had happened to my baby. I could see that same hand poised above him, holding a pillow, and I saw it come down, cover his little face. I'm not making excuses when I say that then I just blanked out. The next thing I was aware of was standing over Isobel, pressing a pillow down over her face. I lifted it away and saw that she was dead. I was quite calm. There seemed to be a kind of poetic justice in the fact she had died in the same way as he did. I raised her head and replaced the pillow. Then I went back out into the garden.'

'Poor woman,' said Joan. 'What a shock it must have been.'

'What would have happened if she hadn't confessed?' said Mallard. 'You had no actual evidence against her, did you?'

'No. We would have been struck, no doubt about that. But to be honest, although my professional pride required me to bring the case to what might be termed a successful conclusion, I think I would have been relieved. She's suffered enough.'

'So what will happen to her?' said Helen. 'Will she be convicted, d'you think?'

'Oh yes, I should think so. She has confessed, after all, and I can't see her changing her story. But I'm sure her counsel will plead emotional stress and claim that she was temporarily unbalanced by the shock of discovering that her baby had been murdered, so it will probably be on the grounds of manslaughter with diminished responsibility.'

'So what sort of sentence would that mean?'

'Well, on those grounds it couldn't be more than two years, and it's more than likely that she'll either get a suspended sentence or be put on probation.' Thanet pulled a face, remembering. 'D'you know what she said to me, after she'd told me what happened? She said, "I won't ask you what will happen to me now, because frankly I don't care. One prison is much the same as another." '

The other three were silent. Outside, dusk had fallen while they were talking and the birds had stopped singing. Beyond the trees at the far end of the garden the sky was still stained with streaks of red, apricot and pink from the reflected glow of the sun which had long since set. The brighter flowers in the garden seemed to have vanished, receding into the background with the passing of the light, but the paler ones loomed ghostly on their stems, as if suspended from invisible wires.

Mallard rose and began switching on the lamps.

'Better close the doors, darling,' said Helen. 'It seems a pity, but the moths will all be coming in. I'll make some more coffee, shall I?'

At the door she turned. 'What about the nanny? She won't get away scot-free, will she?'

'I hope not,' said Thanet grimly. 'We'll have to put the case up to the Director of Public Prosecutions, but under Section 4 of the Criminal Law Act of 1967 she might well get up to ten years.'

'On what grounds?'

'Helping to conceal the crime of murder by giving false evidence at the inquest.'

'I see. And what about the blackmail?'

'A bit more complicated. But we're working on it.'

Next morning, Sunday, Thanet was in the kitchen making an early morning cup of tea for Joan when the telephone rang. He went into the hall to answer it.

'Dad?'

'Bridget! How are you? What are you doing ringing at this hour on a Sunday?'

'You weren't still in bed, I hope?'

'Certainly not! I was making a cup of tea for your mother.'

'She tells me the case is over. Well done!'

'That's right.'

'You don't sound too pleased about it.'

'It wasn't a very pleasant case.'

'Are they ever? Anyway, that's why I was ringing. You were so busy we hardly saw you last weekend. We tried to ring last night, but you were out.'

'Yes. We went to dinner at the Mallards'. Helen was asking for you.'

'I must go and see her next time I'm down for a weekend. But as far as today is concerned, Alexander is suggesting that we drive down and he takes us all out to lunch. What d'you think?'

'Ben too?'

'Yes, of course. Dad?' There was a touch of anxiety in Bridget's voice now. 'You did like him, didn't you?'

Thanet glanced at the hydrangea. It looked healthy, expensive, handsome. Just like its donor, he thought. He remembered that uncomfortable moment of insight, the thought that his prejudice against Alexander might have arisen from his own feelings of inferiority. The Mallards were right. He couldn't think of a single reason why Alexander should not be a suitable suitor for Bridget, should it ever come to that. He took a deep breath. 'Of course I did. He's a very nice young man.'

'I thought you would.' Her relief came over loud and clear. 'So what d'you think, about today?'

'It's a lovely idea,' said Thanet. 'Your mother will be delighted at not having to cook Sunday lunch.'

'That's what we thought. Good. We'll be down about 12.30, then. Can we leave it to you to think of a nice place to go and book a table?'

'Of course. We'll look forward to it.'

And he meant it.

ABOUT THE AUTHOR

DOROTHY SIMPSON is a former French teacher who lives in Kent, England, with her husband. This is her eleventh Luke Thanet novel. Her fifth, *Last Seen Alive*, won the 1985 British Crime Writers' Association Silver Dagger Award. Her other books include *Doomed to Die*, *Dead by Morning*, *Suspicious Death*, *Element of Doubt*, *Dead on Arrival*, *Close Her Eyes*, *Puppet for a Corpse*, *Six Feet Under*, and *The Night She Died*.

BANTAM MYSTERY COLLECTION